CODE NAME:
CRESCENT

A MATT PRESTON NOVEL

PAUL SHADINGER

CODE NAME: CRESCENT

A Novel by:
Paul Shadinger

IBSN-13: 978-0692698891
Title ID: 6222961

Edited by
Ellen Campbell

Cover Design & Formatting by
Kevin G. Summers

Also by Paul Shadinger

Fiction

Houseboat (2016)

A Matt Preston Novel

I would like to dedicate this book to all of you who read my first novel, *Houseboat* and still encouraged me to keep writing. This book would never have existed without your words of inspiration and support. Positive words are food to an author and I cannot begin to describe the number of banquets that so many of you provided.

This book is also dedicated to my wife, Sandy who saw things in my writing that I never saw. Through her reassurance I was able to finish this novel.

And finally, this book is dedicated to my beloved rescue Cocker Spaniel, Buttons who started me on this adventure. My daily faithful companion who became Blackjack in *Houseboat* I know she is waiting for me somewhere over the rainbow. I will always miss you little one.

Please note *Code Name: Crescent* is a work of fiction. Names, characters, places and incidents are the product of the author's imagination or are used fictitiously. Any resemblance to actual persons living or dead, events, locales or timelines are entirely coincidental.

TABLE OF CONTENTS

PROLOGUE

Winter had slipped in early from the frigid north, and the swirling winds drove the already sub-zero temperatures into double-digit sub-zero temperatures, leaving the flat, bleak central Illinois countryside covered in windswept snow. The desolate cemetery standing next to the freeway was bereft of any trees, just a few rows of markers standing in staggered alignment. The gray cement of the freeway provided the only color in the white landscape as far as the eye could see. Considering the weather and where the man was, it was probably the last place in the world he wanted to be.

When his youngest sister had called and told him their father was dead, he wasn't surprised by how little grief he felt, considering the way things had ended between the two of them. When his mother had passed away a few years before, he'd briefly thought about returning for her funeral, but finally decided he still wasn't ready to face his father. Now, after all this time, he found himself standing in the frigid cemetery staring down at their graves.

When the first settlers had created the small resting place for their loved ones, it was centered on the corner of land between four farms, each family giving a bit of their land for the graveyard. When the land had been set aside as a cemetery, there had been no cars, let alone any freeways. The passage of time had changed it all and now the small cemetery stood right next to a four-lane freeway. As the man stood there bareheaded with his head bowed, the roaring behemoths with their full loads and the occasional swish of an automobile passed just a few feet behind him and kept him company. The man addressed the two markers, speaking to them as if they were alive.

His voice was choked with emotion. "I'm sorry I didn't come to your funerals... I wasn't ready to return. Actually I'm still not ready to be here, but now it seems I have no choice. The night of each of your services I went down to the ocean and I watched the sunset. I thought about all of you and how it was. I just thought about you... I knew both of you wanted me to try and make good with the family, but you had to have known it was a waste." As he stood there at the graves, he was aware of the tears in his eyes, but he had no idea if it was due to the blowing wind or the pain in his heart.

Finally, the frigid weather made it impossible to stand there any longer and he returned to his rented vehicle. As he slid into the warm car, he was grateful he had left the motor running and the heat turned on full force. How long he sat in the warm car with his eyes closed as the memories flooded his mind, he had no idea. Happy memories of his parents along with fond memories of his sister and twin brother comforted him. Finally, with a deep sigh, he slipped the car into gear and drove back down the white path, and as he retraced his way, he noticed his tracks coming in were the only tracks in the virgin snow.

The man paused at the crossroads, trying to decide what he needed to do next. Finally, with a deep sigh, he turned left and headed towards his sister's place. Even though it had been far too many years since he'd been down the old country lane, he had no trouble finding her house. As the man turned into the driveway, he stopped and looked up at his destination. The trees marking the drive and those surrounding the house were bare, and the wind whipped their branches. The snow had long since been blown away by the strong winds, and now the bare trees resembled sentinels guarding the entrance to a castle.

The car turned onto the parking pad next to the house and before he even turned off the engine, the front door flew open and his sister was running out across the hard crust-

ed snow. She lunged at him and wrapped her arms around his neck. As he held her tight against him, he felt her hot tears burning his neck. She sobbed in his arms until he gently mentioned they needed to go inside before both of them were frozen in place.

After they were ensconced in the kitchen, she started plying him with questions.

"How long can you stay?"

"When did you get in?"

"Where are you going to stay?"

"Do you want to go and..." he held up his hand to stop her barrage of questions.

"I have no idea how long I'm going to stay. I was able to wrangle an extended vacation and since it's been a long time since I took any, I can more or less set my own work schedule."

As they sat in the kitchen, the old wood stove in the corner filled the room with warmth. He chuckled and pointed at the old stove. "That looks like Mom and Dad's."

She smiled. "Yeah, Pop converted the house to propane and wanted to throw this away. I told him I would take it. We built a brick chimney and vented the smoke up and out. I swear nothing heats like this old stove. Pop kept bitchin' up to the end how he wished he had never given me the old stove. We told him, but you know how Pop was..."

He nodded, of all people, Sis would know exactly how the old man could be. His sister poured him a cup of coffee, fixing it just how he liked it. It pleased him to see she still remembered. As they sat in the warm kitchen, they caught up on the years until finally she finished, "The service was nice. We all wished you had been there."

He still didn't know how he felt about seeing his sibling. His twin brother had always had hard feelings about him leaving, but his brother didn't understand how it was... how he was the one the old man had always singled out.

3

He never understood why the old man had expected him to live the perfect life. His brother was never expected to be so perfect. His brother was never the one that Pop would hold up to the rest of the kids. It didn't matter he had been the star at school, the starting center on the basketball team, or the quarterback on the football team, or being selected as all-state pitcher on the baseball team... even being a straight 4.0 student wasn't enough for the old man. Nothing was ever good enough for the old man. The worst had been when his brother had gone to fight in Viet Nam and after becoming a helicopter pilot, had returned a war hero.

He could still remember seeing his brother coming off the plane with his chest covered in medals for his bravery. Bradley had watched his parents fawn over Burt and treat him like a hero. It didn't matter that Bradley had stayed home and kept the farm going. It didn't matter that Bradley had been the one who had worked hours on end when their father was no longer able to work the farm. Watching Burt return and be heralded as the boy wonder had been the last straw. Bradley had gone back to his small bedroom, packed his bags and left home that afternoon. The note he left had been brief, "Now it's Burt's turn." Bradley had tacked it on the front door and left—left and never returned until today.

He knew he had to see Burt one more time. He asked his sister, "How's Burt?"

"Brad," her eyes started to mist, "he only has a few weeks to live, at best. The doctors think the cancer is from all of the shit he was exposed to in Nam. Even though he came back a war hero, now he's paying for it with his life."

Brad sat for a while staring down at the floor, his hands clasped together. He could still feel some of the resentment, but there was also a new feeling; a feeling of deep sadness. Burt had gone off to do what he felt was right, and now it was killing him. Even though Brad had been stuck on the farm working day and night to keep things going, he was still alive. There was no cancer moving though his body robbing him of his life. So who had been the lucky one? The favored son who was dying of cancer or the son who felt he was always used as the example of how the boys were supposed to act? His sister's voice cut through his reminiscing. "Brad... Brad? Are you at least going to go and see Burt before he dies?"

"I don't know, Sis. I hated him so much. All the time I lived here Pop always picked on me. Burt could do no wrong. Nothing I ever did was right. Who kept the farm going while Burt was off playing war hero?"

His sister snapped at him, "Goddamn it, Brad, Burt is paying for it with his life. What more do you want from him? Get over it. Yeah, Dad was a shit at times to you. But he also loved you..."

The man's voice rose as he interrupted his sister, "Then why didn't he ever tell me that? Why? All I ever heard was 'Burt this' and 'Burt that' Pop never came to one of my games and watched. I never heard the words 'thank you,' or 'I love you.'"

Brad started to stand and his sister raised her hand to stop him. "I'm sorry. Please sit. It's been way too long since I saw you and I really don't want to fight."

Brad settled back in the wooden chair. He looked around the room and smiled. Many of the things that used to be scattered around his parents' kitchen had found a home in his sister's. In a lot of ways, it felt like he was back home in the house he had grown up in. His sister asked him again in a soft voice, "Are you going to visit Burt?"

"Yeah... I kinda have to."

"Why do you feel you have to?"

"I feel bad I never came back and saw Mother before she died... I don't want to live the rest of my life feeling that way about my brother."

"And me," the pain evident in his sister's voice.

"You've been the worst. I've missed you the most. It was always you standing up against Dad when he was fussing at me. It was you who would warn me when there was trouble brewing. I really have missed you, Sis. I asked you so many times to come out and visit me, but you never would."

"Brad, how could I leave the kids when they were little? Or Howard?"

"I know. I do understand, but I want you to know I have really missed you."

"And I've missed you as well. When do you want to see Burt?"

"Where is he now?"

"Over at Valley General."

"You mean Death Valley General."

"Brad!" She laughed at his remark. The name for the hospital among the town's people had always been Death Valley General since it seemed if you ended up there, you were as good as dead. His sister continued, "There's a brand new hospital now, not the old crappy one you remember."

"How about tonight?"

"Sounds good."

~ ~ ~ ~

The new hospital was just as modern as his sister had said, but Brad thought it still felt like what it was, a hospital. They entered the room and when he saw his brother lying there, it was all he could do not to show his surprise at how bad Burt looked. When Burt opened his eyes and saw his brother standing there, a huge smile crossed his face. With great difficulty he extended his hand. "Brad, it's so good to see you again. Thanks for coming."

"I wish I could say it's good to see you, but seeing you here makes me so sad. How do you feel?"

6

"There are good days and bad days. Today has been one of the good ones. I have had no pain and for that I'm grateful. Please sit."

For the next couple of hours, the two brothers tried to catch up on what had transpired over the last years. Brad watched as Burt grew more and more weary from his visit. Finally, he took Burt's hand and told him he thought it was best if they left and Burt got some rest. Burt tugged on Brad's hand, pulling him closer. In a raspy whisper, Burt said, "Come back and see me tomorrow... alone. There's something I need to discuss with you."

"I'll see."

A look of fear filled the dying man's face and his hand trembled as he stretched it towards his brother. "No! You have to come back. I have to talk to you." The agitation frightened him. Brad didn't know what Burt wanted to talk about, but he could see how distressed he'd become.

"I'll be back tomorrow morning. We can talk then."

"Promise?" Burt used all his strength to push himself up off his bed as he pleaded with his brother. "You have to promise. It's so important."

"Yes. I promise." The sick man dropped back on his bed and let out a deep sigh.

~ ~ ~ ~

As Brad entered the hospital room the next morning he was shocked to see how much his brother had deteriorated during the night. Burt's bloodshot eyes slowly opened and when he saw his brother standing in the room, he reached out his hand and beckoned his sibling to come closer. His voice was strained and almost a whisper. "Sit down. Come close. I need to talk to you."

"Burt, maybe I should come back later." He turned as if to leave.

Burt's face turned red and his body shook as he tried to speak. "No! Don't go. I have to talk to you." The outburst frightened Brad and he pulled up a chair and sat beside his brother. "I know I don't have much time left. It's funny, some of the guys I flew back to the medical station in Nam would look at me and tell me they knew they were going to die. They could feel death looking over their shoulder. I used to laugh at them, even though so many of them did die. I thought it was a silly old tale or something. But now I understand, I can see him waiting here for me. You might not see him, but he's standing there at the foot of the bed."

Brad couldn't help himself as he turned his head to look at the end of Burt's bed. He saw nothing there. Brad wondered if perhaps it was the drugs playing tricks on his brother's mind. "It's okay Burt. I'm here. Talk to me. What did you want to tell me?"

"I've been hiding. I know this is going to sound like I'm crazy or out of my mind on the drugs, but what I'm going to tell you is the truth. I've known I was dying for some months now and I also know there's a man who's been looking for me. If he knew I was dying or dead, he'd take all the gold for himself. Half that gold is mine... and I want you to have it."

Brad was sure now the drugs had started to take their toll on Burt's mind. He was positive his brother was delusional. As Brad sat there holding his brother's hand, he decided the best course of action was to just let his brother ramble. "Why do you think there's gold somewhere?"

The tone of Brad's voice showed Burt he didn't believe any of what he was being told. "Listen shithead, don't patronize me," Burt snarled at his brother. "I know you think I'm all fucked up on drugs and I don't know what I'm saying. I've been lying here waiting for you to come so I could share this with you. Now are you going to listen to me and believe me, or are you going to think this is some drug-induced hallucination?"

Brad was stunned at the clarity of his brother's words. He wondered now if perhaps his brother might know something real. "I'm sorry Burt, go ahead."

"I may ramble a bit, but what I'm telling you is God's truth." Brad nodded. "You think I don't know how crazy this sounds? This is true!" Brad continued to nod his head, partly to keep his brother talking and partly to keep him calm.

"When I was in Nam, a captain came to me one day with a secret mission I was supposed to fly for him. He was some super-spook and he had some village chief all believing he could deliver war materials for some gold. The deal got set up by a couple of guys I think were gay... Anyway, they were friends with this village leader and they were the go between. I was supposed to fly in the stolen stuff and the captain would get the gold. The gold was supposed to be split up between the two gay guys, me and the captain." Burt had started to breathe faster and Brad noticed the device that kept track of his brother's heart rate had started to beep faster.

Brad reached out and took Burt's hand. "It's okay. Just take it easy. I won't leave you till you're finished. Just take a deep breath."

Brad watched as Burt slowly calmed. Burt inhaled slowly and then started talking again. "The whole deal turned out to be a setup. We never did learn if it was done by our side or their side. The captain and the two gay dudes took off with the gold and I took off with the supplies. The damn bird was so heavy I barely got off the ground but I did get it back to the base. Somehow the captain had squared the deal with somebody because I was never asked any questions about taking the stuff or bringing it back.

"The gay dudes got the gold out of country. The captain met them on Nevis Island in the Caribbean. I had a buddy

there who deposited the gold for us. I got the name of the bank where the gold is deposited. The captain knows the box number and the two gay dudes have the key. As I understand it's a special key... weird shaped and you have to have it to get into the vault as well as open the box." Burt closed his eyes and for a moment he appeared as if he had gone to sleep. Suddenly he started talking again.

"We all went our own ways. The two gay dudes disappeared off the face of the Earth. Then a few years ago a couple of federal agents came to me and asked a bunch of questions. I told them I didn't know a thing. After about an hour they left, but then a few days later I heard from the captain, except now he's a colonel. I have no idea how he found me, but he said he thinks he knows where the key is and wanted to meet me. About that time, I found out I have the cancer and things have gone from bad to worse. I've been too sick to travel."

"You never contacted the colonel?"

"Naw... been too sick."

"Why are you telling me this story? What do you want me to do?"

"I want you to go see the colonel and be me."

Brad couldn't help himself, the words just jumped from his mouth. "What? You want me to do what?"

"Lower your voice. And you heard me, I want you to go see the colonel and tell him you're me."

Brad leaned forward and hissed, "How the fuck do you expect me to pull that off?"

"The colonel hasn't seen me since Nam and because we're twins, we still look enough alike he would never question it. I can tell you any details you might need to know. All this guy wants to know is the name of the bank. He has the box number and he says he has the key. Go with him and you can divide up the gold and you take my share. Share it with Sis."

Brad sat back in his chair, deep in thought. By the time he stirred, Burt was asleep. Brad watched as his brother lay in his bed fighting for every breath. It seemed strange now... strange that he had been so jealous of his brother and now his brother was dying. He had returned the war hero, but look what it had cost him. Brad's mind moved on to the story he had just heard. Was it true? Or was it just Burt's mind playing tricks, a drug-induced dream? He had heard stories about Burt's ability to fly a helicopter. He had read the report about Burt returning with his chopper overfilled with wounded and the aircraft was so shot up that when it landed it had literally fallen apart.

Brad stood and quietly left the room and then stopped by the nurse's station. "Is there a place I can get a cup of coffee?" The duty nurse told him where the cafeteria was and Brad left in search. When he returned to Burt's room with his cup of coffee, he found his brother awake.

A peaceful look had settled over his brother's face. "I'm glad you didn't leave. There are still things I need to share with you. There's so much I need to tell you." Brad sat down again and Burt started to tell him as much as he could remember about the mission. Finally, he finished his tale and looked at his brother. "So, will you do it?"

"You mean pretend I'm you?"

"Yes. You can do it. I know you can do it."

"The bank is on Nevis Island?"

"Yes. It's called the Fifth Third Bank of Nevis."

"The what?" Brad's voice had risen in volume.

"Shut up, you heard me. The Fifth Third Bank of Nevis."

Now Brad was positive his brother was having dreams brought on by all of the medications he was taking. To humor his brother, he nodded his head and told him, "I'll take care of it. Don't worry. I'll take care of it."

"Promise?"

"I promise." Brad thought for a moment, "Burt, by the way, what's the captain's name?"

Burt's voice was weak now. "He's a colonel now and his name is McNaulty. Colonel Jacob McNaulty. He wrote me a letter. It's at home under the pad on my desk. Call him and tell him you're me. After you meet him, come and tell me what happens. I'll help you pull this off. Trust me. You can do this." Again his brother fell back on the bed and fell asleep. Brad stood and quietly left the room.

~ ~ ~ ~

Brad stood at his brother's desk. He looked over the mess and thought to himself about the differences between the two of them. Brad's desk was clean with everything in place. Burt's desk was covered with layers of papers. Brad carefully lifted the blotter and just under the left corner he saw an envelope. The letter was short and to the point, just giving his brother a phone number to call and instructing him to call him at once.

Brad picked up the phone and dialed the number. After the third ring a voice answered. "Hello."

"This is Burt. Burt James.

"You took your sweet time calling," the voice on the other end of the phone snapped.

Brad was taken aback by the abrupt tone of voice. "Well excuse me! I was busy with other things."

Some of the anger seemed to have left the voice, but it was obvious the man was still pissed. "Okay. At least you called." There was a moment of silence and then the voice continued, a bit more excited, "I may have found out where the key is located. The good news is it looks like it will just be divided between us." Brad was concerned to say too much since he didn't know what he needed to share with the man on the phone. The voice continued, "How soon can you get out to Seattle?"

"Seattle? A couple of days I guess. Why?"

"Because that's where the key is. Shit, James, you don't seem to be very excited about finally getting to the gold."

"Well, it's been so long I kind of figured it was a dead issue."

"You want to give me your share then?"

Brad hesitated. "Not really. Is this the number you want me to call you on when I get to Seattle?"

"Yeah. Make your arrangements, call me and let me know your plans and I'll meet you there."

"Okay." Brad heard a click and the line was dead.

~ ~ ~ ~

As Brad entered the room, he was surprised to see a couple of new machines sitting next to the bed. A nurse bustled in and Brad asked her what was going on. She frowned at him and motioned with her head for him to step away from the bed. When they were a few feet away, the nurse whispered to him, "His signs aren't good. We don't expect him to live much longer."

Brad thanked the young woman and then pulled a chair next to his brother's bed. Taking his brother's hand, Brad started speaking, "Burt. Burt can you hear me? It's Brad, your brother."

Slowly the other man's eyes lifted, and when he saw Brad there he smiled. "Brad... you're here... Well, I need for you to call somebody. There's an envelope on my desk..."

Concerned, Brad interrupted, "Burt, you told me all this. I just talked to your colonel. I'm supposed to meet him in Seattle in a couple of days. He said he has the key. Does that mean anything to you?"

There was a new light in the dying man's eyes. He squeezed his brother's hand and whispered, "He has the key? Really?"

"That's what he says. What is the key to?"

"It will unlock the deposit box. McNaulty knows the number of the box. The box is located on Nevis Island. It is at the Fifth Third bank... remember that."

"I know Burt, you told me that already. What else can you tell me?"

"I never talked much. I was too scared to talk." Burt started to laugh and then his laugh tuned into a coughing fit. A bell sounded and the nurse came rushing back into the room. She took a quick assessment and darted out. When she returned she had a hypo in her hand and she slipped the needle into Burt's IV. Almost at once the coughing stopped and Burt's eyes started to droop. He motioned for his brother to come closer. As Brad leaned over the bed, Burt whispered, "The colonel doesn't know anything about being a pilot... just don't say anything about flying. Keep quiet... say nothing. You'll be fine... you'll be fine... you'll..." Burt was asleep.

Brad asked the nurse how long his brother would sleep and the nurse told him she didn't know. They had increased his pain medication and the combination was unpredictable. Brad thanked her and went out to his car. It had stopped snowing, but the day was still cold. He started the car and turned the heat on full blast. As he waited for the car to warm, he pondered his brother's story. He wondered if Burt had ever shared the story with their sister. The way the man had acted on the phone tended to make Brad feel there was some truth to Burt's rambling.

Brad drove back to his sister's place and they sat in the kitchen. She asked about Burt's condition and Brad slowly shook his head. She commented that it would be the best thing for him to go ahead and pass away; she knew how bad the pain was and felt it was time for him to let go. She smiled at Brad and ended, "He just seemed to be waiting for you to show up. He kept telling me he had to tell you something really important."

"That brings up a question I wanted to ask you. Did Burt ever mention anything about gold from Nam? Anything at all that gave you an idea he might know where there was a treasure left over from his duty in Nam?"

"That is so weird you're asking that. A few years ago there was some story on TV about somebody finding a treasure, and Burt said he knew of a treasure a lot bigger than that.

"I asked him what he meant and he just smiled at me. I asked him a couple more times and when he finally told me it was like he was scared to death. He looked so frightened and he motioned for me to lean close to him. He whispered 'It was called Crescent.' I said the word back to him and he shushed me. Told me not to say it aloud and he finished by telling me it was the biggest treasure he ever saw. Whenever I asked him about it he wouldn't tell me anything, told me it was safer I didn't know anything about it." His sister shook her head as if to clear away the thoughts. She smiled at her brother and asked, "Why do you ask? What do you know about this?"

"Not much. Not much..." Brad wondered just how much he should share with his sister, but then decided until he knew more, it was best if he kept it to himself. Brad was rising to go back to the hospital when the phone rang. His sister picked it up. Brad watched the emotions play across her face and as she listened to the words coming through the phone, he could see on her face what had happened. Burt had passed away... cancer had claimed another victim.

The funeral service was quick and Brad caught a flight to Seattle the day afterward. The colonel was waiting at the agreed-upon motel. When the colonel opened the door to the room he smiled and held out his hand. "Great to see you again."

"Same here. I really thought Crescent was all over."

Brad was shocked at how quickly the colonel reached out and pulled him into the room. After the taller man shut the door he stepped close to Brad. "Will you shut up! How stupid have you gotten? You know better than to go blabbing about that. Shit, James, you're scaring me."

"Sorry, I wasn't thinking." As the colonel turned and walked farther into the room, Brad wondered what he had gotten himself into. He was flying blind to begin with and the way the colonel had just freaked out had really made him wish he had stayed at home.

"What's the first move?" Brad asked.

"We're going to go and talk to the last person who spoke to the man who had the key. I believe he has the key,. or he knows where the key is hidden."

"When?"

"Now is as good a time as any."

CHAPTER 1
THE VISIT

Almost a year's passed since my last adventure. In the intervening time the media totally forgot that the end of the world was just about upon us, and all computers were going to die a horrific death and in the process remove mankind with them. New Year's Eve of 2000 passed as quietly as any New Year passes, over the past year things had gotten no better with the world, but at least crashing computers were not going to be our downfall.

Once again I'm dealing with a wet and cold November and it really shouldn't be a surprise because in Seattle, we get a lot of wet, cold Novembers. Also, for some reason, my adventures seem to start in November. I guess it really isn't too unusual since fall is my favorite time of the year.

It was a Tuesday night, and those of us gathered around the dining room table to play poker at Tom's house thought it was the best place any of us could be. The howling wind and driving rain outside seemed determined to strip away any remaining autumn leaves still unlucky enough to be left on the flailing branches, while reminding us how lucky we were to be inside all warm and toasty.

It had been a few months since I'd played in one of our games and I was happy to be with my friends again. At one of last year's games, I'd won a houseboat and for a while that had turned into a nightmare. By the time everything finally sifted out, I was in the hospital with a gunshot wound to the thigh, my girlfriend had also been shot, I'd lost my beloved dog BJ, my houseboat had almost lost its moorage and I'd been forced to deal with some of the demons left over from my time in the service. But by the time the problems were over, everything had more or less worked out.

As I settled back in my chair watching Scott shuffle the cards, my mind drifted back to a very strange meeting I'd had a short time ago. After my last adventure, I thought my nefarious past from Nam was over until recently when I received a warning from the military. A warning that really puzzled me, and I was still wondering what the visit was all about.

I'd returned late one evening from seeing Walter, an old Army buddy who lives on the other side of Puget Sound, when I received two visitors. My phone rang and when I answered, I was informed that there were two guests in the lobby who wished to speak to me. Curious, I sent the elevator down to fetch them. When the elevator returned and the door opened, I was presented with a study in complete contrasts as two men stepped out. Reflecting back, I should have known there was something wrong with the two of them since my dog Beanie paid absolutely no attention to either of them. This was not a normal reaction for her to two new callers.

The first man off the elevator stood ramrod straight, trim and fit while the other looked like the "before" ad for Weight Watchers. The tall, slim man was dressed in a United States Army officer's uniform while the other wore an ill-fitting black suit. The uniform had insignia on his shoulders informing me he was a full bird colonel. The colonel was as tall as I am and his short military haircut looked like stubble and was completely gray. Looking at him, my first thought was he seemed to be rather old to still be in uniform, but with the way things are in today's world, perhaps he still had something to offer. As he stood there, he seemed almost at attention with his service cap tucked under his left arm. The uniform was well tailored and from the many decorations, I knew he'd seen a lot of combat action over his career. When I left the Army, I too had several of the same colored ribbons on my chest. But that was a part of my life I would just as soon put away.

The ill-fitting suit was worn by a pasty white man who looked like he spent a lot of time behind a desk. His skin was translucent and he obviously didn't spend much time in the sun. The man resembled a pear. His chinless oval head was perched on a fat neck, and his shoulders were narrow and sloped down to a thick waist and even heavier hips. The pasty man was a good deal shorter than the colonel, and his suit coat looked a few sizes too large while his pants were straining at the seams. The way he wore the suit, I could tell he wasn't used to wearing it, and I didn't think he was military either.

Suit guy was balding and trying hard to cover it up with a very poor comb-over. His few greasy gray strands of hair were clumped together and they did little to cover his bald white head. I fail to understand why balding men do the comb-over thing. My hair seems to be moving up my forehead, and even though I may not be pleased about it, I try my best to ignore it. I think trying to cover it up just makes it stand out more. Do the comb-overs really think others can't tell they're balding and are just growing the sides out to comb up and try to cover the shiny spot? I will curb my tongue; moving on…

The pair offered no pleasantries to start the conversation. The colonel snapped at me as if he was interrogating me, "Are you Matthew Preston?" I noticed the suit just stood there and let the colonel do the talking.

The tone of voice and the way the colonel addressed me put me off. I didn't feel much like talking to this person. "Yeah," I retorted. I paused and then continued, "Excuse me, but who are you and what's this all about?" I noticed the name shield on his jacket read "McNaulty."

The colonel ignored my question and came right to what I assumed was the purpose of his visit. "We know about your military past and we have some questions. Do you know Heyward Hollis or Dennis Price?"

Those were two names I had hoped I'd never hear again. Hollis had shot and killed Price behind my apartment, and later he had shot me before I ended up shooting and killing him. Like I said, I didn't need some stranger coming into my life and waking memories I would just as well leave undisturbed. "Know them?" I replied, "Not really. I knew who they were; we were all in the same outfit back in Nam but our times there didn't overlap very much. They're both dead."

"We know that," the colonel snapped back. He paused and looked over at his companion. I didn't detect any communication between them but when the colonel looked back at me, he continued, "What we want to know is what they told you."

I thought, *this conversation is weird*, but I kept the thought to myself and instead replied, "Told me about what? I don't understand what you want."

"Anything… what did you talk to them about?"

I wondered what they were getting at. I asked, "When? You're not making sense. I have no idea what you know about all this, and I also have no idea why I'm even explaining anything to you. But in the interest of getting this over with, I'll tell you Price broke into my place one evening and when I came home, he ran away. We never spoke. When he tried to escape out my back door he slipped and fell in the vacant lot behind my apartment and broke his leg. I went to call the police and Hollis shot him."

The colonel interrupted, "How do you know it was Hollis?"

"Cause Hollis told me he did." That wasn't exactly true, but it was close enough to the truth for these two. I asked again. "What's this all about?"

Again, the colonel ignored my question. "What all did you discuss with Hollis?"

"When?" I countered.

"Up in the lighthouse…"

They knew about that. I wondered how much they knew about what really happened up there. "Well…" I was stalling for time. There were so many ways this conversation could blow up in my face and I had no idea who these guys really were. I continued, "There really wasn't a lot of conversation going on. Basically we were shooting at each other. The only chatting Hollis did was to make a few comments about some of my friends, and then my dog, and when he raised his gun and took a shot at me and missed, I shot him."

"Between the eyes?" The colonel asked.

"Yeah, the military trained me well." I was really getting pissed at these two clowns. I was trying to be polite, but they seemed to be going out of their way to be rude.

"Is that a joke, Mr. Preston?" The colonel queried.

"No. But you seem to know my record. I assume you know what I did over there. Otherwise, I doubt you'd be here. I was just saying I was lucky and the training the Army gave me saved my life."

"The report we read said that Hollis' pistol was empty. How did he shoot at you with an empty pistol?"

"He used all his ammo. I didn't, so I got the last shot." I figured since Hollis wasn't there to dispute my claim, my story was as good as his.

"That's interesting, since Hollis' military records show he was an excellent marksman. Why do you think he missed you?

I shrugged my shoulders. "I have no idea. You need to ask him." I could feel the smirk on my face.

The colonel snarled at me, "Preston, your attitude leaves a lot to be desired." The suit put his hand on the colonel's arm and when the officer glanced down at him, suit gave his head a small negative shake.

The colonel continued, "At any time, did Hollis ever mention anything about Crescent to you?"

"What?" I was totally puzzled.

"Crescent!" The colonel snapped back.

"Crescent? You mean like what's carved on the door of an outhouse?" I asked.

"Well, yes… you know, a partial moon. A Crescent." I could hear the exasperation in his voice as he traced in the air the shape of a half circle. "What did Hollis say to you about Crescent?"

I had to admit, I was totally confused. "Nothing. He never mentioned that word. This is the first time I've even heard the word in connection with Hollis. Why?"

Again, the colonel ignored my question. "You're sure he didn't say anything about Crescent? Not one word?"

I was trying to keep the exasperation I was feeling out of my voice. "No! I told you, I've never heard the word in connection with Hollis until this evening." I paused a moment and then asked, "When do you think Hollis might have said something?"

This time I wasn't ignored. "When you were up in the lighthouse. You're sure he didn't say anything about Crescent?" Now the colonel sounded exasperated.

"I'm positive! We were rather busy shooting at each other to have much of a conversation. Look, I really don't understand what this is all about. Why are you here?"

Again there was no answer to my question.

"Oh yeah…" For the first time the black suit spoke, "We were wondering about you shooting Hollis so many times. Why was it necessary to shoot him in both feet? Was he going somewhere?" Suit must have been feeling a little bolder since this was the first time he had spoken.

"Well, I'm a poor shot," I popped off.

The colonel scowled at me, "Preston… come on. We read the report. The report where you stated you shot Hollis in the chest while you were lying on the steps after you tripped. That was not a poor shot. Why did you shoot him in the feet?"

I was still for a long time. Finally, I asked. "Truth?"

The colonel said, "Yes, please. The truth!"

"I was pissed. I was in a lot of pain and I was very angry. He had told me how much he'd enjoyed shooting my two Seattle police detective friends and then I shot him." I paused for a moment, wondering if I wanted to continue.

The colonel glared at me as he barked one word, "And?"

"Well, and cause he kept calling me names." Boy did that sound lame now that I was saying it aloud. I was telling a high-ranking officer in the US Army I shot somebody because he called me a name. Talk about back in third grade again, but at the time it was how I felt.

The colonel glared at me a few moments more before he asked, "And what name did Hollis call you that you felt you had to shoot him?"

This was so embarrassing. "It doesn't matter."

"It does matter!" the officer retorted.

"I'd rather not say."

"Tell us now or else…"

My voice was almost a whisper as I interrupted him. "He called me a pussy."

"What did you say?" the colonel barked.

I spoke a little louder this time. "A pussy... he called me a pussy!"

Incredulity colored the colonel's voice. "A pussy!" then louder, "A pussy. Are you serious? You shot him because he called you a pussy?"

"Yeah, well, you had to be there to understand. There was a lot going on besides that. I mainly just wanted to shut him up. And he kept repeating it over and over... so I shot him."

The colonel took an aggressive step toward me. "Isn't the real reason you shot Hollis because he wouldn't tell you about Crescent? You were torturing him to tell you about Crescent," he snarled.

I wanted this to end. What was it with this Crescent thing? I decided I wanted to know so I asked, "What is it with you and this Crescent thing? I told you I've never heard squat about Crescent until now. Neither Hollis nor Price discussed Crescent with me... or anything else. And besides, who the hell are you guys and where do you get off coming here late at night and grilling me?"

They ignored my question. "You're sure?" the colonel asked.

I wanted to scream. "Yes, I'm sure!" I paused a moment, working on getting my feelings under control. "Look, Hollis shot me in the thigh. My girlfriend was in the hospital because Hollis shot her. He also wounded two of my other friends. And, to top it all off, the fruit loop put a zip tie around my dog's neck and watched her strangle to death. I was in no mood to have a social chat with that fucking psychopath. I was pissed as hell and I wanted revenge. I wasn't there to talk to him." Boy, these two were dense.

"So you admit you shot him?"

My voice rose several octaves. "Hell, yes, I shot him! It was shoot him or let him shoot me."

"He would have shot you with an unloaded gun?'

I was totally pissed, but I was still careful to keep my lies straight about what had happened in the lighthouse. "Hollis had one shot left." I held up one finger. "He took it and missed. My shot didn't. That's what happened."

"Oh…" The colonel looked at me and I could tell he was not buying my explanation of what happened up in the lighthouse tower. Disbelief dripped from his next question, "And you shot Hollis in the feet because he was calling you a pussy?" There was a moment of silence. "You expect us to believe you shot him in his feet because he called you a name and not because you were torturing him?"

I said nothing. Until I understood more about what was going on, the smartest move was to just remain silent. After glaring at me for a moment or two, the colonel looked over at the suit and this time I saw the suit nod his head. "Mr. Preston. We are here tonight to give you an order." For a moment I thought about telling them that since I was no longer in the service he had no authority to give me any orders, but I was keeping my mouth shut. "You are never, I repeat, never to discuss anything you know about Hollis or Price with anybody. You have never met Hollis or Price. You do not know anybody named Hollis or Price. Am I making myself clear?"

I'd already had this conversation with some other uniforms when I was in the hospital after the lighthouse incident. I had a thousand smartass comebacks flitting through my head, but I knew my next answer might have a lot to do with me staying a free man or ending up going somewhere I didn't want to go. I took the high road. "Yes, sir. I have never heard of either of those two gentlemen. I wish I could help you more, but I have never heard those two names in my life."

Suit grunted and the colonel snapped, "And you've never heard anything about Crescent either!"

"Sir, I can honestly say, I know nothing about this Crescent thing either."

While the colonel glared at me, the suit pushed the button for the elevator. The colonel ended our conversation with, "And don't you forget it. Understand?" Again, there were witty comebacks I wanted to use, but I knew better.

"Yes sir," I murmured. The two men turned and stepped back into the waiting elevator. As the door slid shut, my dog Beanie gave a halfhearted bark. I looked down at her and laughed. "Hey killer, where were you when I needed you?" I joked.

The visit nagged at me for many reasons. I thought I knew where I might be able to go to get some answers, but the problem was I really didn't have the complete question. For several days I considered going back over to see my old Army buddy Walter regarding my late night visitors, but in the end I decided not to do it. I didn't want to inadvertently involve him in something neither of us knew anything about or understood. For the time being, I was content to let things lie.

CHAPTER 2
THE LOST STUDENT

As I felt somebody tugging on my sleeve, bringing me back from my daydream, I was a little embarrassed. I looked around the table and saw everybody had picked up their cards but me. I quickly picked them up and fanned them out. Now that I was playing cards for the first time in a long time, it felt good. Well, kind of. I was enjoying being with my friends, but so far the evening had not gone well for me card-wise, and I figured I was down about sixty bucks. Looking over the cards I'd just been dealt wasn't helping. Not one pair, and I couldn't even scrape up a flush. I was trying to keep a good attitude and not move around too much in my chair, but I just couldn't settle down and concentrate.

Tonight there were eight of us gathered to play: Wheeler, Randy Ralph, my best friend Scott, Tom who was hosting tonight's game, a black gentlemen named William Tate, two newcomers to our game and me. Lamenting the money I'd lost so far, I remembered that old song and I decided it didn't matter if you were ahead or behind, it wasn't a good idea to count your money at the table unless you were trying to cover a bet.

When Wheel showed up for the evening's game, as always he was wearing a bespoke suit complete with vest that was well tailored to fit his stout form. All the way around, Wheel looked a lot better tonight than the last time we had played poker together. Tonight seemed to be his night. I remembered when it was my night and I won the houseboat, and Wheel had stomped off mad at all of us. Tonight he kept getting great cards and when a couple of us started raising the pot, he was the winner.

The hand we were playing ended with me throwing my cards in early. And like so many other hands for me this evening, I would have lost anyway. Scott started pulling in his winnings and a couple of the other players went back into the kitchen to grab a fresh beer while Randy Ralph stepped outside for a smoke. I had noticed William Tate looking at me off and on all evening. Now that we had a break, he asked if he could speak to me alone. I stood and motioned for him to follow me into the next room.

The year William "Tubs" Tate left college, he was considered the top professional basketball prospect of the year. Since his hobby was playing jazz drums in a band, his nickname was Tubs. Because of his size, one of the top drum manufacturers had made him a custom trap set. The bass drum was almost twice the size of a normal one and every piece of equipment was made to fit his 6'11" frame. His quintet had recorded a couple of CDs and he had given all of the poker players copies when they were released. Bill was almost as good at playing drums as he was at basketball, and that's saying something.

We entered the next room and I quietly closed the door behind us. "What's up, William?" I asked.

"Bill. Come on Matt, please, call me Bill or Tubs." He continued, "I know you're buddies with a couple of Seattle detectives," he paused and I nodded, "and I've heard stories about your time in the service." This time I shrugged. I wasn't being uncommunicative; I just didn't have much to say to Bill's comments. My service days were a long time ago, and I would just as soon keep those memories behind me.

To be polite, I interjected, "Yes, I'm friends with a couple of Seattle cops and normally I tell folks I was a musician in the band during my time in the service. But just between the two of us, yeah, I did some strange shit when I was in Nam. But Bill, that part of my life is long past. 'Sides, I'm not really supposed to discuss any part of what went down, even to this day. Anyway, why'd ya bring it up?" While I was in the service, I'd been selected for some special training and during my time in Viet Nam, I had been places that even today our government claims we were never in and I did things there our government says were never done. It's a part of my life I don't like to either discuss, or think much about. I am not proud of the fact I took some lives over there, but at the time it was either them or me. Guess who I chose.

I could tell Bill was nervous about something, and I watched as he fiddled with his watch, and then straightened the large, jewel-encrusted ring on his finger. It was obvious he had more to say, but he seemed to be having a problem getting to it. Finally, to help things along I said, "Tubs, it's obvious you want to tell me something." He mumbled something and I continued, "How about you just start talking and if I don't understand something, I'll ask questions. Okay?"

Bill gave me a fleeting smile and then started, "Thanks. This is tough. Well, it's about my daughter Kim. She was doing so well at the U, then last semester she took an incomplete in every class but one, and she got a D in that class. Matt, she was a 4.0 student."

When he paused, I interrupted him. Family problems are something I have no desire to get involved with. "Look guy, excuse me for interrupting here, but I'm afraid I don't see why you're talking to me. My GPA in college was a negative number." He smiled at my little joke. "What makes you think I can help?"

He looked down at the floor for a moment and then back at my face. "Well, I know you never talked about the house-boat you won from Slim, but we all heard the stories. We all know Ralph likes to talk and we all kinda knew Slim."

I said, "Okay, Randy Ralph likes to talk, but I still don't see why you're coming to me. What is it you think I can do?"

Bill finally took a deep breath and then blurted out, "Well, Samara—that's her mother—Samara and I think she's doing drugs of some sort. I know she was taking something to keep her going when she was doing finals and all, and maybe she got hooked or…" Bill stopped.

I knew I wanted this conversation to end. For one, it was embarrassing for both of us, and reason number two was I didn't see how I could help. To be honest, I didn't want to get involved in anybody's family difficulties. I ran my hands through my silvered hair and as nicely, but as firmly as I could, I told him, "Bill, I still fail to see how I can be of any help. It sounds like you and Samara think your daughter dropped out of school because of some sort of drug addiction?" He agreed and why I asked the next sentence I'll never know. "What would you want me to do about your problem?"

"I don't know." And with that, the huge man standing before me bowed his head again and this time I saw his shoulders were shaking. Oh shit, Bill was crying. When he looked back at me there were tears in his eyes and on his cheeks. "I really don't know what to do, Matt. You know I played professional ball." I knew Bill had been the top basketball prospect the year he was drafted into the pros, and once he was playing professional ball, he'd been mostly responsible for two different teams ending up with a couple of championship seasons each.

Bill continued, "Not to brag, Matt, but I had ice water in my veins at the end of some of those games we won. Put me in with seconds to go, give me the ball and I would bring you the win, bank on it! Not conceit on my part, it was how it was. I knew I could do it and I just made it happen, but right now I feel so helpless. I just thought you might have an idea, something you thought you could do to help. I know I'm just grasping at straws."

I felt a little badly about wanting to sweep his problems under the rug. And now it seemed like with every question I asked, I was getting in deeper. "Where is Kim right now?"

"Neither her mother nor I know," he paused. "And that frightens both of us."

"Have you filed a missing person's report?"

Bill fidgeted. "Well, we don't actually know if she *is* missing. Sometimes she shows up at her mom's and spends the night, but she hasn't been there for a few days. Kim hates my new wife so the only time I get to see her is when we have lunch or dinner. It isn't so unusual for me not to see her very often. Besides, I live over in Bellevue, and Kim doesn't come that way at all.

"Both her mother and I have tried for several days now to call her but it goes straight to voicemail. I spoke to her about five days ago. Her roommate says she hasn't seen her either," Bill grimaced and he continued, "but then her roommate has a new boyfriend and she's been hanging out with him a lot. Kim could have been back to her room and left without her roommate knowing."

I understood Bill's daughter's attitude about Bellevue. Between Seattle and Bellevue is a large lake called Lake Washington. When people refer to the east side everybody around here knows what the reference is. Bellevue is on the east side of the lake, it's difficult to get to and a lot of people also call it the "evil side," and because of the horrible driving conditions over there, I tend to agree. I took a deep breath and knew I was going to regret my next question. "So what do you want me to do?" I asked.

"Matt, I've watched you. The other players respect you. You've always been a straight up person, someone you can trust. From what I heard about Ross Island and what you did, well, I thought if there was anybody who could poke around, it was you."

I was not happy to hear about any rumors about what happened up on Ross Island. I wanted to end this part of the conversation right now. I held up both hands, palms out. "I have no idea what you heard about Ross Island, but I'm telling you what you heard are probably some half-truths and some embellishment. Let me tell you this, I did some stupid things and I was really lucky that day. I could have just as easily been pushing up daisies right now, so if what you think happened on the island has anything to do with your request, please forget about it."

"Fine," he paused, looking for the right words. "But you still, umm, well, you seem to know your way around, if you catch my drift? Please look into this for me," he quickly added, "and Samara."

I knew I was going to regret this, but seeing this dark handsome mountain of a man humbling himself before me, how could I say no? "Oh shit, Bill. Give me her cell number and her address and I'll check around tomorrow. Okay?"

The next thing I knew I was wrapped in two arms of steel and the breath was being squeezed out of my body. "Thanks Matt!" Bill clapped me on the back. "Thanks. I owe you!"

"Okay Tubs!" I tried to breathe. "Then how about letting go of me?" I managed to gasp. The pressure around my chest eased.

We went back to playing cards, but the cards didn't get any better for me and my mind wasn't on the game anymore. I was trying to figure out how I was going to help Bill. Or should I say I was trying to figure out how to let Bill down without hurting his feelings. I really didn't want to get involved in anybody's family problems, even the famous Bill Tate.

Trying to wiggle out of helping Bill wasn't because of any time restraints on me. I'm semi-retired and life has been really good to me. Over the years my dad had bought a lot of real estate and one of his basic concepts is to never sell any real estate... ever! Due to his incredible forethought, I am able to live a very good life. That and one of my sister's boyfriends once called me many years ago and told me there was going to be a new stock coming up soon and I had to put every dime I could get my hands on and purchase mass amounts of this stock. He assured me that it was going to make me one very happy camper. I did what he told me and he was right. I ended up being one very, very happy camper. Oh, the name of the stock? Some dinky little company called Microsoft. I purchased 1,865 shares on the day it was issued at $21 a share and over time it's split nine times. Best forty grand I ever spent.

~ ~ ~ ~

It was late when I finally got back to my place and my puppy was ready to go outside. I opened up the back door and Beanie took off at a run down the walkway. I thought it was strange how Beanie stayed away from the spot where I had buried my last dog, Blackjack. It was as if she knew the spot was hallowed, somehow very special to me and she didn't want to disturb BJ. I was grateful.

Halfway across the vacant lot Beanie came to a stop, squatted down, and started to pee. It lasted a long time and I was so proud of her; she had held it in all evening. She was working out so much better than I could have hoped. Much better than things had with my kind-of-ex-girlfriend Sharon.

33

I know, you ask what is a 'kind-of-ex-girlfriend?' I was still madly in love with Sharon, but the two of us living together just didn't work out. It takes a lot to make a relationship work, and we both knew it, but for some reason, we just couldn't. We still saw each other and dated, and just a couple of nights ago she had spent the night. I can hear you all now, *just like a male, only thinking about sex!* We do care for one another, but on a day-to-day basis, we rubbed each other the wrong way. We had never really sat down and discussed where things were with the two of us, we just lived in different places. I figured we were both too headstrong to live together. At work she was the head nurse in the emergency room at the local hospital. All day long she was in charge and when she came home, she found it difficult to give up control.

As for me, I've been on my own for too long. I just can't find it in me to check with anybody about what I want to do. When we finally decided to live separately, both of us were relieved. The sale I thought I had on the houseboat I had won fell through, and I was still stuck with it. A couple of weeks ago when it was obvious things were not working out between us, I offered it to her to use since her apartment downstairs had been rented. She moved in right away and really loved the houseboat.

Beanie pawed at my foot, letting me know she was finished with her visit to the lot and we went back inside. Beanie went straight to the pantry and sat down, staring at the door. She was ready for her treat. She had been outside, done her duty and now it was time for a reward. She knew the drill and was always upset when I didn't perform my end. I opened the fridge, removed a jug of orange juice and drank straight from the container. After I put the jug back in the fridge we headed off to bed. As I lay there trying to fall asleep, Bill's request came floating to mind.

I mulled it over, wondering why I'd ever agreed to try and help him. I guess seeing a guy cry is even more disturbing to me that seeing a woman cry and I felt I had to say yes. But what did I know about finding missing girls? As sleep drifted over me, I decided I'd spend a couple of hours tomorrow going over to her apartment so I could tell Bill I'd tried, but wasn't successful.

At least I could honestly say I had tried…

CODE NAME: CRESCENT

CHAPTER 3
KIM'S APARTMENT

The next morning, weather-wise, was a little better than the night before. The storm had passed and the rain had stopped, but the pale, anemic sun trying to peek through the cloud cover was alas not having much success. I was standing in the vacant lot watching Bean explore, musing over what possibly could have happened overnight that she would feel it necessary to check out the lot in such careful detail. I decided to call the phone number Bill had given me for his daughter the night before. The call went straight to voicemail and since Kim would have no idea who I was, I could see no reason to leave her a message. Finally, Beanie finished with her inspection and started walking down the walkway headed back to my unit. I followed her.

My coffee had finished percolating and I poured a cup, finishing it off with a good dollop of half and half. After Beanie got her treat, I took my cup to the front room and curled up in my favorite chair. As I sat there, I thought about my conversation with Bill the night before, and I figured I had two ways to attack the problem. The first was to drive by the address Bill had given me and see what I could find. The second was to call my friend at the cell phone service and see if she could at least tell me the last time Kim had turned on her phone, and maybe even the location of her last call. I decided to try the apartment first.

I finished my coffee and took the empty cup to the kitchen and rinsed it out. As I headed down to the garage, Bean was right at my heels and when I opened up the door to my truck, she jumped into the passenger seat and settled herself. Pulling out of the garage, I found myself glancing over at where Sharon used to park and I felt a small tug at my heartstrings. I really did care for her, but we seemed to keep pushing each other's buttons and we just couldn't leave well enough alone. As I pulled onto the street, I decided I was going to stop by the houseboat and see her tonight.

Have you ever felt like somebody was looking at you? Maybe you were sitting in a restaurant and you just knew somebody was looking at you and when you looked over, they were. You didn't know why you felt that way, but you did and you were right. When I pulled out of the garage, I got that feeling. When I looked left and right to pull out, there was nobody standing on the street, but there was still that creepy feeling I was being watched. I thought to myself, "But why? Who would be watching me?" All the way over to the U, I tried to figure what was setting off the alarm in my head.

I remember from the days back in Nam, the times when things didn't feel right and your instincts told you something was wrong. Those who developed those feelings and trusted them came home alive, those who dismissed them often went home in a body bag. It had been a long time since my internal alarm had gone off, and I wondered what had set it off this time.

Kim's apartment was located a few blocks from the U and when I parked the truck, I left the windows down a little so Beanie would have fresh air. I walked up to the apartment and knocked on the door, not expecting to find anybody there. I was very surprised when the door opened a sliver and an eye peeked out at me. The thing that surprised me even more was that it was a male. "Whadda ya want?" a voice growled at me.

I could see no reason for any pleasantries. "I'm looking for Kim Tate," I told the eye.

"She ain't here," the eye replied, still no more friendly than when we started.

The door moved a little as the eye started to shut it and I quickly asked, "Do you know where she is?"

"No."

"Who are you?" I asked.

The eye blinked and the voice replied, "Who the hell are *you* and why do I have to answer you?"

"I'm a friend of Kim's dad and her parents are worried about her. They've tried to call her without any success. They're trying to find her. Let me ask you again, do you know where she is?"

"No," the voice said and the door started to shut again. I reached out and gave the door a swift, hard push. My action caught the person behind the door off guard and he fell backwards. I stepped in as the door swung open. Once inside, I realized the young man lying on the floor was naked. As he started to get up I could see he was a tall, scrawny kid and not very attractive naked, at least not to me. He growled at me, "Who the fuck are you to barge in here? Get out!"

A voice came from the back of the apartment. "Who is it Bennie? Who's here?" A young woman wearing only a pair of panties stepped into the room. Since she was Caucasian, I assumed she was not Kim Tate. She didn't seem to be the least bit ashamed of standing in front of me wearing nothing but a pair of panties so sheer I could see her little trimmed strip of hair, as she just stood looking at me and asked, "Who are you?"

"Hello, my name is Matt, Matt Preston. I apologize for busting in but I'm a friend of Kim's dad and he asked me to try and locate her. Her parents haven't heard from her for six days now. I assume you're her roommate?" She nodded as she smiled at me. I waited for her to tell me her name and when she didn't, I asked, "Do you have a name?"

I got another quick smile as she responded, "Samantha, ah Samantha Pierce. My friends call me Sam."

I could tell she was not a boy kind of Sam. She had a reasonably cute body, small breasted with nipples hard from the cool air. I was just going to ignore the young lady who was all but naked and keep on with my conversation, but it was extremely difficult. I told myself to stay focused. "Do you know where Kim is?" I asked her.

The young lady was making no effort to cover herself and the way she stood there looking at me, I wondered if she was perhaps stoned. Her dark hair was long and she had a pretty face. I thought her figure was pleasant overall but she was oh so young. Kind of cute but way too young. I swear I was never that young.

She smiled briefly at me again and answered, "She left a few days ago. I have no idea where she went."

I started in with a barrage of questions, "Do you know if she's okay? Do you remember the last time you saw her?" From the look on Sam's face, she wasn't following my questions. I decided to focus on just one question at a time. "When was the last time you saw her?"

I watched Sam's face as she thought over the last few days. "I think I saw her five nights ago. Me and Bennie have been hanging at his place but that was the night we came over cause I needed to get some things."

"If you don't mind, how come you told Kim's dad it was six nights ago? Do you remember which one it was?"

Her face looked puzzled. "Bennie keeps me kinda busy and I lose track of stuff." She giggled as she grinned at me as if I understood what that meant. I thought I did, but I really didn't want to delve too deeply. She continued, "Now that I think about it, it was five nights ago. I stop by here during the day to get books and stuff, and once in a while it looks like things are moved around, but then Bennie might have moved things too." Sam stood there for a moment and I could see she was thinking about something.

"What is it?" I asked her.

"Well like, Kim has a really neat sweater and a sexy bra that you wear under it and it sort of shows through, ya know. We trade stuff once in a while. I wanted to wear it the other day and I couldn't find it. I know it was here last week, so I guess Kim is coming in and getting fresh clothes." She was still again and then made a little jump which started things jiggling. "I'm sure some of the food is gone from the fridge cause Bennie hates what we have and I know there's stuff missing."

"Does Kim have a boyfriend?" I noticed that Bennie was heading back toward the rear of the apartment, I hoped to put some clothes on. He had a skinny butt and the sight of him from this view was not any more attractive than his front.

Sam paused for a moment, perhaps wondering what she wanted to say to me. "There was a guy she was dating, but she dropped him."

"Any idea why?" I asked.

"Oh yeah. He tried to rape her. Besides that, he actually did rape one of Kim's friends." The young lady said it like it was no big deal. She was very matter of fact and the way she told me made my skin crawl. It seemed irrelevant to the roommate Kim was almost raped and another girl actually was.

"Sam, you don't seem to be very upset about it." I really hadn't planned on being so blunt, but her attitude bothered me.

41

Sam shrugged her shoulders and the way things swayed forced me to concentrate. "Nothing I can do about it. I told her not to go out with him. I told her I knew girls who went out with him and they ended up regretting it. I told her he was nothing but trouble." Sam frowned. "I'm not her mother. Shit, can you believe he even raped Kim's best friend? He claims she wanted it. Kim caught the two of them together and she said it looked like rape to her. Kim told me she was going to try and do something about what he did to her and her friend. I told her to just forget it.

"Anyway, the word around school is he's done stuff like that more than once. The rumor is he likes his sex rough. But, he's a player so the school looks the other way and it all gets swept under the rug. The women are told to keep still and that's the end of it."

"Player?" I asked, and I was sure I had a puzzled look on my face.

"Yeah, you know, like he's a big time football star... a player. Where you been? I don't know the position, but he's supposed to be drafted next year. Anyway, like I said, I told her to stay away from him, but she didn't listen."

"How long ago did Kim's attempted rape take place?"

"Couple of weeks ago or so." Again she shrugged her shoulders.

"Did she tell anybody else besides you?"

Sam shook her head. Her standing there almost nude made it really difficult to keep my mind on what she was saying. "I don't know exactly. I know she complained to his coach and some people at the main office like the men's dean. Kim told me she was going to find a way to get even and see if maybe she could get him charged with something. She wanted to see if she could at least get him suspended from the team, but I kept telling her there was no point. Like I said, he's a player. Can't touch him." Her wry smile seemed to say, 'what are you gonna do?'

"May I ask you another question?"

"Sure."

"Was Kim doing drugs?"

I thought there was a slight hesitation before she answered, "Nope. She tried some pot but didn't like it. I even made some brownies and she wouldn't eat them," Sam paused and then her face lit up. "Hey, do you want a brownie? I got some in the fridge. Me and Bennie just had a couple and they're really good." She giggled.

That explained a lot. This young lady was stoned out of her gourd. "So, Kim didn't do any drugs at all?" I asked again.

"Well, she did speed when we had to pull an all-nighter, but everybody does speed. That ain't doin' drugs," she explained to me like I was mentally deficient.

"Can I leave my card and if you see Kim, please ask her to call me or her parents? It really is important."

"Sure, put it over there," and she pointed to a countertop. As I turned to go, she reached out and grabbed my arm. "Are you sure you don't want a brownie? They're really strong!"

"Thanks!" I smiled. "Next time, okay?"

"Okay, next time. I'm going back to bed. I'm tired."

The young lady turned and as she started to head in the direction Bennie had gone, I noticed a tattoo at the base of her spine. A tramp stamp. I thought to myself if there was one gal who deserved her tattoo, it was this one. And even before I finished that thought, I felt badly. Who was I to judge this young lady? It was her life and she was entitled to live it as she pleased. Maybe she was an honor student and had a 4.0 grade point average. But to be honest, I kinda doubted it.

I thought of one last question. "Before you go, what was Kim's boyfriend's name?"

Sam turned back to look at me. "Claude Cox," she said and then added, "But they call him Bud." She smiled sweetly at me and turned away. As I left the apartment, I was totally rattled. I knew who Bud Cox was. Bud Cox was the star running back on the varsity football team. Bud Cox was most of the reason the U won the national championship last year.

Last year I went to several games, and one of my favorite memories of Bud was when they played Alabama and all by himself he rolled right over *The Tide*. It was beautiful! I had really enjoyed watching Bud run up and down the field, but after what I had just heard, now I wasn't such a big Bud fan.

~ ~ ~ ~

I sat in my truck for a while, going over the conversation with Kim's roommate. Her information about Bud really upset me. I really liked watching Cox and it bothered me to think he might be a rapist.

Normally when I want to think about things, I head over to my man cave, as it would be called nowadays. My man cave is the top floor of a building where I store my collection of old cars. The city recently sent me a letter notifying me the building had been condemned, but several property owners on the block have taken the city to court and are fighting it. The city wants to raze all of the buildings in a two-block area and build new multi-use fancy condos with retail space in the lower levels. As I said, we're trying to fight it, but just in case, I'm looking for a place to move my collection. I'd also sold a couple of the cars to make it easier in case I have to find temporary storage. I decided I wanted to head for my hideout.

I reached out and turned the key in the ignition to start my truck. The motor didn't catch right away and in order to restart the vehicle, you have to turn the key to 'off' and then turn it 'on' to try and restart. In the quiet between turning the key to off and then on again, I heard the sound of another vehicle starting. Most Chrysler products produce a very distinctive sound when you engage the starter. I always thought it sounded like a threshing machine. By the sound, I knew somewhere somebody had just fired up a Chrysler product.

Looking back down the line of cars I spotted a dark gray van sitting on the other side of the street facing my way. It was a large Dodge with darkened windows. I waited a few seconds longer to see if it pulled out and when it didn't, I started my truck and pulled away from the curb. When I turned left at the end of the street, I saw the gray van had pulled out behind me.

I kept looking back as I drove and the van matched me turn for turn. Remembering my feeling from earlier this morning, I decided to see if this van was actually following me. When I got to a street that would take me over to the freeway, I turned. The van followed. I got on the freeway, stayed in the far right lane, and watched as the van did the same. This was getting too weird. I took the next exit and tried to time a couple of lights to turn red just as I was going through. When I looked up, the van was still back there. I decided to drive through my old neighborhood where I knew various strange little streets and if you didn't know what you were doing, you could get lost fairly easily.

I came to the alley I was looking for and quickly sped up. A fast left, then a right, then a left and down another alley. Partway down the street I had entered from the alley I made a quick left turn, which headed down a steep hill and turned into a sharp right turn. Another right turn and back up a little hill and another tight right and I pulled into Mrs. Spring's old garage. Mrs. Spring had been our next door neighbor when I was a kid. She had since passed away and her house burned down shortly after her death. The old stand-alone garage is still there and it was this garage I was using to hide from the gray van. I shut off the motor, slipped out of my truck and waited. Unless you pulled in behind the garage, my truck was totally hidden. I was not surprised when the van drove by one way and then minutes later drove back the other way. As the van passed by, I copied down the license number, thinking I would ask my buddy down at the cop shop to run the plate through DOL. I waited for about fifteen minutes and then pulled out carefully. I kept to as many back roads as I could and when I got close to my apartment, I parked a block up behind it, near the vacant lot.

After somebody looking for some information had broken into my place, I'd had the steel mesh door fitted with the best lock I could buy. I was told that no lock was totally foolproof, but the lock I purchased was as close to pick proof as possible. Beanie and I crossed the lot and entered my apartment through the steel mesh door. Once we were in, I locked the thing back up again. I summoned the elevator and took it up to my rooftop. Stepping as close to the edge of the roof as I could manage, I looked down at the cars parked on the streets below. Halfway down the block, I saw it; a dark gray Dodge van with the windows blacked out. I wondered who was following me and why. I was planning to go to see my police friend, Jeff L. the next day and this was one more reason to do it. I wanted to know who owned that gray van. Who was taking such an interest in my life all of a sudden?

I discovered I was hungry and I went back down to my apartment and opened up the fridge. I moaned as I looked over the slim pickings in front of me. I was going to see Jeff L. tomorrow, but right now I needed to do something about my empty larder.

And then the phone rang and that idea went out the window.

CHAPTER 4
THE MEETING

The deep rumble from my motorcycle rolled around the hills surrounding the abandoned multi-purpose track and field as I rode up to the gap in the deteriorated fence that encircled the entire field. This was the field from my youth at my outdated and now vacant junior high school. Once upon a time the grassy patch in front of me had been a football field with a track surrounding the perimeter, but now the track was choked with weeds and completely overgrown, while the field was full of holes and rough sod. There would be no more games played on this field. The uprights for the goal posts still stood at each end of the field, but the crossbars were long gone. This was where I had watched my old friend Jeff quarterback the varsity team back in the day. This was a field loaded with a ton of memories.

I stopped my bike in front of the bent and twisted remains of the dilapidated gate. One side was totally missing and what was left dangled on one rusty hinge. I leaned forward and turned off the bike and just sat there, looking around at the deserted field. It was quiet and the only sounds marring the evening were the "tink… tink" of the cooling metal of the bike's motor.

I looked around at what was left of the old school. The windows of the junior high were boarded up, and the doors covered with steel mesh, all padlocked to keep out unwanted visitors. The whole structure was just sitting there waiting to be demolished. The problem was there wasn't even enough money in the budget to pull the old structure down, so there it stood, once a proud school built just after the war to educate the baby-boomers,a but now it was no longer needed or wanted. I thought it was sad to see what "in the day" had been such an important part of my youth, now deteriorated and waiting to be razed.

It had been a surprise when McNaulty, my visitor of the other night, had called me and told me they wanted to meet me, but when he told me to meet at my old junior high football field, I was flabbergasted. It seemed like a very strange place to have a meeting. On the phone, the colonel had told me he would meet me in the bleachers. Since there was only one small portion of the bleachers still remaining, it wasn't difficult to ascertain where our meeting place was supposed to be. The one thing I did notice as I rode onto the school grounds was the field was empty, completely empty. I debated riding my bike across the field over to the remaining bleacher, but I also didn't want to attract any undue attention. I had the feeling we were not supposed to be hanging around the old school.

I parked the bike next to what was left of the gate and started walking across the field. When I got to the old bleacher, I saw there were only a couple of planks scattered among the remaining stands for anybody to sit on. Time and the weather had rotted out the rest of the wooden seats, and as I climbed to the top of the stand, I wondered if the remaining decayed wooden bench was going to hold my weight. I carefully sat on the top stoop, waiting for somebody to show up, still thinking this was without a doubt the weirdest place I had ever met with anybody.

About twenty minutes later a van pulled slowly onto the field and headed directly toward me. When he turned the headlights off I could see it was a Dodge with blacked out windows. The back door slid open, spilling out the colonel and the suit. As they stepped to the bottom of the stand I thought to myself that that was one question answered. I now knew who the mysterious van belonged to. They stayed on the ground looking up at me for a long time.

With a deep sigh, the colonel asked, "Are you coming down?"

"Naw, I like the view from up here. Come on up and take a load off."

I could see no reason to put myself out. When they called earlier this afternoon they demanded I come to this deserted field and meet them at dusk. They had offered no reason why I should show up, just a veiled threat if I didn't.

The suit stayed on the field while the colonel crawled up to sit next to me. Tonight he was not wearing a uniform, but he made the slacks, shirt and light jacket he was wearing look like one. Again there were no pleasantries to start our conversation. "Do you know why we had you meet us here?" he asked me as he swept his hand, motioning towards the abandoned field.

"I doubt if it's cause you want me to turn out for the football team." My smart assed remark got neither a smile nor a comment. I continued, "No, I don't. But I'll admit, I was wondering."

"This is where you went to junior high," McNaulty told me as if he was sharing some great new revelation.

"No shit." I looked at him with as much disdain as I could. "I knew that, and if you had asked me on the phone I could have told you and we wouldn't be out here now."

"Don't get smart. We wanted to talk to you some more and we also wanted you to understand there's nothing about you we don't know. Your past, your present and your future." I had to admit having me meet them out here on my old deserted junior high school playing field had rattled me, and it did make me wonder just how much they really might know about me.

I shrugged my shoulders. "Okay. Let's say for the sake of argument I'm impressed. Why did you bring me out here, other than to show off your knowledge about my past?"

"We want to ask you a question, and your answer will have consequences. We demand that you tell us. What do you know about Crescent?"

I stared at the colonel with contempt. I could see no reason to hide it. "You have got to be fucking kidding me. Are you telling me that's why I had to meet you here?" I waved my hand towards the deserted school. I couldn't hide the anger in my voice. "*This* is why we're sitting here on a rotten old bleacher? You know, you two are really starting to piss me off. I told you before, I don't know anything about Crescent."

I looked down at suit and raised my voice, "I don't know a darn thing about Crescent. Can you hear me?" Suit just stood there looking up at me so I said it even louder. "Hello! Listen to me! I don't know a darn thing about Crescent. Did you hear me this time?" Suit nodded and I looked back at the colonel as I continued, "I'm assuming it was some code word for something you think I was involved with in the past. But I'm telling you, as somebody famous once said, 'read my lips.' I know nothing about Crescent."

"What's your involvement with Bill Tate?"

That question surprised me. It surprised me because of the abrupt change in subjects and their knowledge of my assistance to Bill in finding Kim. But, I was still flipping them shit. "That's none of your business."

"Preston, I won't ask you again. What's your involvement with Tate? Why are you asking around about his daughter?"

I wondered how much they knew. I now knew it was the two of them who had been following me in the van. Is that how they had found out I had been looking for Tate's daughter? I was just about out of patience but I told them, "I know Tate from our poker games. He plays with us from time to time. At the last game he asked me to help find his daughter."

"Why you?"

"He thought I might be able to learn more than the police have so far."

"Why doesn't he just file a missing person's report?"

"He doesn't really know if she's missing. The mother thinks Kim—that's the daughter—has been home when she wasn't there and picked up some of her clothes. The roommate also thinks she's stopped by, but the roommate has this new boyfriend and spends all her time with him. Nobody's seen the daughter for several days and Tate asked me to check it out."

"And…?"

"And nothing. I'm going to leave messages in a couple of places for her to call me when I get a chance. Right now I'm trying to get the address where she may be hiding and convince her to come and stay at a better safe house than where she might be now. A place where she has access to somebody who can help her with the problems left over from her attempted rape."

"You mean your nurse friend."

I was impressed and dismayed by their knowledge of my life. "Yeah. Sharon works in the ER at one of the hospitals up on Pill Hill. She has a lot of training in dealing with rape victims." I let the colonel stew on this bit of information for a while. Finally, I couldn't stand it anymore and I asked,

"Why did you call this meeting? Other than to impress me you knew about my past?"

My question was ignored once again. "Have you discussed Crescent with anybody?"

I had enough and I exploded. "DAMN!" I screamed. "Are you guys some kind of 'tards'?"

The colonel looked at me with a quizzical look on his face. "Tards? What are tards?" he asked.

I was still shouting. "You two! You're both 'tards. You know. 'tards —as in retards, the people who ride the little bus to school and lick the windows. You ride in a van, do you lick the windows too?" I know I wasn't being very PC, but I was pissed. I shouted my next question at both of them. "What is it with you two? How the hell can I discuss something I know nothing about?"

"So you say…"

I snapped back, "Well it just happens to be the truth."

"Did you discuss this with Walter McLaughlin?" the colonel asked.

"Walter?" The colonel nodded. "What does he have to do with this? Why are you asking about him?" I was concerned when they asked about Walter, my old friend from my time in country, as he didn't take to outsiders well and they could cause no end of trouble if they tried to go and talk to him.

"Because you went and saw him right after you got out of the hospital." I should have been surprised they knew this, but I wasn't. I did wonder how they found out I was over on the peninsula.

I wanted to keep Walter out of this if possible. "I just went over to check on him and see if he was doing okay, and also to talk to him about stuff. I do that every so often."

"Like what stuff?"

"I fail to see how it's any of your business," I retorted.

"Seems a bit strange you would go and see him right after you were released from the hospital. Did you discuss Crescent with him?"

I sat for a moment and stared at them. When I finally spoke, my voice was dripping with anger. "Both of you, besides being really lame, are totally pissing me off." I raised my voice. "I know nothing about Crescent." A thought came to mind. "Why, do you think Walter knows something about Crescent?"

"That's none of your concern."

By now I was well beyond pissed. I exploded, "What is it with you two? I keep telling you I don't know a thing about Crescent. You demand I come to a rundown, abandoned sports field at dusk just to prove you did your homework, and now you're threatening me. I'm done with you two." I looked at the colonel and then down at suit. Raising my voice, I said, "Leave me alone, both of you. I'm not military and you cannot give me orders." I started to stand.

"Sit down, Preston." The colonel's voice was cold.

"No! I'm done with you two." As I started to walk down the rickety stairs I saw suit reaching inside of his jacket. "What's this, now? Mr. Pillsbury is going to shoot me?"

Suit finally spoke, "What do you mean, Mr. Pillsbury?"

This dude was dense. "I mean, as in Pillsbury Doughboy." Normally I would never have been that cruel, but I was not in a good mood. The colonel looked at the suit when I mentioned him shooting me and he frowned and shook his head.

The colonel said, "Mr. Preston, do you still have the papers you signed when you were assigned to your unit in Viet Nam?"

Somehow I didn't like where this conversation was headed. "No. I threw them away a long time ago."

"That's a shame." He shook his head. "Perhaps if you read them again you would find the clause where you agreed to be subject to the military until you reach the age of seventy. And then you can also read the part about being called back to active duty at any time during that period. Does that ring a bell?"

I remembered signing a lot of papers when I was shipped out. And when I got to my unit as well. Maybe I should have read them more closely, but I didn't. Hey, I trusted the military… then. "I'm not calling you a liar, sir, but I would like to see a copy of those papers, with my signature."

Suit was doing the talking now, "We can provide them for you. What we are telling you—"

The colonel interrupted suit, "Mr. Preston, as far as we know, you were the only one who had any contact with Hollis towards the end of his life."

I shook my head at the colonel. "That's not quite accurate. There was a stripper named Lan who knew both Hollis and Price back in country. It was my understanding that both Hollis and Price stayed with Lan for a time. I have no idea what they discussed, but she might have known something about Crescent."

"Do you know where this stripper is now?" suit asked eagerly.

"Not exactly. She's buried somewhere."

Their eyes got wide and they spoke the one word at the same time, "Buried!"

"Yes, buried." I couldn't help it, I'm a smartass. "That's what they do with dead people."

The colonel asked, "How did she die?"

"I believe Hollis killed her. I was with a police detective when we found her and he held her as she died."

The colonel continued, "Did she say anything before she died?"

"Yes." I waited. I just knew they were going to love my next answer.

"Well, what did she say?" The colonel finally exploded.

"She talked in her native language. The cop spoke her language and he understood what she was saying. I just know it wasn't any dialect I understood."

Both of them asked at the same time, "Who was the cop?"

"Sakol."

Suit asked, "Who or what is a Sakol?"

"Sakol is the name of the Seattle detective who was with me when we found Lan. He knew the stripper's father back in country and he knew her when she was just a baby. They talked for quite some time as he held her before she died."

"Did you hear either of them say anything about Crescent?"

Again with the Crescent thing. "No, I didn't hear the word once. From what Sakol said, I got the impression she was asking him to tell her parents she was dead."

Suit asked, "Where can we find Sakol?" As an afterthought he added, "Is Sakol his first name or his last name?"

"I don't know. I've only heard him called Sakol."

"Where can we find him?" they asked in unison again.

"At the main Seattle police station."

"What?" the colonel shouted.

This was really going to be fun. "Yeah, Sakol is a Seattle cop. Remember, I told you he was a detective? He works homicide and I'll bet he'd really like you two."

The two of them glared at me for a moment and then looked at each other. It seemed I might finally won this round as the colonel swore and then they climbed back into the van, started it up and drove back across the field.

As I walked across the field behind them, I saw a police car arrive and turn on his flashing lights. The squad car partially blocked the exit and the officer was waiting for the van. I was too far away to hear anything, but I saw a hand extend from the driver's side of the colonel's vehicle and hand a piece of paper to the cop. The cop looked it over and then handed it back so quickly it could have been on fire. I had no idea what the piece of paper was, but it sure scared the hell out of the cop. The cop jumped back, made a very sloppy salute and then motioned for the colonel's van to leave.

I continued over to my bike and once I was there I flung my leg over the seat, flipped the switch and then started it. While it warmed up, I slipped on my helmet. When I drove past the cop I saw he was still standing there staring after the colonel's vehicle. I had no idea what went down between the colonel and the cop, but it sure left an impression on the cop. Once I was out in the street, I hightailed it back to my apartment.

Beanie was overjoyed to see me and I took her out back in the vacant lot. I waited for her to do her business and I wondered if I should give Sakol a heads up. When Beanie signaled me she was ready to go back inside, I followed her in. Once we were inside she got her treat and I rounded up my cell phone. I found Sakol in my contact list and pushed the send button.

He picked up on the third ring. He answered in his normal manner, "You talk, I listen."

"Sakol, it's Matt."

He sounded pleased when he heard my voice. I explained why I was calling him and that I wanted to give him a heads up. I ended with, "I don't really know who these two guys are, but they're obsessed with something called Crescent." The phone was still. So still I finally asked, "Sakol… you still there?"

In a very quiet voice Sakol asked, "They said Crescent? Are you positive?"

"Hell yes, Sakol, every time they talk to me all they do is question me about this Crescent thing. What do you know about it? Did Lan mention it before she died?"

Sakol answered quickly, "Matt, I have to run now. I will call you later." The phone went dead in my hand. I went to the fridge to get something cold to drink and when the door opened, once again I saw vast emptiness. Damn it, I still needed to go to the store and shop. As I stood there looking into my empty fridge, it dawned on me. Sakol had not used his pidgin English. Whatever Crescent was, it made him forget all about the Charlie Chan way he usually talked.

I was curious before, and I'd wanted to know what Crescent was, but now it was becoming an obsession. I was starting to think it was time to go and visit Walter. It was time to find out exactly what he knew about this thing.

Since the elves were not going to stock my refrigerator, I decided that it was time to head to the grocery store before I did anything more regarding Crescent or Kim.

CHAPTER 5
GLADYS

The line at the grocery store checkout stand was longer than normal. A lot longer. If my cupboards hadn't been so vacant, I would have left the store and returned later. But the total contents of my refrigerator consisted of a dried up lemon and half a bottle of catsup with some fuzzy green stuff growing inside. If I wanted food, I was stuck standing in line waiting to pay. Everyone seemed to have finished shopping at exactly the same time and there was just one harried, over-worked checker trying to process the customers as quickly as she could. I felt sorry for her plight and I was not going to make things worse by making a comment regarding the store's poor staffing.

Standing in the long line, bored out of my skull and with nothing better to do with my time, I started checking out the lovely, shapely bottom of the woman standing in front of me.

I know, I know. I'm a pig! But, in my defense, it was a nice butt, it deserved to be contemplated. You have to admit checking out a shapely bottom in a dress is much better than looking at the tabloid trash sitting in front of the checkout stand. How many times can anybody read about the president of the United States being the love child of a space alien and some TV star? Oh wait, that one was true. Anyway, the bottom that held my attention was far more interesting than any tabloid story.

Being a guy, I couldn't tell you what the fabric of her dress was, I just knew the garment clung to her body in a suggestive way and since it was a dress, not pants or shorts, but a dress, I was doubly entranced. I believe the correct term is draped, as in the dress draped well on her body. The woman may have been considered a bit heavyset when compared to today's idea of what women should look like, but the way her dress molded to her body made her very sensual. And since I hadn't seen her face yet, I had no idea how old she was. I didn't care. I was just scoping out her lovely round ass and very appealing presence, and waiting for the minutes to pass, thank you very much.

It seemed like every person in front of us was purchasing something that wouldn't ring up properly so the checker had to keep asking for a price check. It was taking forever to get out of the store, but at this point I didn't care. I was having an enjoyable time fantasizing about the lady in front of me in line. See what mischief a guy can get into just standing in a checkout line?

When it was the woman's turn, as she lifted her basket up onto the checkout counter, her purse caught on something and several items fell out onto the floor. The woman was busy trying to keep anything else from falling out of her purse, so I knelt down and started to pick up some of her stuff off the floor. I picked up a couple items and put them on the counter and then got the rest rounded up. As I placed these on the counter, I had an opportunity to look up into the woman's face. Looking down at me was a woman somewhere in her thirties and her long dark hair, soft brown eyes and sensual lips made her most pleasant to look at. When I put her things down, she smiled at me and in that instant she went from lovely to breathtaking.

She was tall enough so that we were almost looking at each other eye to eye. Her face seemed familiar and I had the nagging feeling I knew her, but I couldn't figure out why. Any woman this attractive I should remember. The front of her dress was cut low and showed off her soft voluptuous chest and an excellent amount of cleavage. Some women who carry extra weight are disproportionate, but this lady, even though larger than average, was perfect.

Her posture was good, in other words she was standing up straight. Sad to say, I have found that many heavier women seem to stand round-shouldered, as if to say they are ashamed of their bodies. This woman stood with her shoulders back and as I looked at her, I thought she looked great. Her attitude was sexy. She stood there proudly and totally comfortable in her own body. She just looked so at ease with who she was and what she was that it was one of the sexiest sights I'd ever seen in my twisted life.

The woman paid her bill and turned back to look at me. As she thanked me she smiled again and I thought to myself again what a really sexy woman she was. That was it. That's what set off the memory switch. As she picked up her bags to leave, I knew where I'd seen her before. The last time I had seen her she had been topless and was dancing at a strip club called Robbie's in North Seattle. It seemed that life was providing me all kinds of reminders about my escapade on Ross Island and my acquired houseboat.

I paid for my groceries and picked up my bags and when I got to my truck, I noticed the lovely woman was parked next to me. When she saw me, she put her window down, gave me that million-dollar smile and said, "One more time, thanks."

"You're welcome, it was no problem." And Beanie took that moment to get up and look out the window. The dancer was immediately taken by my cute little puppy.

"Oh my God, what a cute puppy. What's its name?"

"Brenna, but I call her Beanie. She's my baby."

"What a doll," she gushed.

I smiled back at the woman. "Thanks." I reached inside my truck and picked Beanie up. I moved over to the woman's car and held Beanie out. She reached out and took my puppy from my hands and as soon as Beanie was close enough, she reached out and licked the woman's face. The woman laughed as she tried to hold Beanie out of reach. Her eyes looked a little moist as she looked up at me. "She's adorable, what a sweetie." There's something about a puppy that just appeals to women, and Bean was the epitome.

"Thanks, she's very special to me." I paused for a moment and I felt this was as good a time as any to say something, since Bean continued to try and lick the woman's face. "Do you mind if I say something?"

She gave me a puzzled look and replied, "No, why?"

"Well, for starters, you are stunning." She beamed. I paused, not sure if she would appreciate that I recognized her from the club. "Well, I know who you are, or should I say I know what you do. I saw you at Robbie's a while ago."

She had a really cute grin on her face. "Really?" At that moment Bean managed to get in a good lick and because of her grin I felt more comfortable continuing.

"Yeah. And the reason I remember you so well is because you were by far the best dancer there the day I was there. Most of the other dancers just kind of moved and jiggled and made no effort to keep time with the music. They just took off their clothes and if there happened to be music playing, the two events were totally unrelated. You stood out in my mind because you actually danced, and kept time with the music, and," I was embarrassed now, "well, obviously your dancing made an impression on me because I still re-member it." I looked down and I felt like a dork.

"My, aren't you the silver-tongued devil?" She laughed and I liked the way she sounded. "Do you go to Rob-bie's often?"

"No, that time when I saw you I was trying to meet one of your fellow dancers because she knew the location of somebody I needed to find. And the last time I was there it was a real downer. We were trying to find the other dancer before somebody else did."

"What was the problem?" she asked, surprised.

"She knew some men from back where she came from and one of them was after her."

I watched as her face fell and I wondered if I should remove Bean from her car. She sighed. "Oh. Do you mean Lan?"

"Yeah." I noticed she had a tear in her eye and I stopped. "Hey, I'm sorry. I didn't mean to upset you." I felt bad I'd made her cry.

The woman sat looking forward for a moment and then looked up at me, and I could see she still had tears in her eyes. "Most of the girls are over it, but I was very close to Lan. It really hurt when we lost her. I also knew her parents. She took me up to Canada once to meet them. They were very special." She paused and looked back out of the wind-shield. Bean carefully reached up and gently licked at one of her tears. The dancer buried her face in Bean's coat and then kissed the top of her head. I could see she had been thinking about what I said and as she held Bean out to me, she asked, "Are you a cop?"

Bean squirmed, trying to return to the dancer's arms as I held her tightly. "No, I was just helping out." I was sorry to bring up unhappy memories for her and I found there was nothing more to say. I took a chance; holding Bean in one hand, I reached out with my other hand and touched her face, wiping away the tear that was sliding down her cheek. She surprised me and reached up and held my hand against her cheek, and then turned her face and kissed my palm.

Her smile was bittersweet and she whispered, "Thanks, you're sweet." She looked at Bean and said, "And your puppy is just as sweet."

I was still holding her face in my hand and I looked at the ground for a second. When I looked back at her, I had a tear in my eye as well. "For what it's worth, I've had a hard time with it as well, and the cop I was with that night is also having a hard time with it. He knew her parents back in the old country."

Her face perked up. "Are you talking about Sakol? You know Sakol?"

I took my hand away. "Yeah, we're friends."

"He is such a teddy bear. All of the girls just adore him. And that cute way he talks…"

I could see no reason to punch a hole in her balloon. I knew the truth about Sakol and the way he spoke. I had heard before that women thought he was sexy because of it, but this was my first encounter with women and Sakol. Funny, I've just never thought of him as a sexual being. I guess that proves you can't judge a book by its cover.

"What's your name?" I asked.

"My stage name is Sadie, but my real name is Gladys. The management doesn't like the girls to use their real names and they really don't like the name Gladys for a dancer." She grinned up at me. "Please let me hold your puppy some more." I decided the longer she held Bean, the longer I was going to be able to stand there and talk to her. I thought it a fair trade.

Between her comments and Bean's happiness in returning to Gladys' arms, all of it made me laugh. As far as watching a stripper named Gladys, I could see customers not getting all excited. I extended my hand and we shook. "I'm pleased to meet you, Gladys. My name is Matt, Matt Preston. Gladys, that's kind of an old fashioned name."

"Matt, I'm pleased to meet you, too," Gladys held up Bean in front of her face and Bean lunged forward, planting a wet tongue on the dancer's cheek. Giggling, she looked at Bean, "and I am happy to meet you too, little one.

"As far as the name goes, I'm named after a great aunt or somebody a long way back. By the way, thanks again for helping me back in the store and a really big thanks for not saying anything about me being a dancer. I mean, I have no problem being a dancer; it pays very well and it gives me a lot of free time, but there are times I would prefer people not know what I do for a living. They form an opinion and regardless of what I'm really like, I can't get past their preconceived notions. Anyway, I shop here a lot and they know me, but they don't know I'm an exotic dancer." I watched her face as a new thought struck her. "Hey, we're a long way from Robbie's, do you live around here?" By now Bean had crawled out of Gladys' lap and was exploring the interior of her car.

"Yeah, I live just over the hill. I have an apartment that looks out over Lake Union."

"Cool. I've always wanted to look out over a lake or over water. Must be nice."

"I'll admit, I do enjoy the view."

Gladys reached over and picked Bean up and handed her out to me. "Do you have a few minutes? Can I buy you a drink for helping a damsel in distress?" she asked.

Was she kidding? I'd really enjoy spending some more time with her. "I'd love a drink. Where do you want to go?"

Gladys turned and pointed at a large apartment building just down the street. "That's my building. Why not come over and I'll make you one?"

"Okay. Lead the way."

I got in the truck and followed Gladys into the parking lot of her apartment building. She showed me where to park and when I started to crack the windows for Beanie she told me to bring her in with me. I held the door open for my puppy and told her to come. I didn't have to say it twice as she was across the truck and out the door before I had a chance to repeat myself.

I walked over to Gladys' car, picked up a couple of her shopping bags and followed her up to her unit. It was fun to follow her sweet shapely bottom as it swayed back and forth up the stairs.

Her unit was large for an apartment. It was clean and her furniture appeared expensive. She showed me where to put the bags of groceries and I sat them down. Gladys waved her hand towards the rest of her apartment as she said, "This is it, my home. What none of the other tenants knows is I own this building. Actually I own several apartment buildings and some commercial properties. Dancing has been very good to me." Again with the killer smile. "I don't do any drugs, I don't go out with any of the customers and I figure I can retire just about anytime I want." Once more I was favored with her big smile, and she motioned for me to go and sit on the couch while she put away her groceries, but I elected to sit on a barstool next to a small island dividing the kitchen from the rest of the living space. "The couch is a lot more comfortable," she informed me.

"Maybe, but the view is much better from here." I winked at her.

She laughed. "Thanks for the compliments, but I'm too fat. I wish I was thinner, but for some reason I just can't seem to lose any weight. I try, but—"

I interrupted her, "The way that dress fits and the way you stand and move... you're a very sexy and beautiful woman. If you feel you need to lose weight, then so be it, but

I think you're stunning just as you are. Actually, personally I think women today are too skinny."

"You know, your mama sure did a great job of raising a real gentleman. You say the best things. Makes a girl's heart go pitty-pat." Her laughter filled the room and she winked at me. She continued, "For what it's worth, there are a lot of men who are very enamored with a woman my size. If I choose, my bed is never empty."

I wish I had the words to describe the way her presence filled the room; just sitting there talking with her she was so much larger than life, and I don't mean that as a fat joke. Here was a woman who enjoyed life and you could just tell she lived it exactly as she wanted. I'd been impressed with her the first time I saw her dancing, but today she took on a totally different appeal. I really liked this gorgeous woman, a lot! I couldn't recall ever meeting a woman who was so comfortable with her sexuality. Now I understood why she was so popular at work with so many men, and why they would have her do lap dances for them. Her question interrupted my daydreams. "What do you want to drink?" she asked.

"Any Scotch?"

"Single malt?"

"You mean there's something else?" I retorted.

She laughed. "I did hear once there was some swill where they mix good single malt with other good single malt and ruin both of them."

I laughed in return. "Well, then I need to hurry and drink some before they try and mix it and ruin it."

She turned and stooped down, looking into a lower unit of her cabinet. She named off a couple of different brands and when she named one I liked, I told her to stop. She asked me how I liked it and I told her to fill the glass with ice and then some Scotch. Gladys was kind enough not to mention the way I drank Scotch was not the preferred way of drinking it. Once the glass was fixed, she handed it to me. I took a sip and smiled. "Thanks."

Once she made her own drink, she reached out and took my hand and pulled me over to the couch. We sat down at opposite ends and she turned so one leg was up on the couch. Her dress rode up on her thigh and I noticed she was not wearing hose; her leg was bare. The exposed part of her thigh and her chest were well tanned and I commented she must get a lot of sun. She smiled at me. "I'm funny that way. I can just go from my apartment to my car and I get a tan. I really don't spend that much time lying in the sun. I have a small boat that I take out a lot so maybe that's where it comes from."

"How big is your boat?"

"It's an old 38' Chris Craft. I have it stored up in Anacortes. I try and get out whenever I can. I grew up on one of the San Juan Islands and I love being on the water."

I'm sure my chin must have hit my chest. "You have a 38' Chris Craft?" I asked in disbelief.

"Yeah, an old wooden one."

I was stunned. Those are a lot of work. "No shit! Who does the upkeep on it?"

With some pride in her voice, she replied, "I do."

"I'm impressed. When I was a kid, we had a summer home up on Whidbey Island, that's where I learned to drive a car when I was a kid. I've always liked the old wooden boats. When they're fixed up, they are so sharp."

"If you'd like, we could go for a ride sometime. Let me know and I'll have the boat put in the water and we can go."

"That sounds like a plan. I love boats." We continued to chat. As we talked, we found we both enjoyed opera. She remarked that nobody at the club knew she liked it. She didn't bother to try and explain some things about herself to the girls she worked with. The conversation drifted back to Robbie's and I asked her if she minded if I asked her a question.

She beat me to the question. "Why do I do exotic dancing for a living?"

I chuckled. "Yes, and I know it's none of my business but, I have to admit it, you are a very impressive woman. I'm wowed just sitting here talking with you."

Her voice wasn't exactly friendly, and she made sure I understood her point. "What? If I strip for a living, I must be stupid?" I hung my head and was embarrassed. She went on, "I have a master's degree in sociology and I'm here to tell you that there are not a lot of things you can do with that degree that will let you live the way I want to live." She grinned and I had to laugh as well.

"I started dancing when I was a senior and I kept doing it through grad school. When I graduated, I looked around and found there was nothing that paid as well, gave me the time off I wanted and made me feel as good about myself as dancing does. I know I need to lose a little weight, but I can dance the legs off almost every girl at the club." Gladys took a sip of her drink and made a face as she continued, "I'll admit, I do get tired of being pawed sometimes but, you know, every job has downsides to them. Right?"

I replied, "The one thing I've discovered in my life is judging a person is not a good idea. Either good or bad. People are people and you have to take each one on their own merits. I will admit I'm embarrassed about some of my attitudes about you and your girls. I really do believe that if you develop opinions about things, well like dancing like you do… you can miss out on some really nice people. Like I told you in the parking lot, I was impressed with you the first time I saw you. Now that I've had a chance to get to know you better, I'm even more impressed. You know what you want in life, you know how to get it and you're not afraid to reach out and grab it. Gladys, you're a really neat person."

Gladys sat her glass on the table and took mine from my hands. She turned on the couch so we were face to face and

I took her in my arms. She reached out and took my face in her hands and kissed me. When our kiss ended, I wanted to get up and go look at my lips. I was positive they were blistered from the heat of her kiss. When she leaned back and looked at me, I could see she was breathing hard. "Wow. You really know how to kiss a girl."

I swear I blushed. "Thanks. The drinking fountain at my elementary school had very little pressure and you had to suck really hard." Her laughter filled the room. I paused for a moment; I needed to try and clear the air. I wanted her to know my status with Sharon. "Ah... I need to explain something here. I've been seeing somebody, but we've kind of decided to cool it a little. We were living together, but we're not now. We still haven't come to any conclusions about our relationship. I don't know where this is leading," and I moved my hand between us to indicate me holding her and kissing her, "but I need to be honest with you, and I need to stop until I know more about what my friend has in mind."

Gladys' smile curled my toes. "You need to tell your friend she has competition. You tell me you think I'm sexy, well, I think you're rather sexy yourself." She laughed and added, "You brown-eyed devil."

I explained I really wanted to stay longer, but I also didn't really trust myself. This brought a huge smile to Gladys' face. I asked for her phone number and as she handed it to me, I asked, "Do you mind if I call you?"

"I really hope you do. Why else do you think I gave you my number?"

"You don't think I'm a bit too old for you?" I joked.

"No! I prefer my men a bit older. That way I don't have to spend so much time and energy training them." We grinned at each other. "Seriously, I don't think you're too old for me. And I really would like to take you for a ride sometime on my boat. But since it's fall, that may have to wait.

But I still would like to see you again. I think you're a very handsome and interesting man. Please call me."

I swear I blushed again. I collected Bean and we headed for the front door. At the door, Gladys stepped up close to me and put her arms around my neck. "I like the way you make me feel, Matt." As she pressed her lips against mine, one hand went to the back of my head, holding my face against hers. While she was kissing me, Bean managed to crawl up between us and gave Gladys a big lick on a cheek. Gladys laughed, gave Bean a kiss on the top of her head and gave me one more kiss on my lips. Damn, I liked the way she kissed.

Later when I got to my truck, I checked to see if my lips were blistered…

They weren't.

CHAPTER 6
LET'S VISIT THE POLICE

The next morning, I was watching Beanie finishing her morning rituals in the vacant lot as I sat on the step at the end of my walkway, nursing my cup of coffee. I was waiting so I could pick up after her. I used to just leave my dog's droppings in the lot but ever since somebody had slipped and fallen and had broken their leg, I thought it might be a good idea to keep the area policed better. The fact the man broke his leg due to all the drugs he was taking because of his cancer was beside the point; I just decided it was the right thing to do. Actually, it's the right thing for all pet owners to do!

As I stood there waiting for Beanie to finish, my mind wandered over what I wanted to do today and I decided to check on a few things. One thing for sure I planned on doing at the Seattle Public Safety building was to see my old childhood friend. Now he was the new chief of detectives: Captain Jeff L. Davenport. When Jeff's boss, Frank, was promoted to chief of police, Jeff interviewed for the detective's position and was immediately moved up to fill the vacancy. Jeff and I go all the way back to childhood and I always enjoy seeing him. I thought as long as I was there, I would take care of trying to find out who actually owned the van that was following me. I wanted to know who it was registered to, in addition to spending some time with Jeff.

From the first day I had Beanie, she followed me everywhere I went, and since she stays by my side, I let her come with me. I loved my old dog Blackjack and how well she obeyed, but I believe Beanie is the most obedient dog I've ever seen and I'm very proud of her. When I talk to her I swear she understands every word I say and will mind me without question. I know you're not supposed to have an animal in the police station, but Jeff has never told me not to bring her with… yet.

I was in luck and found Jeff sitting behind his desk talking on his phone. He raised a hand in greeting and pointed at a chair. While I sat down, Jeff held up his thumb and finger a small distance apart, showing me he expected the call to last just a few moments longer. I made sure Bean was curled up under my chair and I settled in to wait. Finally, he said goodbye and hung up. Jeff smiled at me and asked, "Matt, what brings you in today?"

"I just came by to say hi."

Jeff gave me snort of laughter. "Bullshit. You never come by to just say hi. What do you want?"

I placed both hands over my heart and tried to put on the most wounded expression I could. "Jeff, you cut me to the quick," and we both laughed. I shrugged my shoulders and continued, "Okay, now you found me out. Do you know who William Tate is?"

"Bill Tate? You mean as in The Bill Tubs Tate? The famous fabulously wealthy basketball star who is perhaps the greatest player of all time?"

"One and the same."

"Of course I know who Tate is. One of my sons even has an old pair of Bill Tate sneakers. Shit, I even have a CD of his music somewhere. Do you think cause I'm a cop I live under a rock? Back in the day I was a huge Tate fan. Come to think of it, wasn't he part of that big lawsuit that was filed when they moved the Sonics away?"

"Don't know about that, but there were a lot of people who were pissed as hell about the Sonics leaving. And not just Tate."

"So, why did you want to know if I know who Tate is?" Jeff asked.

"Well, he's part of my poker group." Jeff knew about the poker games. I had asked him if he wanted to play, but he begged off, telling me he didn't feel comfortable with his skills playing at our level. He'd heard about some of the pots won and lost at our games. However, Jeff has bugged me several times to invite Sakol to play in our games. I politely refused.

I continued, "The other night we had a game and during one of the breaks, Tate asked me to see if I could try and locate his daughter."

"Why? Is she lost?" Jeff asked.

"Well, kind of…" I hesitated, not really sure how to explain what I was working on.

Jeff interrupted, "What do you mean, Matt? What does 'kind of' mean?"

"Be still. Let me work up to what I'm trying to tell you. Neither this girl's mother nor Bill has seen the kid for about a week now. The kid's roommate has a new boyfriend and she said Kim hasn't been back in the apartment very much lately. It also sounds like the new boyfriend is keeping the roommate busy, if you catch my drift?"

Jeff nodded his head. "I take it you've spoken to the roommate?" he asked.

"Yeah, I went by there. Roommate's name is Samantha, they call her Sam. Anyway, Sam was so stoned she didn't even know she was nearly naked when she was standing there talking to me. She told me she thought some things of

Kim's had been moved in the apartment but she wasn't sure. She also told me that Kim Tate claims she was almost raped."

Jeff was quiet for a moment and then asked, "Did the roommate know who?"

I hated to tell Jeff this part. "Yeah. And you ain't gonna like the answer."

"Come on, just tell me." He rolled his hand in a motion to try and encourage me to go a little faster.

I blurted out, "Bud Cox."

Jeff had been leaning back in his chair with his feet on the edge of his desk. When I said the name, his feet came crashing to the floor, his mouth dropped open and his eyes actually bugged out. "Do you mean as in star running back out at the U Bud Cox? Perhaps the number one NFL draft pick next year Bud Cox?"

"Jeff, I told you you weren't going to like the answer."

"Fuck me. Who knows about this, besides Tate's kid and this Samantha girl?"

"According to Samantha, Kim's roommate, Cox has tried to rape or raped several women. Samantha also told me Kim went to some of the head administrators and complained about him. She was told to keep still and forget it. Anyway, I wanted to run things by you first and see if you'd heard any of the rumors."

"Matt, I really thought you'd learned your lesson." Jeff was referring to my last brush with legal problems. When I won the houseboat, the fellow who lost the boat was murdered. The man who murdered the old houseboat owner turned out to be somebody from my past. I could tell he was suggesting I not get involved and it might be a better idea to just leave things alone.

I tried to explain, "Yeah, well, you didn't have Bill Tate in your face crying and begging you to find his kid. Jeff, do you know how big that dude is? Did you want me to tell him to go fuck himself and I wasn't going to help him?"

"No, but you could have suggested he file a missing person's report," Jeff pointed out.

"I did and that's one of the weirdest things about this so far. He told me he couldn't actually prove the kid was missing. Her mother thinks she might have stopped by and picked up some clothes when the mom was out, and the roommate thinks Kim might have been by; so just because she won't pick up any calls from her dad, it's not really a missing persons thing is it?"

"Well no, but—"

I interrupted, "Look, all I'm going to do is chat with this Bud Cox kid if I can find him. Okay?"

"You know, Matt, I'm not really happy about this. I still remember our last go round. My advice is that you make sure you keep me in the loop."

Behind me, I heard a familiar voice, "What loop? What Matt doing now?" It was Sakol. I jumped up and extended my arms. Sakol wrapped me up in a bear hug and we clapped each other on the back. (By the way, his name is pronounced Say-kol.)

"You're back," I exclaimed.

"Miss ugly face." He pointed at Jeff. "'Sides, he need help. Place all fucked up. Need Sakol badly."

Jeff laughed as he retorted, "Yeah Sakol, without you this place would just dry up and blow away." We all laughed.

Bean had crawled out from under my chair and was now pawing at Sakol's foot. He reached down and picked her up. She immediately started to lick his hand. "Who this?" he asked.

"That's Beanie or as I sometimes call her, Bean. She's mine and I'm going to train her to attack."

Sakol held Bean out in front of his face. "This not killer dog. Too cute. Like you." And we laughed again. Sakol handed Bean to me and she settled down in my lap. For the next few minutes, we chatted about various topics. Jeff explained

77

the reason why I was visiting, and Sakol's eyes opened wide when he learned Bill Tate was one of the major players at our card games. Sakol would love to sit in on a game but so far, I've been able to hold him off. Talk about a poker face. Sakol was the best. With his round moon face and crinkly eyes, I could just see him at our game, blinking and nodding and asking, "Please... how play game?" And we would sit there watching him pull in one pot after another! NO! There was no way I was going to let this man into one of our games. The other players would kill me.

Sakol asked, "Any idea where daughter hiding?"

"Her dad said he was afraid she might be involved with drugs. I know I'm just grasping at straws, but I thought I might pay a visit to an old friend of yours." I looked at Sakol.

"Mouse?" he asked. I nodded. "Need help?" I shook my head. "Call me if problem."

"Thanks." I paused and then looked back at Jeff. "I do have one favor to ask..."

Jeff looked up at the ceiling and swore, "Oh fuck. Sakol, save me! Okay Matt, what do you want now?"

I fished the piece of paper with the license number on it from the van that had been following me out of my pocket. I asked, "Can you run this through DMV for me?"

"What's this?" Jeff asked.

"There's been a van following me, a big gray Dodge van. Two guys that drive the van have been bothering me. One of them wears an army uniform sometimes, but I want to know who it's registered to."

"Who do you think it belongs to?" Jeff asked.

I started to tell them about the visitors I'd had a few days before. I explained that I knew nothing about what the colonel was asking about. Sakol looked at me for a moment and asked, "Is there any way Hollis could have been telling you about Crescent when you were up in the lighthouse tower? Maybe you didn't realize it at the time?"

I got excited, "Sakol, what was it with you the other night? What do you know about Crescent?"

Sakol held up one hand. "Not so fast. I ask. I see if I can tell you. Right now, I can't. Please, leave alone!"

I sat looking at them. I sat for so long they probably thought I had forgotten the question. I had made the decision and I started, "Look, you both know where Sharon was while I was up in the tower with Hollis." Both nodded. "And by the time I got to the top, I knew Jeff was in the hospital, and even though he was supposed to recover, it was still iffy." I pointed at Sakol. "I'd just seen you lying on the ground in a pool of your own blood. And even though I knew you were alive, I had no idea how badly you were hurt or if you would live. Finally, I was shot on the way up there. I was losing blood and my mind wasn't working all that well. I've never told this to anybody, but I shot Hollis several times when I didn't need to. I was hurt and pissed and, well, my brain was not taking in all the info that it might have had things been different." I could see both of them wanted to talk and I held up my hand.

"Wait! Since those two dudes came and talked to me, I've gone over the conversation I had with Hollis repeatedly in my head, a memory I really had hoped I could put away. At no time did we ever talk about Nam, or Crescent or…" We all sat quietly for a while, each of us lost, deep in our individual thoughts.

I started in again, "I need to correct myself. I guess I was a little wrong about us talking about Nam. At one point, Hollis did tell me it had been too long since we were in country and I'd lost my nerve, that I couldn't just shoot him in cold blood. He called me names, trying to get me to shoot him."

Jeff spoke softly, "Then after he tried to kill you, you shot him."

There was a long pause before I said, "Yeah. Like that."

Jeff spoke the words slowly as he asked me, "Did you have to shoot him? I mean to save your life? Was he out of bullets?"

I decided if Jeff really wanted to know the truth, he had a right to it. "Jeff, I shot him because of you and Sakol and Sharon. And I mainly pulled the trigger because he started to describe what he had done to BJ and how much he had enjoyed killing her. Yeah, Jeff. Hollis was out of bullets. I didn't need to pull the trigger." It was like all of the air had been sucked out of the room and we all sat there in silence. Eventually I asked, "So, now what?"

Jeff lifted his feet and placed them on the corner of his desk. He shrugged and folded his hands over his stomach. "Matt, I had guessed that was what happened. Look, the case is closed. As far as I'm concerned, justice was served. It's our belief," he motioned at the two of them, "if Hollis had been brought back here, the government would have stepped in like they did with Price and who knows what would have happened then. I'm not saying what you did was right, but I know Sakol knows this: I've done almost the same thing. We had pretty much guessed what happened up there in that tower and neither of us can really complain about what you did. I think I totally understand why you did what you did and I want you to know both of us are fine with it."

The room was totally silent again. Jeff had just admitted to me he had killed somebody in cold blood when he could have just arrested the dude. That was quite the confession. As we sat and looked at each other, there seemed to be some sort of shared bond between us. This went beyond Jeff's and my childhood and my friendship with Sakol; this was something we all knew had been so wrong at the moment we had done it, but in the heat of things, we'd committed the act anyway. We all understood what the other person had gone through. We knew. We understood.

Jeff dropped his feet to the floor as he held out his hand. "Oh, holy shit, give me the damn plate number and I'll run it through DMV." I handed him the piece of paper with the number written on it and then watched as Jeff tapped on his computer keyboard. After a few moments he looked up at his terminal and asked in a puzzled voice, "What?" He punched something else into the keyboard and when the information was displayed on the terminal he turned and looked at me. "Matt, are you sure about this number? Positive?"

"Yeah, why?" I was confident I'd written down the numbers correctly.

Jeff said as he read off the computer screen, "I need to use an official override. The information here is only for somebody with an access code as high, or higher than mine. Just a second."

I watched Jeff key in several strokes and then start to read off the screen. "Listen to this. It comes up as 'vehicle destroyed.'" He punched a couple more keys. "Hold it, let me read this to you. It says the plate belonged to a red '98 Explorer which was totaled sixteen months ago." He continued to read to himself and then looked over at me. "This is weird. It was a US Government vehicle that was involved in a fatality. Plus, it shows the Ford is actually out in *our* impound lot. I don't understand. It should be gone by now, but it isn't."

Jeff looked over at Sakol. "Why would we even have a federal vehicle in the lot to begin with, and why are we storing it? True, it was involved in a fatality, but that should put it in the Washington State Patrol impound lot, not ours. None of this makes any sense. That car should not have been brought here and for sure it should have been long gone." Jeff continued to look at the computer screen. "Yep! And it doesn't say here why we still have it." I watched Jeff read the information once more. When he looked up at me he had a puzzled look on his face. "Didn't you tell me the van following you was a Dodge?" I nodded. "I wonder why we still have that wreck and even more, how did the plate get out? And what's it doing on a Dodge now?"

"Do you mind if I go and look at the car?"

Jeff closed one eye, shook his head and looked over at me. "Seems to me the last time we let you loose in the impound lot you got both Sakol and me in a shit ton of trouble."

"Yeah, but you weren't in charge of the department then either." I waited a second and then asked again, "Do you mind if I go and check it out?" I paused, "Pretty please?"

Jeff laughed and threw a piece of paper at me. "Go ahead. Here's a pass to get you in. And so help me if this comes back to bite me in the butt, I'll throw your scrawny ass under the bus."

I smiled at him and said, "Hey, I've been under the bus so often now I have a big screen TV under there to keep me company." I called over my shoulder my usual parting remark to Jeff, "Who loves ya baby?" Jeff and Sakol laughed as I walked out of the office.

~ ~ ~ ~

The impound lot was still as depressing as it was on my first visit. Seeing so many people's dreams sitting there all banged up is such a downer. I remembered my last go round with the rotund keeper of the lot, and I had no desire to talk to him again. Instead, I just snuck in.

The color of the vehicle made it fairly easy to find even though it was in one of the back corners. Other than the fact the vehicle was red, it was difficult to guess what kind of a car it had been. The top was squashed down and the driver's door had been pried open to retrieve the body. The air bag had deployed and now hung out of the center of the steering wheel. Every panel was crushed and dented and the car looked like it had rolled over several times. What was weird was there was a license plate still on the back of the car, badly damaged, but still on the vehicle. However, the front plate was missing. I thought to myself if I was going to steal a plate, why not take the one with valid tabs on it? Driving around without tabs just makes you a lot more noticeable. If I saw the Dodge again, I was going to check out the plate as carefully as I could.

As I turned to leave, I heard somebody shuffling up behind me. "Hey!" The voice shouted at me. "What you doin' back here? You ain't supposed to be in here." The voice huffed and puffed.

I turned around and standing in front of me was the caretaker of the lot. I could have sworn he had on the same overalls as the last time I saw him. They were still as filthy and stained and today his stubble had almost turned into a scraggly, white beard sticking out of his fat face. He glared at me for a while and finally asked, "What's wit ya, ya deef? I asked what ya doin' back here."

I handed him the note from Jeff. I had read the note and I knew how many words there were on it. It must have taken him five minutes to read it. I watched his mouth as he sounded out each word and when he was finished, he looked up at me with his rheumy eyes. "Don't give a shit who says you can come here, you don't come in my lot witout checkin' wit me. Now get out." He glared at me as he extended one of his short, fat, grubby fingers towards the front gate. I decided I'd found out what I wanted to know. It was time to leave.

"Yeah. I was just leaving."

"Don't come back here again. I remember you from last time, and you gots me in trouble last time you'se here. Stay out of my lot, hear me?"

I just walked away. This conversation was going nowhere fast and anything I said would just piss him off even more.

When I got back to my truck, I happened to notice my cell phone lying on the passenger seat. I'm not really good at keeping the phone on my person. I've been bitched at a few times about it, but I still keep forgetting it. For more of my life than not, I didn't have a phone you could carry. Phones were something that hung on a wall or sat on a desk and they were connected to an outlet. They were not something you put in your pocket and took with you. It was not a habit I had formed, nor did I think I was going to get very good at keeping the phone on me in the near future.

I picked it up and noticed I had missed a call—from Jeff. I groaned out loud. Did that fat fucking impound lot caretaker call Jeff and complain? I was not really wild about getting my ass chewed, but I decided it would be better to get it over with now than to let Jeff stew about it for a while.

Ring. Two rings. "Davenport."

"Jeff, it's me, Matt. Sorry, I missed your call."

Silence. I waited for a few seconds to see if Jeff was going to respond. I waited until I heard him take a deep breath and I could actually feel anger coming through the phone. "Shit, Matt. What's it been, an hour, tops, and already you've brought down the wrath of God on my head."

"Hey Jeff, I'm sorry the lot dude saw me and got pissed. I really don't know what his—"

Jeff interrupted me, "What the fuck are you talking about?"

"The fat guy! At the impound lot?"

"I still don't know what you're talking about."

This time it was my turn to interrupt, "Then why am I in the doghouse?"

As Jeff talked, I noticed the stress level in his voice had jumped a couple of notches. "When you bring me a piece of paper with the license number of a government vehicle, a vehicle I might add is supposed to be a secret and nobody is supposed to know a damn thing about," Jeff took a breath and I was tempted to tell him to calm down but I didn't. Jeff continued, "Hang on, this gets even better. You come asking about a vehicle that records show has been destroyed on top of being a secret and to top that off, the vehicle isn't supposed to even exist! Matt, that's when I get upset! Do you have any idea what kind of phone calls I've been getting over the last hour?"

I didn't see how any of this was my fault. I didn't tell him to override the ban on his accessing the info, he chose to do that. Things I wanted to say but I sheepishly replied, "No."

"It turns out the reason that red vehicle is in *our* lot is because nobody is supposed to know it exists, including you and me. It is officially destroyed. Key words here, guy, *officially destroyed.* When I asked questions about it, one of the people on one of the many phone calls I received told me it was none of my fucking business. And that's a direct quote. After I explained our interest in the license plate the next thing they wanted to know was what you were doing evading government vehicles that were following you and—and," Jeff finally took another breath.

Jeff was upset. No, let me rephrase that. Jeff was past upset. I quickly told him, "The back plate is still on the Explorer but the front plate is gone!"

Jeff exploded, "What? How do you know this?"

"I was just in the impound lot and I saw it. No front plate but the back is still there. Smushed, but still there."

There was a long silence and then his voice blasted out of my phone. "You were in the lot? Did anybody see you? Why do you keep bringing me these stupid weird cases? Matt—"

"You knew I was going to go to the lot, and yes, the fat old caretaker saw me. What's your problem, anyway?"

"I didn't know you were going straight from my office to the impound lot."

I didn't feel like I'd lied to him. I never misled him in any way in regards to what was happening. This was bordering on spooky. Jeff was talking nonsense. He knew I was going right out to the impound lot from his office. What was his problem? "Jeff, can I speak?" I tried to reason.

"No," he said, "I don't want to hear some bullshit story. Something told me when you came to my office this morning I was going to regret it. And I do!" The last three words were shouted into the phone.

I quickly responded, "Okay, bye." I pushed the end button and then pushed it again to turn off the phone. I needed to get back to my apartment and think things over. I sure had set off a firestorm.

Why do I keep getting myself in these predicaments?

CHAPTER 7
MRS. TATE & AMBRUSTER

I needed some time to think. Basically I just wanted time away from everybody to see if I could come up with some ideas as to what might be going on. I knew if I stopped by the garage Art, my jack-of-all-trades and mechanic, would be there and as much as I enjoyed his company, I wanted to be alone right now. I was also afraid since Jeff knew where I kept my cars stored, he might have an officer hanging around waiting to drag me in. I was concerned he might be so pissed at me for hanging up on him, and then turning off my cell, he was going to have me dragged in front of him in cuffs. I decided the best thing to do was to take Beanie back to the apartment and get my motorcycle and go for a ride. A very long ride to see if I could find some reasons that might make a little sense out of everything going on in my world.

I learned to ride on one of the islands in Puget Sound when I was in my early teens and have been riding motorcycles ever since. A few years back, in a moment of weakness, I went and bought a new Harley Davidson. Even though the bike is now several years old, it only has a few thousand miles on it. I love the bike, but between the not so lovely weather we have around here and my busy schedule, I don't get to ride it all that much. Since very few people know I have it, I thought it would be a perfect getaway vehicle.

I parked the truck out behind the apartment and let Beanie visit the back lot. When she was done, I took her inside and made sure she had plenty of food and water. As I picked up my helmet, I could tell from the way she walked off and climbed up onto the couch she was upset with me. Tough! I pulled on my leathers and went down to the garage to get my bike.

As I pulled out onto the street, I noticed the Dodge van was back. I turned in its direction and slowly drove past. Looking through the front windows was of no use. I couldn't see anybody inside and since the side windows were blacked out, I had no idea if there was anybody in the van or not. As I passed the back of the van, I saw there was now a new license plate on the vehicle. For whatever reason, the plate number I had given Jeff had set off a wave of trouble and now the van was sporting a new plate. What surprised me the most was the plate was still not a government plate. However, the plate did have a valid tag on it. Since I knew the colonel and the suit had something to do with the van, I wondered why the van wasn't sporting official government plates. Another mystery to ponder, as if I didn't have enough already.

I rode off, enjoying the thought that if there *was* anybody in the van, they were in for a long wait. I had no idea how long I was going to be gone, but if they were waiting for me to return in my truck, they were looking at a lengthy stakeout.

I worked my way over to the freeway and headed north. I had no idea where I was going, I just wanted to make sure Jeff, or whoever might be in the van didn't accidentally find me. I decided to head towards one of the islands in Puget Sound connected by a bridge to the mainland. The day was beautiful and the colors of the fall leaves were amazing.

Once I was on the island, different smells teased my nose. It was just the kind of day made for having a motorcycle.

Along the way down the coastline of the island I found a little mom and pop restaurant and pulled into the parking lot. There was a nice table on the front deck in the sun and I settled in for lunch. As I ate, I considered my problems. The first was Bill Tate and his daughter, Kim. I thought I could understand why Kim might want to try and do something about Bud Cox. I thought perhaps one of the reasons she was hiding was to hide from Bud Cox. I could see why she might want to open a can of whoop-ass on his creepy bod. I had no proof. It was a total guess on my part, built solely on the fact that she had disappeared from both of her parents. As I thought this through, I could see no reason to be concerned he might try and retaliate. But since she had fled, I did have to give her credit for wanting to do something to stop him.

As I sat in the warm afternoon sun, my tummy happy from lunch, I decided my next step with that problem was to see if I could find her and make sure she was as safe as possible. I reasoned that was to go and see her mother. If her mother didn't know where she was, I hoped she might have an idea where I could start looking.

My other problem was more of a concern for my well being. While I was worried about Kim and her safety, it didn't directly concern me. But the colonel and the suit seemed to be a potential danger to me. I'd seen firsthand that the Dodge van had something to do with the colonel and his sidekick. Now for some reason, the two of them had sucked me into the whole mess concerning Crescent, whatever the hell that was.

I felt I had not whacked at the bees nest of Kim and Bud Cox enough to cause somebody to want to follow me around. Since I had seen the Dodge van with the colonel and the suit, it had to be the colonel's doing. But if the government was involved, what did that make the colonel? Was his quest for information regarding Crescent his own, or was he doing it for… well, for whom? The government? If that was the case, what branch? I thought about all the different threads I could tug on. Which one was the way to go?

As I sat there basking in a rare sunny warm late-autumn day, another problem came to mind. What was I going to do about Sharon, my longtime friend and sometimes lover? Since she'd moved into the houseboat we had briefly discussed why we didn't want to live together, but we had never really defined our relationship. Did Sharon expect a full-time relationship? Did she expect an exclusive relationship? As much as I dreaded it, I knew we needed to have the talk.

You know those four words a man hates to hear, "We need to talk." The four words that can turn a man's blood to ice. Those four little words are just as scary as a woman's tears. When a woman cries, a man will do anything to get her to stop! When a woman says "we need to talk" I'd rather get my fingers slammed in a car door. The unknown possibilities regarding the outcome is what creates the fear. As a guy, I like to be in control, or at least as much as I can be. In the "we need to talk" talk, all bets are off. There is no program to follow. You're just winging it and sometimes when you wing something, really bad things can happen. I remember a "we need to talk" episode that ended up with me getting my face slapped. Of course, it was my fault. The lady in question was screaming at me about something I had done wrong and I glibly said to her, "Well gee, I guess a blow job is out of the question, right?" Not one of my best moments. But then most males can recall when they were not at their best. It seems to come with the XY thing.

For now, I knew I needed to see if I could find Kim Tate. I also knew I had to have a talk with Sharon. I wasn't in love with Gladys or anything, but I did want to date her and get to know her better. What I didn't have a handle on was what to do about the colonel and his buddy. For that, I decided the best thing to do was get a fresh perspective on the problem. That meant I needed to go over and visit Walter.

Walter is a friend of mine from my days in Nam. We had done a few missions together and he had saved my life. On our last mission I was badly wounded and he packed me out when he could have just as easily left me where I was. I was messed up to the point it was doubtful I would live, and had he not gotten me to an evacuation point, I would have died. Long after I had recovered, back stateside, I saw his picture in the paper in connection with a crime, and I contacted my lawyer's firm and asked them to see what they could do to help him. Eventually I gave him a piece of some land I owned over on the Olympic Peninsula and he built himself a cabin. I use the word cabin, but it's unlike any cabin you have ever seen. The whole house is a work of art. From the front deck and the front doors and throughout the structure, the finish is museum quality and the two of us have spent several evenings on that front deck watching the sun slip into the sea while we sipped excellent Scotch.

The only way one gets to see Walter is to write to his post office box and tell him when you'll be in the parking lot a few miles from his place. I've been to his cabin enough times I think I could probably find it, but Walter still has a lot of issues left over from his time spent overseas and it's best not to show up unexpected.

Now that I had some basic plans to deal with my problems, I was happy, or at least as happy as I could be with the way things were. I paid for my lunch and got my gear. After I was suited up, I headed off. It was still a wonderful day to be riding, but it was starting to get chilly.

The trip back to town was brisk, but it also kept my mind active. When I got back I was going to have the talk with Sharon and I thought taking her to a restaurant called Tony's Hidden Harbor for a nice dinner would be a good start. I would also get the address for the ex-Mrs. Tate from

Bill. Tonight or tomorrow night I would see Sharon and then I was going to make the visit to Mrs. Tate. I settled down into the seat of the bike and with an ear-to-ear grin, I watched the large bike eat up the miles taking me back home.

~ ~ ~ ~

Tony's Hidden Harbor is a wonderful restaurant located in the heart of Seattle nestled among the docks on southwest shore of Lake Union. It's been in existence since 1947 and Sharon and I have shared many pleasant meals there over the years. I felt that another lovely dinner would be a good way to work into the talk.

I decided I was going to drive my old Cad convertible. The Cad is from the last year they manufactured convertibles and when the POS motor gave up the ghost, Art and I installed a Northstar V-8 and the car looked like it had just rolled off the showroom floor. I can never sell the car because of the motor change and no matching numbers, but who cares, I like it. Before I pulled her out of the garage, I put the top down and then I went over to pick up Sharon. Because Tony's wasn't too far from the houseboat, I hoped Sharon wouldn't be too upset about her hair getting messed up. The evening was crisp but the car's heater kept the inside of the vehicle warm and toasty. A lot of people looked strangely at us as we drove by but I didn't mind. My very first car was a convertible and I fell in love with driving with the top down. Unless it was raining or something of equal ugliness, I liked the top down on my cars.

The young man who was doing the valet service that evening was impressed with how nice the old car looked. He pointed at a vacant spot right in front of the door and jokingly told us he had reserved that spot just for us. When I held out my hand for a ticket he said not to worry, that he would remember what car I was driving. I thought he was a nice kid.

Tony was standing at his customary station when he greeted us at the bottom of the stairs informing us if we didn't mind having a drink in the bar and waiting a few minutes, the diners at our favorite table were just leaving, and if we could give the staff a minute, they would have the table cleared and reset for us.

Tony was in his late seventies and his entire family had been an institution in Seattle when it comes to the restaurant business. Tony came from a family of eight kids, seven boys and one girl. I guess the boy genes were strong in that family. Of the eight, seven of them were in the restaurant business and one of the boys became a priest. (Perhaps their religion had something to do with the large number of children. Just a guess mind you!) The priest claimed his siblings fed the body while he fed the soul. I have actually eaten at all of the restaurants, but I think Tony's was the best by far, or at least his ambiance beat out all the rest of them.

Tony was maybe 5'5", completely bald and colored his eyebrows and his pencil-thin moustache a dark black, and even though it could have looked really hokey, he carries it off with great aplomb. Every night, Tony stood at the bottom of the stairs wearing either a white dinner jacket or a tux. With a red carnation placed in his jacket lapel, Tony was ready for the evening. I doubt if there was anybody in the state of Washington who was of any importance that he didn't know by first name. I don't know a thing about his home life other than he never took a night off except for Sundays when the restaurant was closed. Tony had been known to present his flower to a beautiful woman diner every once in a while. Needless to say, getting a flower from Tony was considered a real coup.

Sharon and I headed back into the bar, which was actually a cave carved out from under the street above. As we sat having a small, but nourishing Scotch, I happened to look out at the people who were leaving our table and I almost dropped my glass. It was the suit and the colonel dressed in civilian clothes. We were well back inside of the dark bar and it was impossible for the two of them to view us. But I could see them as they climbed the stairs to the street above. Sharon could tell I was disturbed and she asked me what was wrong. I just shook my head. I didn't want to frighten her.

I tried my best to keep them out of my mind during dinner, and being with Sharon really did help. We laughed and she had a couple of really cute stories from the hospital. She told me about one of the doctors walking in on a couple making love in the woman's hospital room. The fact that they were making love wasn't so strange, but the fact the she had just delivered a baby less than thirty-six hours before was a little over the top. The man claimed it was his wife who instigated the whole affair and she blushed when she admitted it was true. She told the doctor she was breastfeeding her baby and it had put her in the mood. Later, the doctor told Sharon up to that point, he thought he had seen it all, but now he discovered he was wrong. The whole staff was discussing it and Sharon finally decided she had to see this woman. As she told me the story, Sharon paused a moment as she held out her hands with the palms facing one another about six inches apart. Slowly she started to move them apart until it looked like there was a yard or better between them, and she as she nodded her head she told me, "Yep! That was her butt. She was not just fat, she was huge. I was stunned at her size!" I just shook my head and laughed. Sharon never seemed to run out of tales to tell from the hospital.

As usual, dinner was excellent. Tony stopped by the table at the end of our meal and asked how we were doing. When he asked, it came out as, "How y'all this fine evening?" The funny part of all this is Tony was born in Seattle and as far as I know, he had never lived anywhere in the

South. Why he feels like he has to speak like somebody from Gone With The Wind is beyond me.

We told him dinner was excellent as always and Sharon asked him how he was doing. He frowned as he shook his head. "Not so good. They tell me I have the funny spots on my lungs." He went on to tell us he was going in early next week for tests. Sharon asked him if he smoked and he looked down at the ground. When he looked back at us he seemed angry. "It ain't my fault. Back in the war, I mean the big one ya know, we had all the cigarettes we could ever want. We all smoked and when I got back I just kept on. Hells bells, they had ads with doctors telling us to smoke such and such a brand and even ol' Ronnie Reagan was pushing smokes before he went to the White House. Now we find out that this shit is killing us and we're hooked."

"How much do you smoke, Tony?" Sharon asked.

"Dunno, about two packs a day, I guess."

"What brand?" Sharon followed up.

"Lucky Strike. But it's okay cause I don't smoke them with those filters on the end. That shit will kill ya! You know, them filters are made outta that fiberglass stuff."

Sharon asked, "Have you ever tried to stop smoking?"

"Why? It's too late now." He shrugged his shoulders. "If something's wrong, no point in quitting now. But thanks for the suggestion."

After he left we smiled at each other and shook our heads. We had commented in the past as we wondered how people can still smoke after all of the research shows how dangerous it is. I did at one time and I was grateful I had that monkey off my back.

Tony brought us the bill personally and after he handed the bill to me, he reached up to his lapel and removed his flower and handed it to Sharon. When she extended her hand to take the flower, he took her hand and kissed the back of it. "Lovely lady, you actually deserve a whole bouquet. My biggest wish is that I was thirty years younger." Sharon actually blushed.

When we came out the front door the valet tossed me the keys to the car. I went over and opened the door for Sharon and then walked over to give the kid a tip. As I turned to leave, the colonel stepped out from behind the valet's booth. He said, "I thought that was your car when I came out of the restaurant."

I was not happy to see him. "What do you want?" I snarled.

Pointing a finger at me, he said, "I just wanted you to know that we're keeping an eye on you. I know you know something about Crescent and you're lying to us."

I could feel the anger surging through my body. "You know, you really are an asshole. You keep asking questions and I keep telling you I don't know what you're talking about, and you still won't give me any information. I wonder how difficult it would be to get a court order to keep you away from me."

The colonel glared at me for a moment before he spoke. "Preston, if you have an ounce of smarts, you will not do anything that stupid. I'm telling you I am just the tip of the iceberg and you do not want to know how much trouble that would cause."

I leaned towards him and in an angry tone of voice, I told him, "McNaulty, I am telling you now, stay away from me. I don't want to see you again. If I do, I am going to see what I can legally do to keep you away."

"That would be a stupid move, Preston. I still believe you know something about Crescent. I know you do, and I'm going to follow you until I find out what." The colonel glared at me for a second and then did an about face and marched off. I watched him turn the corner and then went over to the Cad. After I opened the door, Sharon asked me what was going on. I told her it was okay and not to worry.

When we got back to the houseboat Sharon invited me in but I declined. The run-in with the colonel had put me in a bad mood and I wanted to go back to my place. I just couldn't get over how insistent McNaulty was about Crescent. Talk about your dog with a bone. Even if I had some idea, which I didn't, because of the lack of information they shared with me, how was I to know if, or what I might know?

Seeing McNaulty had really disturbed me. I knew I needed to have the talk with Sharon and I had planned to, but seeing the colonel and his little buddy had put me in a mood where I didn't want to talk to anybody. I for sure didn't want to have the talk with Sharon tonight. I walked her to the front door and gave her a peck on the cheek. She reached up and put her arms around me. Looking up at me with a wicked grin on her face she said, "The offer still stands if you'd like to come in." She rubbed her pubic bone against me to drive home her point.

"Thanks baby, but I need to get on home. I have a full day tomorrow." It was a lie, but I needed to go. Somehow I was getting a feeling for movement and it would help me deal with the feeling that the colonel was closing in on me. I knew it wasn't real, but I was feeling trapped. It seemed like every time I turned around the colonel was looking over my shoulder. I had no idea what Crescent was, but just to satisfy my curiosity I wanted to know what it was all about. How was I going to figure this out? Walter was quickly becoming my last resort.

All the way back to my apartment I kept looking in the rearview mirror. I'm not usually a paranoid person, but knowing the colonel was keeping track of me didn't help my outlook on life. When I took Bean out for her nightly walk I kept seeing dark-colored vans either driving by or sitting along the street. I knew I needed to do something about the colonel and friend, but the problem was I didn't know exactly what. At least I knew what I was going to do tomorrow. I had to get the address for the ex-Mrs. Tate and see what she could tell me about Kim's disappearance.

~ ~ ~ ~

All my life I've been impressed with all the lovely homes along Sand Point Drive, but as I turned off and started up the large hill into Highlands Park, I was really wowed. The homes just seem to get bigger and better the higher up the hill I went. Eventually I crested the hill and turned left onto—surprise, surprise—Hillcrest Drive.

At the end of the block with a commanding view of Lake Washington and the mountains to the east sat the home I was looking for. I am a real pushover when it comes to mid-50s to 1960s style homes, and this was something right out of the 1962 issues of Better Homes and Gardens. With exposed beams, massive windows with lots of stone and cedar, swooping rooflines and cantilevered decks, the house looked like a large bird of prey just getting ready to take flight. When I pulled up in front of it I sat in my truck for a moment and just took in the view. I was in love with this house.

I stepped up to the massive twelve foot high double doors and pushed the button for the bell. Deep inside the house I heard what sounded like a mallet striking a large gong. It was the coolest doorbell I'd ever heard. After a few seconds wait the door was opened by an Asian man in a dark red jacket. His jacket looked a little like a cook's jacket, but the cut was more Asian than a cook's coat. Even though the man was shorter and looked older than me, he appeared to be in excellent shape. His jacket wasn't tailored, but you could still see his body was well toned. The way he was dressed and the way he opened the door indicated to me he was hired help. We said hello and he asked me what I needed. I told him I was there to see Mrs. Tate. The servant stepped back and motioned me to come in. He told me to wait and he would get her.

I could see into the front room and then off across the lake. We were high enough so that I could see way beyond it, all the way to the mountains in the distance. The view was amazing and I thought it put my view to shame, and I had always felt mine was a knockout. A tall Eurasian woman stepped into the foyer and walked up to me. Extending her hand, she said to me, "Hello, I'm Samara Tate. My man tells me you wanted to see me about something?"

I took her slim hand, noticing her long fingers and well-manicured nails. "Thank you for seeing me. My name is Preston, Matt Preston. I wanted to talk to you since your ex-husband has asked me to see if I can locate Kim. Has she been in contact with you?"

I watched the lovely woman for a moment and I thought I detected a flicker of fear in her eyes. "Who are you? Why has Bill asked you to find Kim?"

I tried to put the best 'aw shucks' look I had on my face. "Bill and I play poker together once in a while. Some time ago I won a houseboat and as I was taking possession, there was a murder in it. I was involved and Bill was aware of my involvement. I guess he thought since I know a couple of Seattle cops and I was able to help the cops catch the bad guys, I might be able to help him, and you, find Kim."

Her almond-shaped eyes widened as she took half a step back. "That was you who won the houseboat?" Mrs. Tate slowly looked me up and down and with a certain respectful tone in her voice, said, "Bill told me about that. He said you ended up on one of the San Juan Islands in a shootout and then ended up in the hospital. I think he also told me you were a spy or something in Viet Nam."

I grinned as I explained, "I was not a spy, Mrs. Tate. I normally tell folks I was just a bandsman in the service but to help explain things, I was in a very secret group that did some very secret things, but I was never a spy. I guess Bill thought I might be able to help find your daughter."

"I'm sorry, what did you say your name was?"

"Preston, Matt Preston."

Mr. Preston, won't you please come in and sit for a moment." She turned and walked deeper into the house. I followed her into the front room and continued to be blown away by the grandeur of the vista through her front windows. She motioned for me to take a chair and when I sat down, she sat across from me on a sofa.

"Would you like something to drink? Coffee, soda?"

"No thank you, Mrs. Tate."

"Please call me Samara," she invited.

"Thank you, Samara. Have you seen your daughter recently?" I asked.

There was a long pause and I could see she was trying to decide just what she wanted to say to me. I leaned back and looked her over. Her black hair was cut short, I believe the correct term is a pixie cut. Her almond eyes were very attractive, her lips full and lush. Even though her blouse was a loose fit, being a guy I noticed her breasts were full and the rest of her body was trim with just the right curves in just the right places. This was a very attractive woman whom I assumed to be in her mid-forties. She was more than just an attractive woman. This lady was class, and from the way she dressed and acted, she probably was also a very expensive woman. For sure, this lady was way over my pay grade.

I couldn't help but wonder what the problem had been between Tubs and Samara. I know from my personal experience that one can never really tell what a marriage is like. Even though both parties are really nice people, once they're together, things don't always work out. But I still wondered what Bill's problem was with this woman. I thought she was both exotic and erotic. Finally, Samara spoke, "Mr. Preston—"

I spread my arms and as I held my palms towards her, I interrupted, "If you're Samara, then please, I get to be Matt."

Samara smiled. "Okay, fair enough. Matt, ah, I saw Kim three nights ago. She came by here to get some clothes and she asked me for some money. I told her until she told me what was going on, I wasn't going to give her anything. We had a fight, no, let me rephrase that, we had an argument and eventually she told me a boy she had been dating tried to rape her. When she went to the campus police they more or less laughed at her. She also went to the dean of men and they told her she was just overreacting. I understand the boy plays football, and she even went to his coach. He told her if she was wise, she would keep it to herself.

"What seems to scare her the most was that she got a call from the boy telling her if she didn't let things go, he was going to find her and do a lot worse things than rape her. Kim said he has some very scary friends. He grew up in the Central LA area and from what Kim said, he can be very intimidating. Anyway, she came here to get some clothes and money and said she was going to hide until the police finally did something about all of this." Samara took a breath.

"Do you know where she's hiding?" I inquired.

"No, I don't." Samara stared at me for a moment and then asked, "But how do I know you aren't working for this boy, trying to find Kim?"

That was easy enough. "Just call Bill. Ask him who Matt is and what I look like." At first I thought she was going to get up off the sofa, but then she relaxed. I could see she was struggling with her decision. Gently I told her, "Samara, I really think you should call Bill, right now. I need for you to trust me. Call Bill and ask him why he asked me to look for Kim. Go ahead. I'll wait right here."

She called out, "Ambruster… Ambruster…" from the kitchen I heard somebody say, "Coming ma'am." When the man who had met me at the door came into the room, Samara instructed him, "Ambruster, please get me a phone." We waited for Ambruster to fetch the phone. Once she had it in hand she started punching buttons. There was a pause while the phone rang. "Hello Bill. It's Samara." There was some buzzing from the phone but I couldn't understand the words. "Yes. The reason I'm calling is there's a man here. He says his name is Matt. Matt something…"

"Preston," I supplied her with my last name.

"Matt Preston. Do you know him?" I could hear the buzzing on the phone get more excited. I still couldn't make out the words but during Bill's talk, her eyes never left my face. When he was done, she thanked him and hung up. Ambruster was still standing next to the couch and she handed the phone back to him. She smiled up at him. "Thank you Ambruster." Next she turned her lovely smile on me. "According to Bill, the only thing you can't do is walk on water, but you're working on that."

I had to laugh. "Samara, I was really lucky up in the islands and what happened got blown all out of proportion. Bill seems to think I am some super… well, I don't know, but he did ask me to look into Kim's problems."

"Did you really shoot a man between the eyes up in the lighthouse?" I nodded. "Well, since Bill seems to, I trust you as well. But I don't know where she went. She wouldn't tell me. I didn't really like it, but she was so scared and there was nothing I could do. She flat out refused to stay here. And I know she won't go to Bill's place. I know she's determined to bring this rape thing out in the open. She told me the boy had tried to rape other women and that he had actually succeeded a couple of times. I don't understand why nothing happens to him. Why is he still free? Why isn't he in jail where he belongs?"

"Samara, I wish I understood better myself. All I can tell you is sometimes when a boy shows he has some prowess on the athletic field, people look the other way when he does bad things. When he isn't punished, then he thinks he can get away with more. The problem is that over time he just beleives he's above it all. I know it's an ugly part of our society, but sports are big business and this young man is becoming a major player. A lot of people are riding his coattails and he knows it. I'm trying to find him as well and settle all of this in my mind."

"I hope somebody does something about him. I'm so afraid for Kim. I can't get her to listen to reason. She's determined to see that boy pay for his crimes."

I tried one more time, "You have no idea where Kim is? A phone number, perhaps?"

Samara paused a moment and I could see in her eyes when she decided to confide in me. "Yes, she does have a new cell phone, one that this Cox boy doesn't know about. Just a minute, I'll go and write it down for you." When she returned she handed me a small piece of paper with a phone number written on it. "Please go and see if you can bring my baby back safe." I saw there were tears in her lovely eyes. It made me sad to see her cry. I didn't say it to her, but I promised to myself I would do everything I could to bring Kim back safely.

As I stood to leave, Ambruster stepped to the front doors and opened one of them. When Samara and I got to the door, she extended her hand and put it on my arm. "Thank you for doing this, but are you safe? From what Kim says, I'm worried for your safety as well as hers."

"Samara, I appreciate your concern, but I can take care of myself. If nothing else, I keep a pistol in a handy place in my truck. Will you be okay here? Is there any way Cox—by the way, the boy's name is Bud Cox—is there any way Cox can find out where you are and try to harm you?"

I watched a bemused look come over Samara's face. She glanced over at her servant in his handsome red jacket and then back at me. "Ambruster might not look intimidating, but trust me when I tell you I'm very safe. Bill found Ambruster when he was in college. Bill's school had played a game somewhere and Bill got separated from the rest of the team. A group from the local 'hood' trapped Bill in an alley. Bill was lucky, as Ambruster was walking past the entrance to the alley just as one of the men pulled a knife on Bill. Neither Bill nor Ambruster will talk about it much, but one time I did hear that out of the six men who were in the alley, only one of them lived. When we divorced, Bill demanded that I keep Ambruster as... well, he's everything for me. He's an amazing cook, when I need him to be, he's my butler and also my driver. I don't think this boy, Bud Cox did you say?" I nodded my head. "I don't think he wants to meet Ambruster."

"Okay, if you think you're safe."

Even though she smiled, there was a look of worry on her face. "I only wish that he was with Kim. He wanted to go with her, but she refused. In a way he was her nanny. When Bill and I divorced, Ambruster was the one Kim turned to for support. She seemed to blame me for the divorce, but she also blamed her father. I think Kim was worried something might happen to me and she wanted Ambruster to stay here." She stepped back and as she shut the door, she added, "Please call me and let me know what's happening. I trust Bill, but still..." her voice trailed off. I assured her I would let her know everything I could.

I got in the truck and fended off Beanie trying to lick my face. I kept telling her I had only been gone a few minutes and she didn't need to lick me every time I returned. After a lot of fussing she settled down and I started to pat her. As I sat there, I watched a side door open and Ambruster came out with two sacks of garbage, lifted the lid of one of the garbage cans in the garage, and dropped the two sacks inside. Ambruster glanced over at me and nodded. I held up one hand and acknowledged his greeting.

I drove the truck slowly down the hill, still gawking at the amazing houses along the way. I thought to myself there was some very serious bread living on this hill. Even with the way things are today, these homes had to be at the top end of seven figures, maybe even as high as ten million for a couple of them. At the bottom of the hill I met with a rent-a-cop sitting in his car, watching who was going up and down the hill. As I stopped at the stop sign, he got out of his car and held up his hand. I put down my window. "Good afternoon, officer," I greeted the wannabe cop.

He didn't smile back. "Good afternoon sir. May I ask you what you're doing here?"

I thought to myself how this was a free country and as far as I knew, I was allowed to go anywhere I wanted. But I also realized there was no reason to piss this guy off since I had no idea how much connection he might have with the Seattle Police, and I still hadn't called Jeff back. "Yes, sir. I was just up visiting Mrs. Samara Tate. Her ex-husband and I are friends." It might be stretching the truth a bit, but I was still going to try and use the "Bill Tate" card.

"Oh. Well, excuse me, sir. We try and keep a watch on folks living up here. Sorry to bother you. Good afternoon, sir." He still hadn't cracked a smile, but at least his tone had improved a bit. I wasn't too surprised to see there was a private security car patrolling the neighborhood. Given the amount of money living up on this exclusive hill, I was sure those living in the Highlands wanted to know they were safe.

As I pulled back onto Sand Point Drive, I looked in my rearview mirror and saw the security cop was still watching me drive away. After I thought about it for a while, I realized there weren't a lot of pickup trucks in that upscale neighborhood. I didn't look like construction or yard maintenance, so it shouldn't have surprised me to be stopped. I thought to myself it was too bad there was no way to hire a security firm to protect Kim Tate. Protect Kim Tate… that thought brought me to my next thought. Ambruster was Kim's go-to person when her parents split up. When Kim was hurting, she went to Ambruster to protect her, to help her cope. I wondered if Ambruster knew where Kim was stashed. How could I get him to confide in me if he actually did know where she was?

I pulled over and stopped. Did I dare go back into Highlands Park? I didn't want the security guard to get suspicious and perhaps call the police. So how was I going to get to Ambruster? I wondered what Bill Tate could tell me. It sounded like he knew Ambruster better than anybody else did, except maybe Kim Tate.

I called Bill on my cell. He picked up on the second ring. "Bill, it's Matt Preston."

"Did Samara tell you what you wanted to know?"

"Well... Yes and no. She did tell me she *has* seen Kim in the past couple of days. But she also didn't know where Kim might be hiding. The reason I'm calling is to ask you if you think Ambruster might know where Kim is."

The phone was silent for a while and I was starting to wonder if I had dropped the call. When Tate started to talk it was slowly and thoughtfully. "I never thought of that. When Kim's mother and I were going through the divorce, Kim went to Ambruster for moral support. Since neither of us really knew what to do for her, we were both grateful he was there for her. I think he just might know where she is."

"How can I get ahold of him?"

"Give me a few minutes; I'll get back to you."

"Thanks, later." I hung up. I knew Jeff was probably still looking for me so I decided to drive around until I heard back from Bill.

My cell phone went off a few minutes later. I recognized Ambruster's voice. "Mr. Tate asked me to call you. How may I help you?"

I hate dealing with people on the phone. That's always been one of my pet peeves. I want to see the face, the eyes, the way they either look at you, or don't. It all tells you something about them. All of this is lost on the phone. I remember from some movie where they were discussing what people said vs. what people's body language was saying. As I recall, less than twenty percent of what people tell you is contained in the words. The rest is all in body language. "Ambruster, thank you for calling me. I was wondering… ah… if I could see you for a few minutes. I would rather not come back up to the house if you don't mind. Is there any place you can meet me?"

The silence stretched so long I was starting to wonder if he was still on the phone. "Why? Why do you want to see me?"

I figured the best way to play this was to be honest. "One of my quirks is I hate phones. I need to talk to you and I don't want to do it on the phone. Can we please meet someplace?" I didn't exactly answer his question.

"There's a coffee stand at the corner of 84th and Sand Point Way."

"I know where it is," I said.

"Give me fifteen minutes. I'll meet you there."

I ordered my drink and when the barista put it on the counter, she told me it would be $3.85. Since I had a lot of change in my pocket, I dug out enough to pay for my latte and put it on the counter. The young lady stood there staring at my pile of coins sitting on the counter. She finally looked up at me and asked as she pointed at the money, "What's that?"

"It's change, for my drink."

"I don't do change," she said peevishly. "Do you have a credit card?"

I was stunned by her comment. "I don't do credit cards," I retorted. "All I have is change."

She snapped at me, "Whatever!" Without even counting the money, she glared at me as she swept it into her till. I briefly considered speaking to the manager about this young lady's attitude but then realized she just might be the manager. Whatever happened to the service you used to get from a clerk? When did it become acceptable, (that is if you could find a clerk who can make change) to just hand over a stack of bills with your change balanced on top of the stack without even so much as a thank-you. Forget having the change counted back into your hand, that's way too much to ask. Pop told me one time that the world was going to hell in a handbag. No shit pop! You are correct.

It was less than fifteen minutes later when Ambruster rolled up. I had secured us a table and as he walked by he asked me if I wanted something. I told him I had already ordered. Once he had his drink, he returned to the table and sat down. He took a sip, put his drink on the table and looked at me. "Why did you want to see me?"

"You know that Bill has asked me to look for Kim. I know you saw her a few days ago and I was wondering if you would tell me where she is."

Ambruster looked at me for a few moments before he spoke. "Why are you asking me?" This was why I wanted to talk to him face to face. I could see from the look in his eyes and the way he sat in his chair he knew exactly where she was.

"I know Kim looks up to you, that you're almost her second father." I watched as his face relaxed and I swear his eyes changed, somehow they were softer, more compassionate. "It seemed to me that if she needed a place to hide, she might go to you." I paused a moment and then in a soft voice I asked again, "Do you know where she is?"

Ambruster sat looking at me for so long I started to wonder if I was even going to get an answer. He took a sip of his drink and then looked down as he slowly sat it down. When he looked up he said, "Yes, but she's safe."

I tried to sound as reassuring as I could. "I believe I have a place that might be a little safer than where she is, but I need to know where she is so I can judge if that's true. Also, if I'm correct, I want to go and fetch her."

Ambruster leaned back in his chair and stared at me. "Why did Bill ask you to find Kim? Not to be rude, but what makes you so special?"

I considered how much I wanted to share with Ambruster regarding my life, but I felt I had to at least put some of his fears to rest. "I've done a lot of strange stuff in my life. I've knocked around and Bill knows things about my past, about my time in the military. I guess he thought I might be able to find her, and even more important, perhaps help her."

Ambruster surprised me with his next question out of the blue, "Did you know she was raped?"

Even though by now I was pretty sure she had been raped, it still saddened me to hear it for certain. "I heard she was *almost* raped, do you know different?"

Ambruster looked down at the table and when he looked up at me he had tears in his eyes. "That asshole did actually rape her. I held Kim in my arms and she broke down and told me the truth. I don't know why she's telling people he almost raped her, maybe she's too ashamed to admit the truth. I really don't know. But she was raped and she wants to see him pay for it." The man took a deep breath and his bottom lip quivered when he told me, "I want to find him and just beat the shit out of him."

"Ambruster, please don't take this the wrong way, but this kid could really put a hurt on you without even trying."

Ambruster leaned back in his chair and a cold look dropped over his face. "Mr. Preston, I know you mean well, but that little punk is no threat to me, trust me." Just the way he said it made my blood run cold. I had no idea what skills the man possessed, but I felt at that moment he was undoubtedly proficient in all different manners of violence. He continued, "The boy called her and told her he was going to kill her if she told anybody. He also told her when he was finished with her, he was going to come and rape and kill her mother as well."

As softly as I could, I asked him again, "Do you know where Kim is hiding?"

"She's safe." He insisted.

"Ambruster, I don't doubt that, but I have a place that's safer. But more than that, there's also a nurse there who can help Kim. This nurse is a very good friend of mine and Kim needs a woman to talk to, a trained professional. The nurse's name is Sharon and she's a head nurse in the ER up at one of the hospitals on Pill Hill. Sharon can help Kim deal with her rape. Please let me take Kim to her."

Ambruster sat and sipped his coffee. I knew there was no point in prodding him for an answer, he had to decide on his own. Either he trusted me or he didn't. Eventually he said, "I agree that Kim needs help. All I have to do is touch her and she shudders. She couldn't stop crying the last time I saw her. It's killing me to know how she hurts and there's nothing I can do to stop the pain." He took a deep breath and his voice was tight and strained. "Go and get her. Take her to your friend and see if she can help her. I'm worried about her."

Ambruster reached inside his jacket and pulled out a pen and small pad of paper. He wrote down an address and handed it to me. I could see the pain in his eyes and his hand was trembling as he passed me the paper. It was obvious he cared for her, and obvious he wanted to say something. I waited as I held the paper in my hand and finally he spoke. "Mr. Preston, it's a dangerous neighborhood for a person of your color." He grimaced as he continued, "I would advise you to be careful. Very careful. I know you will be, and I know you're armed, but it's just not a place where you'll be welcome."

"Thanks for the warning. I hate to say this, but I've been in any number of places in my life I was not very welcome."

Ambruster said, "Sounds like both of us have led checkered lives."

I thought to myself, "So true, so true." and I just smiled.

CHAPTER 8
KIM

Several years ago I was vacationing on an island in the Caribbean called St. Kitts over New Year's, which by the way, for them is their Carnival time. And during the festival, my lady friend and I had an excellent time. One morning around three AM as we were partying downtown in the main square in the capital city, we realized there was a huge crowd of people around us who were all partying with us. Normally no big deal, but there were hundreds and hundreds of black folks and the two of us whites. It could have made us a bit apprehensive but at no time did we feel any fear or concern for our safety. The entire time we felt as safe as if we were in our mothers' arms. We were all there to do the same thing, have a good time and party.

This morning as I drove through the Central District, or the "Ghetto District" as some might refer to it, I wished I could have made the same statement. The deeper I got into the neighborhood over Capitol Hill, the more I felt I was intruding. Driving down some of the back streets, I thought I saw a lot of hostility on the dark faces of several of the men standing on the street corners.

When I found the street I was looking for, I was happy to see there was nobody standing around. I pulled up in front of the address and parked my truck. I debated leaving the windows down a crack for Beanie, and I decided she needed the air more than I needed to feel secure nobody was going to try and break into the truck. I knew my fears were probably unfounded, but I couldn't shake the feeling I was someplace I really didn't belong.

The house looked clean, but it was badly in need of a coat of paint. The lawn needed to be mowed and there were two bicycles on the front porch. An old car sat on bricks in the driveway and I walked around it as I stepped up to the front door of the house where Ambruster had said Kim was and knocked. I could hear noise inside, but nobody came to open the door. I knocked again and still nobody came to greet me. I stepped off the front stoop and moved around to the back of the house. As I rounded the corner, I saw somebody carefully shutting the sliding glass door. I waited for her to get the door shut and when she turned, I recognized her from the photos I'd seen; it was Kim Tate. She looked at me and I saw fear flit across her face. As she turned to run, I spoke to her in the gentlest tone I could muster at that moment. "Kim, please stop. Don't run. All I want to do is talk to you."

She spoke to me with perfect diction. "Who are you?"

"My name is Matt, and I'm a friend of your father's. He asked me to see if I could find you and Ambruster let me know where you are."

Her dark eyes flashed. "I thought I could trust him." She stared at me for a moment and then asked, "What do you want?"

"First off, you can still trust Ambruster." She scowled at me and I quickly continued, "He told me because he was worried about you. Secondly, I'm begging you not to run from me. Call your mom and ask her about me, or call your dad. Honestly, I just want to talk to you. I promise I won't hurt you, actually I think I may be able to help you."

"How are you going to help me?" The skepticism was evident in her voice.

"Your father is concerned about your well being." I felt that was the best response I could offer.

"I doubt that," she snarled.

Her hostility surprised me. "Why do you say that?"

"He has his new bride." The way she said the word 'bride' made it sound like a swear word. "He's just like all the rest of the men I know, thinking with his cock. He has this new wife with her big plastic tits and all she wants to do is fuck him for his money—"

I broke in, "I don't mean to make light of anything, but it seems like you have a lot of hate stored up for both your father and his... ah..." I searched for the best word, "his new mate."

"Ha, good word for her! I know my mother isn't the easiest woman to live with, but he was still a shit about the way he left her."

I didn't know much about how Bill's divorce went, other than a couple of comments about how he was paying dearly for his freedom. But since I knew he had some multi-million years when he was playing ball, and not counting all of the various endorsement deals, I didn't think his ex-wife was too bad off. I asked Kim, "Doesn't your father pay any alimony?"

"Yeah, and he gives me money too. But it seems like now that he has this new wife, I don't count."

I was getting a little tired of her attitude. "If he didn't care about you, why do you think he asked me to find you? When he asked me to find you he was actually crying." My voice had risen in volume. I stopped and took a breath. "Do you think he'd be so worried if he didn't care?"

That question seemed to stump her. She looked at me and then I saw a couple of tears running down her cheeks. She hung her head and I could barely hear her. "I don't know what to do, I'm so scared." A sob and then her shoulders started to shake.

As gently as I could, I said her name and I extended my arms and invited her to come over to me. She looked at me for a moment and then slowly stepped over. I carefully put one arm around her and I felt her body tense. I lifted my arm and she reached up and took it, placing it back on her shoulder. I could feel her shoulders shake. A sob escaped from deep inside her and she buried her face in my chest.

I didn't know what else to do so I just stood with one arm resting lightly on her shoulder and let her weep. When she looked up at me she noticed my wet shirt. She touched the wetness and looked back up at my face with a sheepish grin. "I'm so scared. Sorry," she gave a slight hiccup and then continued, "I didn't mean to get you all wet." Even with tears in her eyes she was a beautiful young woman. "I just don't know where to turn or what to do."

As we stood there, for the first time I really had an opportunity to look at her. Her eyes were almost black and almond-shaped. Kim's mother was of Asian descent and the combination of ethnicities had made her a very lovely lady.

"I think you had this stored up for a long time. Can we go someplace and talk?" I wanted to talk to her, but I also didn't feel comfortable in this neighborhood.

"Yeah, just a minute." She walked over to the sliding door and opened it. She called into the house that she was leaving and would be back later. As she passed me she said, "Let's go."

When we approached my truck, there were three young, very large black men standing between me and the driver's door. The one in the middle had his arms crossed over his chest, trying his best to look menacing. I asked, "Can I help you, gentlemen?"

The one with his arms over his chest spoke, "What you want wit her?" He motioned towards Kim.

"We were going to go and have a cup of coffee and talk. Why?" I replied.

"She been cryin," his dark face looked flushed with anger, "why?"

"If she wants you to know the reason, I think she'll tell you."

The man uncrossed his massive arms and took a step towards me. "Hey," his hands were clenching and unclenching in frustration, "don't give me no shit or I mess you up so bad…"

Several plans went through my mind and I discarded them as quickly as they formed. I was getting worried and I wondered what I was going to do. Kim spoke up and asked them to just go away and leave us alone. The man in the middle whom I had considered to be the leader said, "Shut up bitch," he glared at Kim, "we be helpin' you."

"I'm okay," she gave him a weak smile, "Just go away, please." Her voice had a tone of worry in it now.

I felt sure I could seriously hurt a couple of them, but I didn't like the idea of having to deal with all three. The odds were not in my favor. Suddenly the cavalry came around the corner. A long, black, top of the line S-class Mercedes rolled to a stop next to the three young men. As the driver got out of the vehicle and opened up the back door, all three of the men who were detaining us stood with their mouths agape. From the back seat of the car emerged a diminutive man I was not unfamiliar with. He was a childhood friend of Sakol's with a shady history that went by the moniker Mouse. I knew the miniature man's real name was Steve Fox, but everyone knew him as Mouse, and he had been introduced to me as Mouse and all I had heard him called was Mouse.

Mouse walked up to the large man in the middle who now had his arms folded across his chest again. "What's the problem, gentlemen?" Mouse asked in a rich, deep voice that didn't go at all with his size.

"This honky was fuckin' with a sister. He thinks he ta-kin' her with him," the leader said to Mouse.

Mouse stared at the big man until he uncrossed his arms and looked down. In a voice as cold as an Alaskan morning, Mouse said, "You know who I am. This 'honky,' as you call him, is a friend of mine." Mouse glared at the larger man. After a short pause, he continued in the same cold voice he had started with. "A very good friend, and you are in his way. What are you going to do about that?"

I noticed the other two black men who had been with the large man had disappeared. I hadn't even seen them leave. The man who was left looked at me and spoke with a lot of respect in his voice now, "I'm sorry. I didn't know you knew Mouse. I hope I didn't trouble you too much. Please accept my apologies, sir." The man spoke now with no trace of ghetto in his speech.

I wanted to let him save face so I tried to ease the sit-uation. "I admire you watching out for your women. I un-derstand you were just trying to protect Kim. Everything is cool, okay?" I could see no reason to make any more of an issue out of this than necessary.

The large man just looked at me and then turned to Mouse. "I'm sorry for any inconvenience I might have made for you or your friend. I'll be on my way." The man never offered his hand to me and I was not going to make an issue out of that either.

After the man left I turned to Mouse. "Thanks, I don't know how that was going to turn out, but I do appreciate you stopping by. How did you know I was here?"

Mouse laughed. "The right thing for me to say is I know everything that goes on around here, but the truth is I saw you and I had my driver follow you. I wondered what you were doing down here."

I motioned towards Kim and said, "This is Kim Tate. I know her father."

Mouse's eyes opened wide, "Tate… you mean as in William Tate?"

Kim asked, "You know my father?"

"Hell yes—excuse my language—yes, I know who your father is. I've never had the privilege of meeting him but I followed his career very carefully. I thought he was one of the best to ever play the game. The day he retired was a very sad day for the game of basketball."

"Funny. Him being my father, I never saw him that way. I mean I knew he was a famous player and all, but to me he was just Dad."

Mouse extended his hand and when Kim took it, he bowed. "It has been an honor to meet you, my dear. I'll leave the two of you now." Mouse looked over at me. "Matt, I would suggest you take her out of here as quickly as possible." He winked at me and then climbed back into his limo. Kim and I got into my truck and we departed as quickly as we could. As we drove away Kim asked, "Who was that little man?"

I replied, "Believe it or not that little man is actually a very scary little man. It's a good thing he was there and that he's on our side."

Once we were underway, Beanie crawled out from behind the seat and settled into Kim's lap. Kim held Beanie against her face and Beanie tried to lick her. Kim laughed. "Is this yours?" she asked. I smiled. "I always wanted a dog. It just never seemed to be the right time to mother and father for me to have one. This is a really cute puppy. What's her name?"

I told her and we talked about dogs for a moment. I told her about my last dog and when she asked me what happened to BJ, I tried to keep the story brief. I almost got through the story before a tear escaped and rolled down my cheek. Kim looked at me with alarm and asked me if I was okay. I explained that most of the time I could keep the memories in check, but from time to time I really missed my old dog. For some reason seeing me upset about BJ changed Kim, and for the rest of our journey she just sat in the seat looking out at the passing scenery, petting Bean, who was overjoyed to have so much affection.

I pulled into the parking garage of my apartment before Kim said anything more. When I parked, she looked over at me and asked, "Where are we?"

"This is my apartment. Actually I own the building. I have a place I'd like for you to stay. It's with a friend of mine and she'll take really good care of you." We got out of the truck and stepped into the elevator.

"Why can't I stay at the place I was at?" she asked.

"I'd really like for you to be some place a bit safer. Nobody knows about where I want to take you. Also, my friend is an ER nurse and she'd like to talk to you." The last statement was a bit of a lie, but I knew that once Sharon found out about Kim's rape, she would definitely want to talk to her.

"Why are we here, then?" Kim asked with some suspicion. The elevator opened and we were standing in my lobby.

I had to smile, "I need to chat with my friend first. We're having some issues and—"

Kim asked, "Is she your girlfriend?"

"Yes… and no." I laughed nervously. "I mean… well, we do love each other but when we're together for too long we seem to end up fighting."

Kim stared straight ahead. "My God, can I relate to that. It seemed like Mom and Dad would be just fine for about three days, and then they would start to fight about everything. The stupidest thing would set them off. It drove me frickin crazy."

I explained to Kim, "Well, I need to go and talk to Sharon about you. I know she'll want you to be with her, but I need to discuss it with her first."

"I take it you two used to live together and now you don't?" I agreed. "And when you broke up, you didn't talk things over, you just moved out, like a typical male."

I held up one finger. "Just to keep the record straight, Kim, she moved out on me. I own the place where she lives, but Sharon moved out."

"Whatever…" God I hate that saying. I hate to sound like an old grump, but I absolutely hate it when kids say, "Whatever!" Like I said, I hate that word, but it seems to be part of today's young people's vocabulary.

I know, get used to it old man!

I said, "I'm going to leave you here. I'll leave Beanie with you if you want?" Kim shook her head no. I continued, "I'm asking you not to leave. Please stay here and I'll be back for you. There's some food in the fridge and drinks, too. Help yourself. Can you stay here alone? Will you be okay?" Kim agreed. I wrote my cell number on a piece of paper and gave it to her. "Call me if you have any problems."

I took her to the front room and then showed her around. Kim really liked the view over the lake and up the canal. "I'll be fine here," she assured me. "Go ahead. I'll be okay."

CHAPTER 9
SHARON

I decided to leave Beanie in the truck since the last thing I needed was any sort of distraction during this visit with Sharon. I've always joked about the four words that strike terror in a man's heart, "we need to talk." But, to be fair, I think it goes both ways. When a guy says those words, I suppose a woman is just as frightened as we are when we hear them.

Anyway, not only was this a talk I dreaded, but somewhere along the line I also needed to try and convince Sharon to let me stash Kim with her. Not to mention, I wanted Sharon to have some time with Kim to talk about her rape. I knew to pull this off, I had to keep all my wits about me and the last thing I needed was for Beanie and Sharon's dog Max to get together. They were littermates and to this day, when they get together they run through the house, barking at each other and then play fight on the floor until it just drives me crazy.

I have never wanted to hurt Sharon, but not talking about the elephant in the room was actually hurtful to both of us, and not addressing the issue was creating larger issues. We had danced around our problems for too long, and it was finally time to decide what we wanted to do with our relationship. I felt like an ass since we had just had dinner together the other night and it had been my intention to have the talk with her.

My feet drummed on the wood decking of the wharf as I walked out to the houseboat—the houseboat that had caused me so much grief in the past. But every time I see it now I like it more. The dark green shade is appealing and all of the exposed light-colored wood had been varnished. I really like it now.

I stepped up onto the barge the houseboat is built on and knocked. I waited a few minutes and was about to leave when Sharon cracked open the door. It was obvious she hadn't expected me. Mentally I kicked myself for not calling first. I realized since we were really no longer an item, it would have been polite to call first, but I didn't, and now here I was asking her if I could come in for a minute. She stood there looking at me with a troubled look on her face. She seemed to be ready to say something to me when from deep inside I heard a male voice call out, "Who is it, darling?"

Her face turned red and as she put her hand on my chest. I noticed it was shaking. I stepped back down onto the dock and as I turned, I called back over my shoulder, "I'm so sorry. It was really rude of me not to call first. I had no right to just show up. Forgive please."

She raised a hand and begged, "Stop! I want to talk to you. Can you come back in fifteen minutes? Please." Her last word was a plea.

"Yeah, sure," I said and I turned and started to walk away. I heard Sharon step onto the dock. I stopped and looked back at her. Her hair was messed up and I could tell she was naked under her robe. She stepped up to me and put her hand on my chest again. "Matt, please come back. I want to talk to you… no, make that I need to talk to you."

"Fifteen minutes?" I said it as both a question and a statement.

"Yes! Please. Will you come back?"

I nodded and she mouthed the words, "Thank you." I headed back to my truck. Bean was overjoyed to see me. I moved my truck to the far end of the lot to wait out the fifteen minutes. I knew it was childish, but I wanted to see who her visitor was.

As I sat there petting Bean, who by now was snuggled into my lap, I thought about what had just happened. When Sharon had moved out, we never discussed seeing other people. I had wanted to take Gladys to dinner but I didn't because I felt it would be cheating on Sharon. From what I'd just seen, it would seem she was doing a lot more than just having dinner with somebody. I knew I had no right to be angry, or hurt, but it was still painful to know she could move on so quickly after we parted ways. But I also try to be fair about things and I know I had been putting off having a discussion about our relationship, so I really had nobody to blame but myself.

After about ten minutes I saw a man walking up the dock dressed in a suit with his tie untied, just draped around his neck. He appeared to be in his late forties or perhaps early fifties. He didn't seem too upset about getting the bum's rush and I thought he was handsome in a rugged kind of way. His suit looked expensive. When he got to the parking lot, I watched as he climbed into a new BMW 700 series car. Whoever this dude was, he had money. I knew that the BMW with all the right bells and whistles could run well over a hundred grand, not to mention what the custom made suit cost.

I watched as he started his car and then pulled out into traffic. Once he was gone, I put the windows down a little for Bean and then locked up the truck. When I knocked, Sharon opened the door immediately. "Come in, please." She stepped back and motioned me in.

"Thanks," I said, and stepped into her living room. Sharon pointed towards the couch and asked me to sit down. She asked me if I wanted a drink and I almost said yes, but then I declined because I really needed to keep my wits about me. As I dropped onto the couch I noticed she had changed her bathrobe to sweats. Being the horn dog I am, I also noticed that she wasn't wearing a bra. Unfettered breasts made it difficult for me to maintain focus. See, I told you I was hopeless!

I knew I had screwed up big time and I hoped I could mend this fence. Looking up at her with a most sincere look on my face, I started in, "Sharon, I am so sorry I didn't call first. I didn't know—"

Sharon, facing me, held up her hands to interrupt, "Stop! No, Matt, this is so embarrassing. This is all my fault for not talking to you. I just dreaded having this conversation and I am such a chicken. I kept putting it off and now..." her voice dropped. She shrugged her shoulders and continued, "Oh shit! I was just looking for the right time to talk to you and it just never seemed to happen. I'm the one who's sorry." She was hanging her head and she directed the last few words at the floor. "Matt, I never wanted to hurt you."

I could tell she was upset with the situation and I wanted to let her off the hook. "Hey, look! Sharon, please look at me." She slowly raised her head and finally looked me in the eye. I explained, "I can't let you take all the blame. I'm just as guilty for not having the talk about us. I understand how it is, I know why you put it off. It's the same reason I kept putting off talking to you. I didn't want to hurt you either. It had been so easy to just let things float along." I sat there looking at her. I didn't care how it happened, I just was sorry I had embarrassed her. I continued, "Look kid, you have nothing to be embarrassed about, and anyway, regardless of when we should have had our talk, I was wrong not to call first. That was just rude and thoughtless on my part. For that I ask you to forgive me." I was serious and I hope she realized how I felt.

Sharon shook her head and gave a halfhearted laugh. "Okay, it's agreed, we're both at fault for today happening. I forgive you if you'll forgive me for having somebody here?"

There was really nothing to forgive her for. Sharon had only done what I wanted to do, which was to be with another person. I'll admit I was a little hurt to find her with another guy, but to be honest, if I could have dealt with my guilt about being with Gladys a little better, I'd have done the same thing. Just because I had been too chicken to try and define our relationship was in no way her fault. I smiled at her and replied, "Nothing to forgive, is there?" Sharon shrugged her shoulders. In a way, I was relieved that she had made the first move, and now it was just necessary to figure out where we wanted to go from here.

I leaned back on the couch and put my arms across the back. Sitting there I kind of wondered who the guy she had been with was. I briefly considered and rejected making a smartass comment about how I had just discovered her, but that wasn't really fair of me; since I had met Gladys, and I was interested in pursuing a relationship with her, I needed to do this. Since I felt this was the best time to finally work something out between us, I decided to ask Sharon about her visitor. I would get to the real point of my visit in a second, but first I asked, "It's none of my business, but who was the dude who just left?"

Sharon looked down at the floor for a second and then back up at me. "He's a doctor I know from the hospital. His name is George. Before you and I were involved, I dated him a few times. Lately he's taken me to dinner a couple of times. When he stopped by this afternoon… well, things happened and…" her voice trailed off.

There was no point in not addressing what was going through my head about the two of them. I asked, "So, I guess my question is: are we through, then?"

Sharon looked at me with a really sad face. Her chin was quivering and I saw a tear slowly slipping down her cheek. From the look on her face, I knew she still didn't have an answer yet. "Matt... well, yes and no."

"Yes and no? Care to explain that?" I asked with apprehension.

As she stood there, I still thought she was lovely with her hair all messed up and her eye makeup smeared. She really was a very sexy woman. As she spoke, her words were slow and soft. "Well, yes in that I would like to see others. I want us to be friends, but I'd like to date other men..." I shifted on the couch as I prepared to stand up. I was getting ready to leave. She extended her hand towards me. "Sit! Listen to me, please. To finish my thought, no we're not through, because I still want to see you as well." She walked over to a chair across from me and sat down. She sat for a long time just looking at me. Sharon took a deep breath and then asked, "Is that possible?"

It was my turn to just sit and wonder about things. I leaned back on the couch again for a while with my legs extended in front of me and my ankles crossed. I didn't really know what exactly to say and I just started rambling, "I think I understand why you want to see others," I thought about my next words carefully, "but I fail to understand why you still want to see me. What did I miss here?"

Sharon answered immediately, "Because I really do love you in so many ways, and you're my best friend." She snickered, "What I want, is what I think is called friends with benefits." Her face turned beet red and she looked down at her lap. She continued, "Matt, nobody understands me like you. I can tell you anything and you always understand.

And," her voice was barely a whisper, "Nobody satisfies me like you. Nobody can do the big nasty to me like you do!"

She looked directly at me and smirked as she continued, "You must think I'm really a slut." I shook my head no. I know I'm a slut, so how can I cast stones at her? Sharon continued, "George, the guy who was just here, he's very nice, but as a lover… well, let's just say he leaves a lot to be desired. As a surgeon he's the best, as a lover he is way too fast." She gave me a cute grin. "I was feeling so randy this afternoon and just as I was about to call you, he showed up. As you can tell, we had sex. But, the problem is, it wasn't all that satisfying."

In a way I was still hurt to find out about George, but I was pleased to hear she still wanted to see me and if she was going to start dating others, then that should make it permissible for me. I know it sounds so weird, but her admission to me that she still wanted to be with me was a turn-on. I guess I'm a typical male, because once she told me she still desired me, my cock went from a little lump in my pants to wide awake in seconds. I wanted her more in that moment than I can describe.

I know! I know. I really am a sleaze. The morals of an alley cat and all that. In my defense, I offer this: You had to have been there. There are certain moments in life that defy explanation and this was one of them. I'd ask for your forgiveness, but I don't deserve it. However, forgive me this time please.

Looking at her sitting there, I had to admit, Sharon was really something. It didn't matter to me Sharon had just been with somebody, I was pleased she was still interested in me. But more important, I was happy she wanted to continue to be friends, that meant a lot!

Eventually she looked at me and I could see the question forming., "By the way, just why did you come over?"

Caught! Now I was going to have to explain my feelings about the two of us. "Well, this is a bit difficult. Seeing as how I caught you and now you're going to think that's the reason…"

Her eyes grew large and she interrupted, "Were you coming over to break up with me just now?"

"Well, remember your earlier answer of yes and no? I have the same." Sharon's eyes were big and I could see she wanted more of an explanation. "Well, in a way it's like your yes and no. It was more like I wanted to discuss exactly what kind of a relationship you wanted with me. Way back in the beginning, I told you being your friend was important, more important than anything else, remember?"

"Yes, and I feel the same way." There was a long pause and when she spoke again, it was almost a whisper, "Are you going to break up with me?" Her voice sounded a little hurt.

I leaned forward, reached out and put my hand on her knee. "I didn't come here to break up with you, I came to see if we could come to a decision on what to do about our relationship. I hate it that we fight so much. But I understand why things are the way they are. We understand what our problems are; it just seems we can't change them. Since we don't live together any longer, I felt we needed to have some sort of an agreement regarding seeing other people. If for no other reason, so something like this afternoon doesn't happen." She smiled at me. I continued, "And as for making love with you, are you kidding? The sex part of us has never been the issue. Like I said, for some reason, after we've been together for a few days, we start to pick at each other, and that I just can't stand."

Sharon's voice was soft and I could tell she felt the same. "I know, and I don't know why we do that either." She added with a smile, "But I'm glad you still find me desirable."

I laughed. How do you explain what a treat it is to make love with a woman as sexy as Sharon, how do you tell her she's one in a million? "Darling, that was never an issue. I do find you desirable. Very desirable."

"Thanks." She paused and then asked, "What are we going to do about us?"

I thought things over carefully. "I think we should still keep an *us* as best we can. I want us to be friends. I also think we need to work on being able to talk to each other more freely in the future." I thought about how I wanted to tell her what I wanted to say. I pushed on, "But I think we should still be free to go our own way. Can you deal with that?"

Sharon was still for a long time. She gave a deep sigh and started talking, "Yeah. Just so long as we can remain friends. I love you so much, but you're such an asshole at times." She chortled. "I'll work on my communication skills with you if you promise to work on yours." I murmured agreement. "We're still friends?"

"Friends. And," I hesitated, "Well, there *is* one other thing,"

"Yes?" Her voice had taken on a slight edge.

"Well… um… I would like for us to still…" I waved my hand between the two of us, indicating my desire for us to be together. "That we'll still make love?"

Laughing she replied, "Oh God, I hope so. But just call me first." And we both broke up laughing.

I leaned back again on the sofa. It was time to get down to the main reason I stopped by. "Okay, now, there's still one small problem…" I tried to get a grip on how I wanted to approach the subject.

"Come on, out with it. How can you tell me in one breath you want to fuck me and then you get all tongue tied?"

I was starting to sweat. "Okay! I need a favor, a really big favor."

"How long are you going to drag this out?" she asked with amusement in her voice. "Can you get to the point sometime today?"

Quickly I told her, "Well, I need a place to hide somebody, and I was wondering—"

Her voice rose in volume as she interrupted me, "Hide somebody? What the hell do you mean hide somebody? Are they dead or alive?"

I was shocked. "Sharon! Alive of course!"

"Then why do you need to hide somebody?" She lifted one eyebrow as she looked at me. "Is it a female?"

"Yes! It's a female. A young woman." I could not believe how difficult it was telling her what I wanted.

"How young?" She looked at me with an amused expression on her face. I could see she was having fun at my expense.

"Maybe twenty. Maybe younger, I'm not really sure."

"Robbing the cradle?".

I heard her snicker when she asked me the question and I knew she was giving me a hard time. "Bill Tate, one of the guys at our poker games asked me to find his daughter. I found her and she's at my apartment now, but she needs a place to stay until I can find the dude who she claims tried to rape her… well, that isn't quite true either. She told one person she was actually raped."

I heard Sharon draw in a sharp breath. "Raped? Oh Matt, is she okay?"

"Yeah she was raped. I really don't know how well she's actually dealing with everything. She was dating this kid and at first she said he tried to rape her, but now she says he really did rape her. Later she found out he's tried to rape several women and perhaps even succeeded a few times. The problem is he's a big-time athlete over at the U and a lot of people are trying to just sweep this under the rug. She wants to make an issue out of this and he's threatened her. I found her and have her stashed for the moment but the problem is I don't feel comfortable having her at my apartment. Can I bring her here?"

"Why here?"

"Couple of reasons. Other than just a few of the guys at the poker game, and you, nobody knows about this place. She'd be safe here, and…" I paused for a moment.

"And what?" she asked with a hint of suspicion.

"I was hoping you could talk to her, you know, like woman to woman." I leaned forward and implored, "Shit, Sharon, you have training on helping women who were raped. See if you can find out if it's true. Was she raped, or did he just try and she got away? I can believe her either way since I've talked to one other woman who said this guy tried to rape her."

"Who is this dude anyway?"

"Claude Cox… Bud Cox."

Sharon leaned forward as she asked, "Matt, are you serious?" I nodded. She leaned back in her chair and took a deep breath. "We had a girl in the ER a few weeks ago, badly beaten and raped. She wouldn't tell us who did it. Even the police came and questioned her and she refused to talk. I spoke with her a few days later in her room and she seemed to open up to me a little. I asked her who had beaten her up and she told me she wouldn't tell. I asked her why she was protecting this bastard and she told me there was no point in telling, I wouldn't believe it if she told me. I asked her several times why she thought I wouldn't believe her and she finally told me he was a big deal jock at the U. I asked her again who it was and she got really frightened. She looked totally terrified and said she had told me too much already. If it ever got out she had said something, she could get beaten up again or even worse." Sharon's eyes were big and I could see some fear on her face. "I wonder if it was Cox who raped her."

"Do you know where to find her?" I asked.

"I guess I could look up her address from the admitting records, but with the laws the way they are today, it isn't something I should be doing. I could get in a lot of trouble."

"I was wondering if you could contact her and ask her if it was Cox."

"Let me think about it. When did you want to bring this girl by to stay with me?"

"In just a little bit, if it's okay with you?"

"Okay, I'll fix up the other room for her." I waited for a moment and then she continued, "And also, perhaps we will call one another before we show up at the other person's doorstep?" I knew she was serious, but there was a twinkle in her eye.

I had to laugh. "Sorry about that, it never occurred to me you might have a guest over. I was worried about the talk we needed to have, and if you would consent to having a guest for a while." I asked, "Does this mean I can date other women?"

Sharon smiled. "Who do you have in mind?"

Telling her a little white lie I said, "Nobody yet, but if I were to meet a woman I might like to take to dinner, are you going to get all wigged out?"

"After how you discovered me today?" We laughed and she told me, "But I'm glad you did come over, this is perfect. I've wanted to have this talk for so long and I feel much better now. I wanted to tease her that now she wouldn't have to feel guilty but I was pleased as well with the way things were turning out.

~ ~ ~ ~

I returned to the apartment and found Kim curled up in my favorite chair. The room was dark and she was watching the boats in the lake and the canal beyond. I told her she was sitting in my favorite chair doing one of my favorite things. We agreed how peaceful it was and the calming effect it had. I told her I had spoken to Sharon and she was ready for Kim to come over.

I decided to take Kim to the houseboat in my old Caddy convertible. The windows are darkened and I thought it was the best car for sneaking her over. I don't drive it very often and I didn't think any of Cox's buddies would have any idea what to look for.

On the way I gave her a brief rundown on how I had ended up with it, and why I thought it was such a good place for her to hide. I asked her if she minded if I told her parents where she was and she asked me to wait until tomorrow. I wasn't too wild about the idea but I agreed.

When we got to the marina parking lot I looked around to see if any cars seemed out of place. Nothing jumped out at me. I had a large parka on Kim and I had her pull up the hood. Beanie came with and the three of us walked down the dock. Sharon must have heard us coming because by the time we were standing in front of the door, she had it open. Kim stepped in quickly, but Beanie was faster. Once Sharon's dog Max saw Beanie, they took off running through the house.

Sharon was still dressed in sweats, but her hair was fixed and she looked very, well, nursey. And if that ain't a word, it should be. Once the door was closed, Sharon smiled warmly as she extended her arms towards Kim. As if the two of them were old dear friends, Kim stepped into Sharon's embrace and Sharon hugged her. Since Sharon was quite a bit taller than Kim, she seemed to engulf the smaller woman in her arms. Kim's shoulders started to shake and a sob escaped. Sharon had once again worked her magic. I don't know how she does it, but people just feel good about Sharon. She can meet total strangers and they'll fall all over themselves telling her things about their lives I just can't believe. Kim had fallen under her spell.

I waited until Kim was settled and I explained that I needed to get going. Sharon asked me if I was coming back and I told her I just didn't know how things were going to play out. I didn't want to tell Sharon in front of Kim I was going to look for Bud Cox, and I especially didn't want her to know about the two strange men who were following me.

CHAPTER 10
AN EVENING WITH GLADYS

I had spent the whole day working on my cars and as I was headed back to my apartment, I realized it was still rather early in the evening. I hadn't heard from Kim or Sharon all day, but I still wanted to touch base with Bill Tate. I made a quick call and explained to him I had Kim and she was safe. He asked me where she was, and I explained my promise to Kim about not divulging her location as one of the caveats I'd agreed to in order for her to allow me to hide her. I assured him Kim would want to see him in the next day or two, but most important, the place she was at, she was getting some counseling. I ended the call by asking him if he would mind calling his ex and letting her know Kim was safe. Bill ended with, "Okay, you know I trust you, Matt. That's why I asked you to help me. Thanks!"

There wasn't anything left for me to do until tomorrow, and now that I had official permission to date whom I desired, I wanted to stop by and see Gladys. I know some of you may think ill of me, considering I had just come to an understanding with Sharon the night before and all, but I felt now I was free, so to speak, I had every right to stop off and see Gladys. Remember, Sharon hadn't exactly been living a righteous life, had she?

When I pulled into Gladys' parking lot, I was pleased to see her car nestled in her parking stall. I parked my truck in a guest parking slot, went up and knocked at her door and waited. When the door opened, I was greeted by her enticing perfume and a sensual vision in clingy velvet. Her full-length bodysuit was tailored to fit and left little to the imagination. She looked really sexy, definitely erotic and most enticing.

Gladys stepped forward, wrapped her arms around me and hugged me hard. She looked up at me, kissed my cheek and said, "Matt, what a sweet surprise. Come in, come in, please." She took me by the hand and pulled me in. Once I was inside, she stopped and then looked behind me. "Where's Bean?" I told her she was out in the truck and after a tongue lashing, Gladys made me go back and fetch her. When I returned and sat Bean down, the dog ran through the house checking things over. Gladys laughed at her antics and pointed to the couch. "Sit. What can I get you to drink? Scotch?"

"Yes please."

"Same as last time?"

"Please."

When she returned with our drinks she sat on the couch next to me and Bean came up and sat on the other side. "To what do I owe this visit?"

"Plain and simple, I wanted to see you again. I was very taken with you last time we were together and you've been on my mind."

Gladys asked with a mischievous grin, "And how are things with your friend?"

I explained, "Well, I stopped by her place and caught her with somebody. We had a really long talk and basically we've come to an understanding. We'll live our lives as we want, but still continue to be friends."

"Friends with benefits?" she asked.

I was not going to lie. "Yeah. Being honest, I'm sure we'll still sleep together sometime in the future. Is that a problem?"

We both took a sip of our drinks and she replied, "No. If it becomes a problem, we'll have a talk. Okay?" I agreed and she leaned over and patted my hand. "But are you here just to get even with her? Is this something you're doing on the rebound?"

Her question caught me off guard. In a way it surprised me. I knew I wanted to get to know this lovely woman, but how much of this visit was some sort of a get even with Sharon on my part? "I won't lie to you. I don't think that's my motive. I'll admit I was hurt when I found them together."

"So, you still care for her?" Gladys interjected.

"Well, yeah. There are still some feelings. After our talk, it seems for now, we mainly want to be friends."

"And if you and I were to get involved, and she wanted you back, how would that play out?"

I was getting very uncomfortable now. What I had thought would be a fun evening was turning a bit dark for my taste. "I haven't lied to you yet and I am not going to start now. I can't tell you what the future will bring. All I can do is be honest about how things are. I told you the last time what was happening. And the reason I'm here is the chat I had with my friend." I took a sip of my drink and added, "Do you want me to leave?"

She placed her hand on mine. "No. And I'm sorry if you felt uncomfortable with my questions. I'm just trying to take care of me. I wanted to see where I stood." She patted my hand and I lifted her hand to my lips and kissed the back of it. She grinned at me and asked, "How did you know I was here?"

"I took a chance. You told me when you worked, you preferred working days, and I hoped you might be home."

Her smile was warm and her voice got husky, "Your timing is perfect. I just finished with my shower and I was wondering what I was going to have for dinner."

I asked, "Are you interested in going out for dinner?"

"Not really. I'm comfortable with what I have on," and she motioned with her hand at her outfit, "and I don't want to have to go and change. I can make us something here if you don't mind?"

"Well, I'd hate for you to change out of that outfit, I love it!" Gladys gave me her sexy smile. "If staying here keeps you dressed like that, it sounds great. Will you let me help with dinner?"

Gladys reached over and patted my hand. "In a little bit. Let's just sit and have our drinks." I settled deeper into the very comfortable couch. As we drank, we discussed various topics and I was once again astounded at the depth of this woman's knowledge of so many different subjects. To be honest, I'd never really known an exotic dancer all that well, and as much as I hate to admit it, most of my ideas were not based on fact. Just sitting next to her and listening to her talk, I was amazed.

Gladys noticed my glass was empty and without asking, took it from my hand. She stood and as she walked from the room, I was delighted watching the sexy sway of her nice round bottom. I know, I know, I'm such a sleaze. But in my defense, remember she does have a magnificent bottom!

She returned with two fresh drinks and handed me mine. This time when she sat on the couch, she was sitting much closer than before. Her warm leg was resting against mine and our shoulders were touching. She looked at me and smiled. "This is very nice. I can't thank you enough for coming over. I was really hoping I'd see you again."

"Why me?" I asked. I was sure, considering what she did for a living that she met a lot more interesting men than me.

I watched as she considered her response. "Let me explain a few things here if I may." I nodded. "Mostly, I like what I do. All in all, I like it a lot. Not to brag, but I make a vulgar amount of money. I have all the time off I want and for that reason I couldn't ask for a better job. I meet a lot of interesting men at work and I enjoy getting to know them— *at work*!" Gladys stressed the last two words. "You wouldn't believe the stock and real estate tips I've gotten from some of my clients. When the social security checks come, we get a lot of older gentlemen visiting us as well. The wise girls let them talk because they have years of business experience. To be honest, sometimes I feel like the girls and I should be paying some of the gentlemen who come to the club for all of the tips on business and investments they share with us."

Gladys took a sip of her drink and then continued, "But out of all the men I meet, there are very few I would wish to see outside of the club for a multitude of reasons. Now, because of the way we," she moved her finger between the two of us, "met, I don't see you as a client from the club. And because you're special, and I don't feel any conflict, I can let myself have feelings for you, which I am very careful not to let myself do with any guys from the club."

Gladys frowned as she continued, "A lot of guys think since I dance, I must be a hooker, that I'll fuck them for money. It is true I let guys feel me up, and that I rub against them, but I provide a service, if you will, I make lonely men happy. I will admit getting pawed is the part of the job I don't like that much but, you take the good with the bad with any job."

She took a deep breath and let it out, "Anyway, you were the perfect gentleman in the grocery store. From the way you helped pick up my stuff off the floor, to you not saying anything about seeing me in the club. Then in the parking lot you complimented me on my dancing, which really made me happy because I do try very hard to do it well. I know many of the girls just take off their clothing and flash the men and call it good. I try and put on a little show, and you noticed that. I appreciated that a lot. Then when we were here, I showed interest in you, but you were up front with me. You didn't try and have sex. You were honest about your... ah, friend?" I smiled. "You just seem to keep doing the right things and I was really hoping you'd come back and see me. It's a real pleasure to have you come back."

Gladys reached over and put her hand on my thigh and squeezed. "Thanks." With that, she leaned over and kissed my cheek. "Sweetie, it's time! I need to eat something. Breakfast was a long time ago and these drinks have done their job."

I watched her walk into the kitchen, having really sexy thoughts that her sweet swinging bottom brought to mind. When I tried to stand, I could tell I had consumed a couple of very stiff drinks. I needed something to eat, too. I walked carefully into the kitchen and asked her what I could do to help. She replied, "Stand there and talk to me. Oh wait, do you know how to start a gas grill?" I answered in the affirmative. "Great, it's out on the balcony. Fire it up."

I did as I was told and once I had all the burners going I came back in the kitchen. There were several chicken strips soaking in some sort of a marinade and she was making risotto in a pan. "Is it going?" she asked when I returned. I agreed that it was. I was so totally enthralled with watching this lovely young woman, speech was difficult. It was either that or the couple of strong drinks she had given me. "Give it a couple of minutes and then put the strips on the grill. Make sure you turn it down just a titch."

I took the chicken out and put it on the grill. After a few minutes I turned it, and when they were ready, I took them off the grill and brought them into the kitchen. While I'd been out, she had set the table in the kitchen, and now there were candles burning in the middle, and the lights were turned off. In the short time she had been working, she had prepared a small fruit salad and had dished up the risotto. The chicken was done to perfection and even though it was a quickly made meal, it was superb.

~ ~ ~ ~

When we were finished with dinner, Gladys cleared the dishes from the table and stacked them in the sink. Once she was finished, she reached out, took my hand and led me back to the couch. She excused herself for a moment and when she returned she had two brandy glasses in her hand. I took a sip and the liquid warmed my mouth and then all the way to my tummy.

"I'm glad I came over. I thought about you a lot."

"Even with your friend?"

"You asked me if this was something on the rebound, me coming here.. When I went to have my talk with my friend, I caught her in an… umm… embarrassing situation, for both of us. I was rude and didn't call and, well... she had a guest. I'll be honest. I was a bit hurt. But I was also kind of relieved that something had finally happened. I guess this makes me a real sleaze, but I thought about you. I realized that I could come and see you and not feel like I was cheating."

We sat sipping our drinks for a while. I could tell Gladys was thinking about something. Finally, it looked like she had made a decision. She reached over and patted my hand and then excused herself. I watched in delight as she walked away. I called out after her, "By the way, remind me to me to tell you about the day in the grocery store when we first met."

"Oh, what about it?"

"When you come back." She smiled and sauntered from the room.

When she returned she had changed. Now she was wearing the most transparent negligee I'd ever seen. If there's such a thing as spun spider webs, this was it. Things were covered, but they weren't. I'm not sure, but I swear my eyes popped out. Gladys picked up her glass and sat back down beside me. "Okay, I'm back. What were you going to tell me?"

I laughed and started to tell her about being bored while I was standing in line. "It seemed to take forever to go through the checkout, and I started checking out your ass."

"Oh really," she smirked. "And what did you think?"

"First off, I adore a woman in a dress and your dress that day was really something. Then there was the actual butt inside of the dress and that was even more enticing." Gladys smiled. "I could have stood in line for another day just checking you out." Gladys reached out and ran her finger softly over my cheek. I said jokingly, "I see you've slipped into something more comfortable."

"Matt, I like the way you make me feel. You've been a real gentleman tonight. I'm going to share a secret with you. Something I've never told a soul." I drew back and lifted my eyebrows. I was ready for her secret. "Usually when I dance, I get really horny. I mean sometimes I have to come home and masturbate for at least an hour before I can calm down. When you rang the doorbell, I was just getting ready to have a drink and then take care of myself." Her voice dropped and became low and sultry. "How do you feel about helping out a lady in distress?" Gladys had wrapped her hands around one of my arms and was leaning against me.

That was a request that did not need a second invitation. I followed as she led me back to her bedroom and a king sized bed. She stopped in the middle of the room and slipped off her outfit. I pulled my clothes off as fast as I could and we met in the middle of the bed. Making love is always good, but once in a while it seems to me that the act goes to a higher plane. I don't want to get carried away here, but being with her was why humans are so driven. Making love with Gladys bordered on a religious experience.

We lay there for some time in a blissful state, both of our bodies just humming along. Gladys sighed and said, "I don't have to work tomorrow. Wanna go up and see my boat?"

"Can't. I have to go and see a friend about a problem that's cropped up. Well, maybe I shouldn't call him a friend... more like an acquaintance. Anyway, I'm looking for somebody and I hope he can help me find him."

"Who are you looking for?" she asked.

"A kid that goes to the U. Football player named Cox." I felt her tense under my arm and heard her draw in her breath with a hiss. "What's the matter, Gladys? Do you know him?"

It was a long time before she answered and when she spoke, it was all I could do to hear her. "Bud Cox has raped at least two of the girls who work with me. The problem is both of them took some money before they went off with him. But it got really ugly and he beat both of them up. He tied them up and raped them both in front and back several times and when he cut them loose, he said them if they told anybody about it, some of his buddies would come and pay them a visit. And after his friends were done, their faces would be so ugly they'd never work again."

"Are you okay?" I asked

"Sorry. It's just that I held one of the gals when we took her to the hospital. Her anus was so torn it needed stitches, and to this day she hasn't been able to dance. I heard about the other one through the gossip at work." Gladys sounded frightened as she continued, "Matt, I think you need to keep away from this kid. He's a really bad egg."

"So you're telling me you want me to let him keep raping women? I don't believe that."

"Matt, don't be an ass, you know I'm not saying that. I just don't want you to get hurt." Her eyes were big and her face looked frightened as she talked to me.

"Baby, I don't want to sound macho, but I can take care of myself. I'll be careful. Very careful." I kissed her on her forehead.

"Please. I want to see you again."

"Really? Like the way I do the chicken, huh?"

She pushed an elbow into my side. "No... not really; your chicken sucks. I like the way you do me." I felt her hand slip down my tummy and gently grab my soft penis.

I wondered how I was going to explain things to her. "Gladys. I have to tell you, there's nothing left in there. I'm spent."

"Oh, really?" she asked. "Do you mind if I check? You might be surprised."

I'm glad I let her check.

~ ~ ~ ~

The next morning over coffee, she asked me again if I was going try and find Cox. I told her I was and she asked how I was going to go about it. I started to explain I knew this fellow down in the Central District. I told her he was a very mysterious man. I went on to tell her he was just a little bitty guy but he dressed better than a GQ model. Gladys piped up, "Do you mean Mouse?"

I don't know why, but I was surprised. "How do you know Mouse?" I asked.

"Please don't make me sorry I ever told you this, but very few people know. He owns the largest share of Robbie's and you wouldn't believe who some of his partners are." I was surprised, but in a way I wasn't. "I've met him on several occasions. He's always been a gentleman and has never hit on me, but I can tell he's interested. He's a very sweet man, but he doesn't appeal to me that way. I do adore him, though. Tell him hello for me please."

"I'll do that."

Gladys reached out and touched arm. "When will I see you again?" she asked in a sexy voice.

I gave her a big grin. "Soon. I have another problem I'm dealing with, too. I'll let you know when I can see you again. I promise."

"Thanks for a nice evening," Gladys purred.

"So you like the way I grill chicken?" I picked up Bean and made my way to the door.

Gladys laughed and answered, "Yeah, but the way you take care of me is even better."

CHAPTER 11
MOUSE

Mouse's real name is Steve Fox, but other than Sakol and me, I don't think anyone else knows that. The reason Mr. Fox is called Mouse is his size. I'm around 6'3" and I must be at least a foot taller than he is. Other than his size, there are two outstanding things about Mouse. The first is the way he dresses. The man is a walking advertisement for GQ. The other is his knowledge of what's happening in not only Western Washington, but around the world. The man knows secrets that I find almost frightening. In addition, he seems to know everybody. I figured if anybody knew anything about Bud Cox, Mouse would.

When Sakol and I visited Mouse at what I refer to as his place of business, I swore I would never go back. It was without a doubt one of the most frightening places I have ever been. Considering where I've been and what I've done, that's a strong statement. I guess the lesson learned here is: never say never.

I parked a few doors down and carefully locked my car. The street in front of his building and the stairs leading down to his den were exactly as filthy as I remembered them. The light at the bottom of the stairs was just as feeble as I remembered from my last visit. The place did not invite unwanted visitors by its appearance.

I'd seen Sakol reach out and turn a doorknob somewhere. I fumbled around until I located it and opened the door. The room was still dark but I thought the stench was worse than last time. This time I knew where I was going and I was able to navigate the dimness. When I touched the door at the end of the room, a massive black man stepped out of the shadows. His voice was a rumble. "What do you want?"

"I'd like to see Mouse," I announced, trying not to show any fear.

"Do you have an appointment?" the rumbly voice asked.

"No, but—"

The man interrupted me, "Does he know you?"

"Yes, I've been here before. And we have mutual friends."

"Just a minute. Stay here." The door opened a fraction and the gigantic man slipped through into the next room. What I found strange was he had not even asked my name. The door hadn't closed completely when it opened up again. The immense man opened the door wide and invited me in.

The overblown elegance of the room stunned me, just as it had on my first visit. Everything about the room whispered luxury. I saw the fire burning brightly in the fireplace and Mouse sitting behind his massive desk. When he saw me, he jumped up and literally ran towards me. He extended his hand and as we shook, he held my hand in both of his and exclaimed, "Matt! What a treat to have you come and visit. I never thought you'd come back here again." I couldn't help myself, I had to laugh. Mouse smiled and continued, "I can't believe I'm seeing you so soon. And how is the young lady you were with?"

"She's doing well, thanks. She's with my friend who's a nurse. The young lady had some challenges she needed help dealing with."

"She's with Sharon?" Mouse asked.

I had to laugh. His face got serious again and he continued, "For you to come here and see me, you must have something very important to talk to me about. Please, come sit."

He pushed a button concealed on his desk and the same lovely petite Asian woman I'd seen last time came into the room. "Coffee with lots of cream for our guest," he told her.

"Very good sir." She smiled at me, bowed and left the room. I was impressed Mouse remembered what I'd drunk when I visited with Sakol. He motioned to one of the over-sized leather chairs in front of the fireplace and I sat down. He took the chair directly across from mine.

He said, "I cannot begin to tell you how very pleased I am to see you again, but I'm also not so stupid as to believe you just came for a social visit. His voice was cordial, but his curiosity was apparent.

I was embarrassed. This man was so outgoing and seemed to go out of his way to make me feel comfortable and here I was making a visit with a motive. "You embarrass me."

Mouse laughed. "Please, I know how people feel about me. To be honest, it's to my advantage and it's something I try and cultivate. I know how people view me, and I do understand how difficult it must be for you to come and see me. Matt, all I ask is you keep in mind that everything you think you see is not as it appears." I wondered what the hell he was talking about.

Mouse leaned back in his chair, folded his hands and put his feet on the ottoman. "Now, tell me, what is it you want from me?"

I decided the best approach was to just come right out and tell the man. "I'm looking for Bud Cox."

He frowned. "Why? What do you want him for?" There were no wasted words, just right to the point.

"I play poker with Bill Tate." Mouse tilted his head. "The last game we played together, Bill asked me to see if I could find his daughter. He had heard about my… ah… my visit to Ross Island and everything that happened, and he knows some of what came out of it." Mouse looked thoughtful. "Tate's daughter was in hiding from Cox when you saw me trying to get her out of the hood. She says Cox raped her, and she wants something done about it. Kim says the school doesn't care, and she's told people Cox threatened her. She's also been threatened by people telling her they'll do her harm if she doesn't back off.

"But it goes deeper than that. I have a friend who works at Robbie's, who by the way sends her greetings, and she told me two of the girls from the club were raped, but because they took money from Cox to have sex with them, they can't go to the police."

Mouse laced his fingers together. He pointed his knuckles at me and asked, "Who's your friend?"

"Gladys. I believe you know her as Sadie."

Mouse's face lit up with a smile. "Ah, what a lovely woman. I have so often enjoyed the way she dances. I mean, she really dances. Lovely woman." The smile slipped off his face as he continued, "Anyway, I'm disturbed she never told me about the rapes, even if the girls took money for sex. I know a lot of what goes on at Robbie's." I didn't think it was wise to tell him I had heard about his connection with Robbie's. He continued, "I've heard the same rumors. And I've also spoken to the lad—not about what you want to discuss with him—but he is impressive." A look of sadness came to Mouse's face and he shook his head. "It seems that you never know who to trust and who to fear." I thought that was one of the most profound statements he could have uttered.

I said, "I've heard so many things. I'd like to find Cox and see what's up. I want to talk to him. I'm told he's an engaging person, but I also hear the kid's an animal. Which is correct? I thought if anybody could put out the word, it would be you."

Mouse smiled. "You flatter me."

"No sir. When I was here with Sakol I was stunned by your knowledge of what goes on in this city. I kid you not, I found it almost frightening. I had no idea our poker games had come to your attention and the fact that you knew about my… ah... difficulties with the men I knew from the service was unsettling."

I went on, "I know you put the word in the right people's ear and things happen. I'm positive you can get Cox to come and talk to me, and that's why I came to see you." I looked down for a moment and concluded, "In addition, I'm embarrassed that I haven't come back for a social visit. That was rude of me."

Mouse laughed and clapped his hands. "Okay, you're forgiven. As for your request, consider it done—with one provision." I raised my chin. "You will not harm him. Regardless of what you learn from him, you will not harm him in any way. Do I have your word on that?" I nodded. Mouse smiled at me and said, "You just go about your business and I'll have him come and find you. Will that work?"

I can't explain how much I wanted to ask how he could get Cox to come and see me. In addition I wanted to know how he was going to keep tabs on me. But I decided there are some things best left unasked. I was asking the man for his help and I just needed to trust him. I replied, "Yes."

Mouse cleared his throat and then held a finger. "Please, there is one more thing I would like to ask of you. After your chat with Mr. Cox, please come back and talk to me. I've heard rumors as well, but I also hear all of the good things about him. I respect your judgment and I'd like to hear what you have to say. Will you do that for me?"

I agreed. There was a rap on the door and the elegant Asian woman returned with a large cup of coffee, just the right color for my taste. She bowed as she handed me the cup and I thanked her. I was surprised to see she actually blushed. She bowed to Mouse and left the room.

"I'm impressed. You seem to have made an impression on Jade. She never blushes when I thank her for her services." I was positive I was blushing now. I took a sip of my coffee and it was excellent.

"By the way Matt, may I make an observation?"

"Of course," I said.

"Do you know much about the two gentlemen that are following you?" he asked.

I was speechless. At first I wondered how the hell Mouse knew about the colonel and the suit, and then I realized this was just Mouse being himself. "You're amazing," I said. "How do you know about the colonel and the suit?"

"The colonel, as you call him—I don't know exactly what his true rank is. I believe he wears the uniform to intimidate you. Anyway, I've known him for a long time and I've never trusted him, or the super-secret organization he works for. I would tell you stories, but I can't." He grinned. "Matt, I'm advising you not to trust him. The man is incapable of telling the truth."

He continued, "The other man, what did you call him? The suit? All I know is there was a chopper pilot with his name in Viet Nam. Rumor has it that he went on to be a chopper jockey for hire. He's supposed to have been all over the Middle East, both flying and teaching how to fly. It's my understanding he's worked for both our military and for the other side as well. The story on him is that it's amazing what he can coax a chopper to do.

"I've heard he doesn't look like much, but then looks can be so deceiving." Boy did I know that. Just looking at Mouse you'd never know he had his fingers in just about every important business deal and every important political happening in the state. He was truly the puppet master, the man behind the scene. I couldn't help it, I laughed out loud. If anybody's looks are deceiving, it's Mouse's. He seemed to understand what I was laughing at and as he smiled at me, he turned his hands over with the palms facing up. The gesture made him more endearing; he knew what he looked like, but he also knew how people viewed him.

Mouse said, "But, that's where the problem comes in. The pilot from Nam and the pilot who was later for hire have been described as looking totally different. To me, it sounds like there may be two people, and the second one is riding the reputation of the jockey from Viet Nam. Anyway Matt, the pilot from Nam is also someone I wouldn't trust. Too many things just don't add up."

I leaned back and stared at him. I was dying of curiosity, I just had to know. "Mouse, may I ask you a question?"

"I think I know what you're going to ask, but go ahead anyway, and I promise I won't take offense." He leaned back in his chair.

I took a breath and then started, "I'm going to ask this right out. How do you know all this… this information?"

In a hushed voice he said, "I guess my answer should be, 'if I told you, I'd have to kill you.'" When he saw the look on my face he started to laugh. I knew he meant it as a joke, but I also knew there was a grain of truth in what he said. The look in his eyes didn't match the laughter in his voice.

"Seriously Matt, let me put it this way. The way I make my living could be considered by some as living outside of the law." I leaned forward to say something and Mouse held up his hand. "Please let me finish. I'm a broker of information. I know many things about, well many things. If I don't keep on top of them, then I have nothing to sell. I gather information, and I'm lucky enough to be in a position where I can sell it. Everyone seeking to purchase this information has their own set of laws. I listen to everybody and make my decisions based on... well, based on my judgment. Because I move back and forth between these groups, I pick and choose the laws I wish to respect. I do not believe in harming others and that is a law I will respect. So many laws are actually rather gray if you think them through. As you were raised, were you taught, thou shall not kill? Yet, if somebody in the correct position decides it's right, then one person kills another. Which law was violated? Which law will you uphold? Do you understand?"

"Yes and no, but it really doesn't matter to me. There have been parts of my life, and things I've done in my past I would prefer not to have anybody judge, so I'm in no position to judge." I realized Mouse had not really answered my question, but I didn't think it was wise to pursue an answer either. "Who you are, what you are, all of it is none of my business. I just wanted to let Cox know I want to talk to him and I thought you were my best resource."

Mouse extended a finger towards me and said, "Thank you for the vote of confidence. And, may I offer you a piece of advice? And since it's free, you know what it's worth. Watch the colonel and the flyboy very carefully. I know you call flyboy the suit, but in reality, if he is who he claims to be, at one time he was a very gifted helicopter pilot. Both of them in their own ways are very dangerous. Looks can be very deceiving. Don't sell anybody short." Mouse leaned back and smiled at me, "And so ends the lesson, grasshopper." He stood. I could tell I was being dismissed.

"Goodbye, Matt."

As I shook his hand, I said, "Goodbye, Mouse. I want you to know I think you're a very impressive individual. I have the utmost respect for you. There are not a lot of people I respect as much as I do you. I fear that when we first met I may have sold you a little short."

He looked back up at with a mischievous look on his face. He asked, "Is that a short joke?"

I was so embarrassed. "Oh no, that's not what I meant. I'm…" He dissolved into a fit of laughter.

"Goodbye Matt." He took my arm and turned me towards the door. "I do hope you come back and see me again. I've enjoyed our visit, more than you will ever know." I stepped through the door and into the darkness of the front room. As I passed through what I had thought of as the drug den, I looked around a little harder this time. There were shapes sitting around the room, but none of them were moving. They tables were empty, just a couple of candles providing the dim illumination. Besides the large bouncer and me, there was nobody else in the room. It was all an elaborate ruse. Why the room looked the way it did I had no idea, just something else to add to the "Mouse Mystique." When I reached the exit, the large black man reached out and opened the door for me. "Have a good day, sir." His voice was warm and friendly.

Even though the light was still dim, for the first time I could make out his features. He looked familiar. In an instant the thought 'football' flashed through my mind and I wondered if his size made me think he played ball, or if I recognized him from his playing days. The door shut behind me with a click. The fortress was now closed and locked.

I had done what I could. I had put out the word I wanted to see Bud Cox. Kim was safely hidden away with Sharon and she would let me know when Kim wanted to meet with her parents. Now I just had to wait for Cox to find me and see just what kind of person he was. I wondered how much of what I had heard was true. I had a very difficult time believing Kim was lying, and an even harder time believing Gladys would lie to me.

Now I was ready to deal with my other problem. I had to get a handle on the colonel and the flyboy. Hopefully Walter would have some ideas. I'd written him earlier in the week and tomorrow I was going to catch a ferry and go over to see him. I didn't know how much light he could shed on Crescent, or my two strange shadows and the rest of the mess, but I'd found in the past talking things over with him seemed to help.

CHAPTER 12
WALTER

I'm always excited when I have the opportunity to go over and visit Walter. I don't know if it's seeing how happy he is with life, or looking at the amazing structure he's constructed to live in, or if my happiness is over something I was involved with that turned out so well. I was the one who saw Walter's picture in the Seattle newspaper and read that he had been picked up for being in a disturbance down in the International District. I'd instructed my attorneys to do whatever was necessary to get him out of jail and deal with his legal problems. Basically, it turned out that after Walter's time in Viet Nam, he never really was able to fit back into society. I gave him a chunk of land I owned over on the Olympic Peninsula where he doesn't have to deal with very many people, and he built what he calls a cabin. It's more like a work of art and calling it a cabin doesn't do it justice, but that's another story. The point is, it never fails to bring me enjoyment to visit my friend Walter and his lovely wife, Thien.

I pulled up to the ferry ticket window, paid my fare and then parked where the attendant indicated. In just a few minutes, a ferry pulled in and I sat in my vehicle and watched as people drove off. Soon it was my turn to drive my rental car onto the boat and then head across the Sound. I considered getting out, but my mind was so full of things to think about, I decided to just stay in the vehicle. Bean crawled into my lap and promptly fell asleep.

As I sat there petting her furry little body, my mind started to wander. My very first concern was about whoever had been following me off and on, and what their intent was. I was sure I had taken the proper steps to cover my tracks, and I doubted if the gray van was following me now. But so far I'd been surprised by the colonel's knowledge about me and I was taking all of the precautions I could. I had no idea what he knew about Walter, but I wanted to keep Walter as safe as possible.

Since the colonel knew all of my vehicles, I decided to drive something neither the colonel nor the suit had seen before. I parked my truck up in my man cave, and then I used a back exit from the building into an alley. I cut down the alley and then walked over a few blocks to a rental car agency. Even though I was now driving a strange vehicle, I was still being cautious. Once I was close enough to Walter, I knew a place where I could pull off and see several miles behind me and make sure I wasn't being followed.

My next concern was a bit more selfish. I have for the most part put away a good deal of what happened back in rice paddy land, and usually I'm at peace with it, or at least as much as one can be at peace having done some of the shit I've done. Basically, I just made sure I didn't dwell on my past very much. I think those who want to relive horrible events need to find a way to move on. We all have to find a way to deal with our past. Having to revisit the past again now, so soon after my last encounter, was difficult. I found myself returning to memories I had worked hard to keep locked securely away. I also wondered if any unresolved issues with Sharon weren't making things difficult as well. And now to cap it off, here I was on the ferry headed to see Walter again. Even as pleased I was to see him, who knew what doors this visit was going to open? And more to the point, did I want those doors opened? Did I really have the choice?

The ferry pulling up to the dock roused me from my contemplations. I was one of the first ones in line. On the off chance I might be followed, I sped through town and headed towards the mountains. When I reached the pull off, I looked in my rearview mirror and there was no traffic to be seen for miles behind me. I parked behind a large rock and got out. I sat on the rock for better than fifteen minutes and watched back down the road. Only five vehicles passed by and none of those was a gray van. As far as I could tell, I wasn't being followed.

When I pulled into the graveled spot where I usually leave my vehicle, Walter was sitting on a stump next to the clearing waiting for me. We hugged and then he teased me, "I've seen you more in the last few months than all the years since Nam. What gives? Did ya miss me?"

I was amused. Walter was correct. "Well, hello to you too. I need to talk to you about something that's come up. Since this is the only way to see you, I had to come over."

"Come on. You can talk while we walk."

I didn't want to tell him my real reason for coming over yet. I had no idea if he knew anything about what the colonel had asked, but I wanted him to be able to tell me what he knew, if anything, without any interruptions. "Sharon sends her love to you and Thien."

"How are the two of you doing?" he asked.

I hesitated for a moment. "Well… she moved out and lives on the houseboat now."

He stopped so quickly I almost ran into his back. He turned and asked, "What! Why?"

"Go on, don't stop like that." I gave him a push to start him walking. He just stood there and I started to tell him what was going on with Sharon. "Well, we just do better living apart. We still see each other and we even spent the night together, but day to day it just doesn't seem to work for us." He was still standing there and I gave him another push to turn around and get going.

"Damn. And I was so happy for the two of you," he said.

"Well damn, why can't you still be happy for me? I'm happy for me." And we both laughed.

Thien was overjoyed to see me; she once told me that if I hadn't helped Walter back in Seattle he probably would have died of a drug overdose, or worse. They now have a son, my namesake, and I was proud they named him after me, but I was also embarrassed. Little Matt was just barely able to walk and he really was a cute little guy. I could see how proud Walter was of his son and it made me feel good. The three of us sat and talked a while and finally Thien excused herself with "I will make us something to eat."

After she left, Walter looked at me and said, "Okay. Now, why did you come over? I'm glad you're here, but I know it isn't because of my winning personality. I know something's up."

I had planned this conversation many times in my head but now that it was time to tell him, I didn't know exactly where to start. "I guess I might as well just tell you the whole story and hope I don't miss anything." I told him about my two late-night visitors and then about the strange meeting we had at the old playing field. I told him about the van that was following me, and its involvement with the colonel and the suit. I told him about the license plate but I also assured him the van had not followed me to his place, and that I was sure he was safe.

I concluded with, "Walter, the two of them keep asking me the same thing every time I see them. It doesn't mean a thing to me, but does the word Crescent mean anything to you?"

He gasped and went pale. It actually frightened me to see the change in his demeanor. "Walter, are you okay?" I asked.

He gulped and said, "Matt, are you sure they said Crescent?" I raised my eyebrows and gave him a grim look. He leaned towards me, the tension apparent. "Listen to me. Listen to me *very* carefully and do what I tell you. Have dinner with us and then take Bean and go back to your car and go home. Go home and forget all about this. And most importantly, never… I repeat… *never,* say that word again. Leave this alone. Do you understand?"

"You mean Crescent?" Walter held a finger to his lips and made a shushing sound. He nodded his head yes and I shook my head no. There was no way I could walk away now. "No Walter, I don't understand. I had a strange vehicle following me. When I asked Jeff to run the plates for me he got a huge ration of shit over it. I had two very weird men come to my apartment and then demand to meet me again at an old deserted sports field, asking strange questions, and, all I know about this is that it's somehow all related. The two strangers are obsessed with something called Crescent. So I'm asking you again, what is this Crescent thing? Come on Walter, talk to me. This is, me, Matt… your friend. What's going on?"

Walter excused himself and went into his cabin. In just a few minutes he returned with his glass pipe in hand along with a lighter and some weed he had grown in his garden. He putzed around cleaning the pipe and then slowly filled it with weed. I have always thought that pipe smokers use their rituals to stall for time to mull things over, and as I watched Walter, he was no different. Eventually the pipe was filled to his liking and he lit it and took a long draw. He took another puff and passed the pipe to me. As I held it in my hand, it dawned on me the only time I smoked anymore was when I was visiting Walter. I wondered if perhaps Walter was a bad influence on me. But then I quickly decided, *Naw!* I can be bad without any influence! Walter slowly let the smoke out of his lungs as he slid down in his chair and put his feet up on the big wooden ottoman.

Just by his posture, I could see he was mentally back "in country." There was nothing to do but wait. Wait until he returned. He lit the pipe again and took another long puff. As he released the smoke, he started to talk. His voice was just above a whisper and I had to listen carefully to hear him. "God, I hope I never regret telling you this." He looked over at me and I could see in his eyes he was questioning himself about talking to me.

"By the way, all of this is AM!" I know I had a questioning look on my face. Walter leaned close to me and said, "After Matt." We both chuckled. "Crescent was the code word for a mission that happened back in Viet Nam after you were gone." I had that part already figured out. "It was top secret; a fucked up very top secret mission. Even at the briefing I knew the mission came from a long way up the food chain... if you catch my drift?"

I murmured agreement and he continued, "It was me, Price, Hollis, some captain Green Beret dude and a warrant officer. The warrant was a hotshot chopper flyboy. Captain was a tall skinny dude, but in amazing condition. I don't remember much 'bout the warrant officer, except he was a dumpy looking little fellow and he was a helicopter pilot... a very, very good one. The story on him was once he went out and picked up a bunch of wounded in the middle of an ugly firefight. Bullets flying everywhere and this warrant knew he only had one shot to get as many wounded out as he could on the one try. His chopper was full and he was ordered to dust off a couple of times, but he ignored them and kept waiting while they stuffed more wounded into his bird."

The way Walter stared off into space, I could tell he was reliving the memory. He took a puff and then handed me the pipe. Finally, he continued, "The helicopter was so overloaded it barely made it off the pad. Those rice balls kept pouring bullets into it and by the time he returned to base, there were so many holes in the bird that when it landed, it actually fell apart. Matt, it was like a cartoon. He got the thing landed, they pulled all of the wounded people off and as the warrant walked away, it literally just disintegrated behind him. There was just this pile of metal. He was a legend. Nobody could understand how he got the thing in the air, or how he kept it in the air or how he ever landed it without crashing. I never did hear how many he had on his bird or how many lives he saved, but he got a big-time medal for it."

Walter got quiet and I knew he was thinking about his story. He gave a short bark of laughter and continued, "Weird looking little dude too. Looked like a pear with legs, but man, could he fly a chopper. Nobody could ever figure how he made it through flight school. I mean, they like would run all the time and there was a lot of physical training. It must have damn near killed him." Walter laughed again at the memory. From Walter's description, the colonel and the suit sounded like the two he was describing.

"Anyway, back to Crescent. The warrant flies us into this remote location to a place that was as off limits as it could be. I was sitting where I could see the compass over his shoulder and I watched our heading for a long time. Matt, we were on a course that took us to a place we were never supposed to go."

"When we got there we met a couple of village leaders. The two chiefs had some gold bars and they wouldn't tell us how or where they got them. They just told us they could get a lot more and what they wanted was stuff… military stuff. The captain promised them everything they asked for and they made a deal for a shit ton of gold.

"When the deal was set to go down, I ended up being assigned to a different mission. I think it was cause the captain didn't trust me. The captain got Price and Hollis and a couple more guys and they all went off in a Huey with loads of military equipment. Later I heard the warrant barely got the chopper off the ground, it was so heavy."

Walter took another deep puff. He exhaled and started in again, "A few weeks later I heard through the grapevine the two dudes that went with them were never seen or heard from again… listed as AWOL. Hollis and Price showed up back at base camp for a while and then were off on a new mission. The next time I saw them, Price was all fucked up and we were taking a powder off the hill and out of country.

"The really weird part is the captain returned with all of the stolen stuff and nothing was ever said. The warrant just landed the bird with all the stuff the captain had pulled and they both disappeared. If you asked any questions about what happened, you were just told it was part of 'Code Crescent' and that meant 'shut your mouth, don't ask questions, it's none of your fucking business.'"

I took a hit off the pipe and as I handed it back to Walter, I asked, "I wonder why the colonel—who I think was the captain in your story—came and asked me what Hollis said up in the tower."

Walter settled back in his chair, deep in thought. Still looking out across the valley, he said, "Well, the grapevine said the gold disappeared. The deposit they got when I was with them, and the payment for the military stuff. Somehow the warrant, the captain and Price and Hollis all got separated. Lots of rumors about that. I heard the warrant flew off with the gold, but I also heard that the captain and the pilot came back together with the stuff. I heard Hollis and Price knew where it was, but there was no way I would ever ask them any questions. I even heard the captain took off with it. But it looks like if your colonel is that captain, he didn't take it either. Either way, I guess we really don't know what happened."

"Why didn't you want me to ask you about Crescent?" I asked Walter.

It was difficult to make out Walter's features in the dusk. He sat quietly for so long I started to wonder if he'd fallen asleep. Eventually he grunted and looked over at me. "I'm happy with my life, Matt. I don't want it to change." I understood, and I had to agree. Walter did have a great life now. "I cannot begin to describe how amazed I am at how my life turned out. I know you get it because you're a big part of why I'm here and because of Thien and all, you know?"

"I understand. I'm happy your life is so good. For a while, I was very concerned about you."

He nodded and continued, "Crescent? Matt, without you being able to read my mind or something, there is no way to explain why I felt the way I did, but from the first moment I heard about Crescent, I knew something was wrong." Walter turned to me and leaned forward. "You know Price and Hollis? You know how crazy weird they were? That was just the start of how spooky Crescent was. Dude, you know we did some weird shit, right?" I agreed. "This was beyond the stuff we were doing. I just knew it wasn't going to turn out well right from the start. I just knew it!" Walter grew still again. "I don't want anybody to know I've even heard the word Crescent. I don't want anybody to think I know anything about Crescent, the gold or who was involved. People have killed, and been killed for a lot less than what the gold is supposed to be worth.

"Everything about Crescent was beyond secret. It took place where we weren't supposed to be and it involved people who were not supposed to be involved. The way people talked about it when we were setting it up made me feel like there was some serious black shit connected to it. I wish I had the words to describe it…" Walter looked over at me. "But I saw fear in the captain's eyes when he told us about it. The fear wasn't about the mission; it was something else. Like I said, I can't describe my feelings right, I just remember it scared the fuck out of me and I was really glad when I was sent off on another mission instead of going on that one."

We sat there awhile and I thought Walter was finished, but then he spoke up "Nope! As far as I know there were only a few people who knew about Crescent. I know of three people who might still be around. Since Hollis and Price are dead, that leaves just the captain, flyboy and me. I don't know what happened to the warrant officer, I don't even know if he's still alive. Well, I guess that leaves me and the captain for sure. If the two cats who came and visited you were the captain and the chopper jockey, it sounds like somebody's trying to find the gold."

We sat for a long time staring off into space. I didn't know if Walter was back in country or just what he was thinking about. Suddenly Walter jumped in his chair, startling me. "Are you okay?" I asked.

"Do you remember the stripper I told you about?"

"Lan?" I asked.

"Yeah. Her father was one of the two village leaders the captain talked to. He was one of the natives who had the gold."

"Are you sure?"

"Positive. Because Price and Hollis knew the family, the captain had to use them to get to the leaders and to the gold."

"Did I tell you Sakol found the father living in Vancouver BC?"

"I think you did mention it. I wonder if the captain knows they live in BC."

We fell into silence again. Considering how the colonel had acted at my place, I hoped he didn't know about Sakol's friend in BC. I wondered why the colonel had waited so long to try and find the gold, if that was what he was really trying to do. I had a thought. "Walter, do you remember the name of the pilot?"

"Dude, please leave this alone. I don't want to see you get hurt. I keep telling you, when they were setting up that mission, I knew it was a lot more than just the captain's involvement. There was something else going on there besides our side trying to arm some of the mountain people. Call it CIA or military intelligence or whatever, but there was something really strange about the whole deal. I'm positive I got left behind because I asked too many questions."

"I appreciate your concern, but I'm getting pulled into this. I've had a gray van following me off and on for the past few days and I think somebody was in my apartment while I wasn't there."

"See? Leave this alone. Matt, go home. Find Sharon and take her someplace fun for a while."

"I'll consider it. But, do you remember anything else about the chopper pilot?"

"The cat's name was James. Chief Warrant Officer Grade 3 James. I don't know his first name, at least I never heard it. Or if I did hear it, I've forgotten. Shit, man, I'm amazed I ever remembered his last name. Oh, and the captain was Mac something, like McNut, or something like that.

"Do you mean McNaulty?"

"Yeah, that's it."

"That's the name on the colonel's jacket."

Walter looked concerned. In a soft voice he said, "Dude, you so need to leave this alone. Please don't make me sorry I told you all this."

I tried to reassure him, "I promise you won't regret it. This is our secret. How's that?"

I could see Walter was not happy with the way things were, but he still smiled and said, "Cool. How long can you stay?"

"Till tomorrow. Okay?"

~ ~ ~ ~

I stayed for another day. I knew there were things I needed to deal with back in town, but since Kim was safe with Sharon, and I really didn't want to deal with the colonel and his sidekick, I stayed.

Thien cooked an amazing dinner that last evening, and afterwards Walter and I were comfortably curled up in the two huge chairs Walter had made. Even with the chill in the air, we were comfortable sitting on the front deck looking off into the distance. Walter lit the pipe and we were passing it back and forth. Like I said, the only time I smoked anymore was when I was visiting Walter, and he had a big patch of weed he'd grown among the vegetables Thien planted. We were both lost in thought as we passed the pipe back and forth. Finally, Walter cleared his throat and asked, "Can we talk about why you came over here?"

"You mean Crescent?"

"Yeah."

"What about it?"

"I've thought about it off and on all day now, and it's my belief McNaulty was going to kill the village leaders once the deal was done. Basically they were going to rip off the gold and then murder the chiefs."

"Is that something you heard or something you just think?'

"I really can't answer that. My memories are all fucked up. Like I said, I kept thinking about it today and that thought just came to me. Don't know why." Walter looked over at me, "Matt, I've tried to forget all this shit. I never told you this, but at the end there I was sent in to take out a leader in some movement. I believe the papers had already been signed over in Paris ending the war and all, but we were still doing our shit before we had to beat feet.

"Anyway, I think they sent me cause they believed nobody was coming back from the mission, and somebody wanted me gone. I did what I was supposed to do, but I almost didn't get away. I got as far as Thien's village and her people hid me. Getting them out of country as everything fell apart at the end, well, it was like my payment for what her people did for me."

Walter took a deep hit on the pipe and as the smoke curled out of his mouth, he continued, "Sometimes I think I missed the dude and he's coming after me, but I know there's no way he walked away. Shit like that bothers me, man. Who was I to snuff anybody? Because some officer told me to kill somebody made it right? You know, the way we were trained, you're never supposed to ask questions, and I didn't. But now when I think about it, it ain't right."

I don't know how long we sat there passing the pipe back and forth. I understood so well what Walter was talking about. Those were the memories we kept locked away. Those were the nightmares I didn't want to remember. Now Walter's excellent smoke had unlocked the door and it was wide open.

The memories started to flow and I found myself back in country. It was so real. I could smell the damp, hot jungle, and I could also feel the fear. These were not happy memories. Finally, I dragged myself back to Walter's deck out in the middle of nowhere. "Why did you bring up Crescent?" I asked.

"Oh… you know it was always my belief that the mission was a lot deeper than anybody was supposed to know. Like for some reason that village was doomed. The whole thing was supposed to blow up and that village was supposed to be wiped out. There were rumors about it. I told you Price had a lover there?" I agreed. "I also think I heard one time Price took Hollis to the village and Price's lover committed suicide. But there are so many things I think I did or heard, and I wonder."

I was lost in my own fog. Like I said, I didn't smoke much anymore and since Walter's stuff was so strong, it really hit me hard. His comments took me back... I remembered how it was that I became involved with the unit I was in back in Nam.

I know I surprised a lot of people when I decided to drop out of college and join the Army. What people didn't know was after two semesters I had less than a one-point grade point average. I had done my best to have sex with every available girl in school, and I wasn't interested in going to class. I knew I was headed for expulsion so I just dropped out and went into the military before I got drafted. What would have surprised friends even more would be the knowledge of what I did in the Army. When I was in school, I was always in the band. I liked being in the band. Besides, I wasn't really good at any sports. I could run and all, but I wasn't that fast to play any kind of sports. I was coordinated, but again, not enough to play any team games.

So for me to end up in a fairly elite group in the military would have stretched their belief. But if the truth be told, I was really just going with the flow. You know, going with the flow... as in you started dating and then you were sleeping together and then maybe living together or at least so close it became assumed you were getting married and then it was happening, it didn't matter if you were screaming in your head as you walked down the aisle, "Fuck no... Fuck NO... I do not want to get married." You just got swept along... you went with the flow because it was easy. At least that was my first marriage.

When you enter the Army, you're given a battery of tests. The tests given in the morning everybody has to take. The tests in the afternoon you *get* to keep taking as long as you pass the previous test. Take one test and if you passed, take a break. Take another test and if you passed, come back and take another. It didn't matter they didn't let you get to sleep until midnight the night before, and then woke your little ass up at 4:40 the next morning. Let me tell you, it was really tough pulling it together and giving some sort of coherent answer.

The group of us who were testing kept getting smaller and smaller. Fewer and fewer guys passed each test and as we moved on, we moved to smaller and smaller rooms. Much to my surprise, I was one of those moving on after each test. I just kept going with the flow. Next thing I knew we're taking the last test of the day. At the end of the day we were allowed to return to the billets and have dinner.

It was towards the end of basic training when I was called into the company's duty office. What transpired in the CO's office I am still not at liberty to discuss, but when basic training was over, I was sent to a school in a place where I never expected to end up, and I was still going with the flow. I was taught a lot of really weird shit and I ended up doing some really spooky things—the things I try and not think about. Again. Just going with the flow.

After I came back to the States, my story was that I was in the band. I was taught what a bandsman would do in the Army and from that point forward that's what I said I did for Uncle Sam. For a long time, it worked just fine. Then one day, Price and Hollis showed up in my life and all of a sudden the memories were back. Now they were coming out at times I least expected. Of course sitting on Walter's deck smoking his killer weed didn't help keep them at bay either.

Walter asked, "Are you sure Hollis never said anything to you about Crescent?"

"Shit, Walter. You know I'd tell you if I remembered anything." Walter murmured and I continued, "Don't you think I've gone over and over that day up in the tower? But nothing was said about anything called Crescent. I know I was pissed and angry, and I was wounded and maybe not tracking as well as I should have been, but I'd remember that. We were up in the tower and Hollis started calling me names after I shot him. He started talking about how he murdered Blackjack and I ended it. You know he didn't have any bullets left?" Walter acknowledged that. "I'd do the same thing again. Maybe he wanted to tell me something about Crescent and never had the chance. Dunno, dude. You know I'd tell you if I knew something, right?"

"Matt, I don't doubt you in the least. All you've done for me and Thien, I trust you completely. It just seems so weird that McNaulty would come out of the woodwork now. Why did Price and Hollis getting killed start him on this?"

I shrugged my shoulders. It *was* weird. I looked over at Walter and asked, "Don't take this wrong, but I could ask you the same question. Have you told me everything you know about Crescent?"

I watched as Walter slumped deeper into his chair. He lit the pipe and took a long pull. Still holding the smoke, he started to talk, "It's just a fluke I even know what I do. When we got back from the first visit to the village, I didn't like the way things were shaping up. I just knew deep down inside it wasn't what the captain was telling us it was. I can't tell you what was said, or what made me feel that way. Even today when I think back on the parts I *do* remember, the one thing that stands out more than anything else are the feelings I had about that mission. It wasn't what we were being told, it was more like what we *weren't* being told."

I could hear Thien in the cabin with little Matt and Bean. From time to time I would hear her talk to him, making baby sounds and laughing. I could tell little Matt was playing with Bean and I could hear sounds of happiness coming from all of them. It made me sad. I think I would have liked to have a wife and children too. I would like to have been sitting on my front porch listening to my wife and son playing with a puppy. But for some reason I was just too independent. I wanted to live my life my way and as much as I would have liked to have had the family and all, I wanted my independence more. I loved Sharon, but after a few days together I started to feel the noose. I could feel it, tighter and tighter until I finally broke. No. A wife and children seemed to work for Walter, but not for me. Bummer!

As both of us sat staring off into the night, Walter suddenly jumped in his chair, frightening me as he exclaimed, "Fuck! Fuck, fuck. I wonder if..." His voice drifted away.

"What is it? What happened?" I asked in alarm.

Walter explained excitedly, "Sorry. But I just recalled something. I think I remember seeing a book. I'm not totally sure, but I think I remember seeing Hollis writing in a book a couple of times. I asked him once what it was and he told me it was none of my business. The problem is I'm just not that sure, but I can close my eyes and I think I see the book in his hands." Walter closed his eyes. "I remember seeing him sitting at a table, book open and he was writing. I asked him what he was doing and he told me to go away. I asked him again what he was writing and he asked me if I minded if he wrote in his diary." Walter stared at me. "He told me it was his diary, then told me to fuck off. At the time I thought it was odd. He was the only guy I knew in the whole unit who kept a diary. And of anybody in the unit, he was the least likely. I knew I didn't want to keep a record of my time over there. When I got back stateside, the last thing I wanted was something to remind me of being in that hellhole."

"If there was one, what happened to the diary?"

"Fuck if I know man. I only saw it a couple of times. I guess he only wrote in it when nobody was around. I doubt if anybody else knew about it. Who knows what happened to it?"

"I'd love to read that diary. Maybe it could answer some questions."

Walter reached over and grabbed my arm. He squeezed it so tight it actually hurt. "No dude, you do not want to read that diary!" Walter's face was serious and he continued to hold on to my arm. "Matt, listen to me. I know you think you did some strange stuff over there. But I'm telling you what you did was a Sunday school picnic compared to some of the things those two were involved in. You do *not* want to read his diary." He leaned towards me and in almost a whisper he said, "I'm positive there are things in that diary that if you ever read, would put your life in jeopardy." My face must have shown how doubtful I felt at what he was telling me. His voice was now a menacing hiss, "I believe McNaulty would shoot you between the eyes and not regret it for a moment. There are probably things in that book that would cost a lot of people their freedom and a few lives to boot. Promise me if you ever accidentally found that damn thing you would never read it." He squeezed my arm again harder, "Promise me." I nodded my head.

I was shocked at the intensity of his little speech. If anybody knew some of Hollis' and Price's secrets, it was Walter. And if Walter told me I didn't want to read Hollis' diary, then I would take his word for it.

"I wonder," I started, "I wonder if McNaulty knows anything about it. Is there any way he might have known Hollis kept a diary?"

Walter sat staring off into space for so long I wondered if he had heard me. Finally, he started in, "If he knew, or if he even suspected something like that existed, he'd be frantic to get his hands on it. I'm not supposed to tell you this, but McNaulty was Price's and Hollis' controller for a while. If Hollis wrote down any of the things McNaulty told them to do, I totally understand why your two visitors wanted to know what you and Hollis discussed up in the tower."

I cannot remember any time in my life when I was more torn over something. I would have given anything to read the diary, if it actually existed, but after Walter's dire warning, I felt my life might be in jeopardy. I sure wished this whole mess would just blow away, but I knew better. The only way it was going to go away was to figure out how to deal with it.

"What's next?" Walter asked. I proceeded to tell him about Kim Tate and the problems she was having. I told him about the Cox kid and the two sides of him I kept hearing about. I explained why I needed to get back to Seattle and help Kim and her parents resolve her mess.

Walter chided me about getting involved with other people's problems. He asked me as he shook his head, "Matt, when are you going to learn not to get so involved?"

"Dude," I reminded him, "had I not gotten involved, where do you think you might be today?" He blinked and smiled at me.

And that question ended our conversation regarding me helping people.

CHAPTER 13
SAMARA'S VISIT TO THE HOUSEBOAT

I was already waiting in the marina parking lot when Mrs. Tate's limo rolled in. I'd seen pictures of that model, but it was the first time I'd ever seen one in real life. If you take a top-of-the-line S class Mercedes, and then put it on mass steroids, you'd end up with the Maybach. The car just screamed big money as it rolled to the end of the lot. It was painted a pale silver-blue on the top and some sort of white with silver metal flakes on the bottom. I realize I am not really doing the colors justice; you just had to experience the car. Since I'm a real car whore, I was ecstatic to see this car, it was beautiful.

The car stopped and I reached out to open the back door. As the door opened, the smell of expensive leather greeted my nostrils, and then continued to flow out of the car as Samara Tate stepped out. Ambruster had opened the driver's door and was coming around the end of the car. I noticed he had on the same style of outfit as the day we had first met. His red jacket was tailored to fit perfectly and even though he was of slim build, he moved with a certain stealth and calm. We acknowledged each other and I extended my arm for Samara to take. By the time we were standing in front of the houseboat, the door was open and Sharon was standing there. Today she had on a lovely dress which looked like it had been designed just for her. She looked like a million bucks. I noticed behind her Kim was peeking around the corner. Sharon invited us all in.

By the time we were all in the living room, Kim had her mother wrapped in her arms and tears were flowing from both of them. Finally Kim stepped back and looked over at Ambruster. She extended her arms and moved to take the man in her arms. "Brue, Brue… I've missed you so much." Kim looked over at me and said, "My special name for him is Brue. I always thought Ambruster was too much to say." I had to laugh. "He was my nanny when I was a little girl." Ambruster turned bright red, almost the same color as his jacket. "He's been as much a father figure to me as my real dad. Brue is my special friend." And Kim gave him another big hug. I could see from the look on his face he felt the same way about Kim as she did about him.

"I would agree, but somehow I don't see myself calling him Brue." Ambruster scowled at me. I could see there was going to be just one person calling him Brue and it wasn't me.

I excused myself and Sharon told the three of them she was going to go with me and leave them alone. We went out and walked to the end of the dock, where one of the residents had put a bench. We sat. Sharon asked, "What do you think is going to happen, with the Cox kid I mean?"

"I went and met with a man Sakol introduced to me about a year ago. This man seems to be able to do all sorts of interesting things. I asked him to put out the word I wanted to see him. I was told to just go about my business and Cox would find me."

"What are you going to do with him?"

"You mean Cox?" Sharon nodded. I explained, "I want to get his side of the story. I heard all these stories about the kid, and I know he's running around loose and nobody seems the least bit concerned some of these stories might be true. I find it difficult to believe he's tried to force so many women, and nothing has happened to him yet. I don't know what to believe about Kim."

Sharon put her hand on my arm and when I looked at her, she said in a soft whisper, "Kim said he did and I believe her!"

I continued, "Kim's roommate told me Cox had tried to force her as well, but there seems to be a question about that. Kim says she knows somebody else he raped and you thought he had raped the girl you met at the hospital. Through the grapevine, I hear stories of others, and a rough count looks like at least ten. One attempt and who knows how many for real. I'd like for him to tell me what's going on. I'm sorry, but my mind just doesn't seem to be able to believe the two totally different stories I am hearing. I want to meet him face to face."

"Why do you think he'll talk to you?"

"This friend I know, actually I don't even know if I can call him a friend. He's more like a very good acquaintance—anyway, he has ah… well, he has ways of getting people to do things. I really don't quite know what to make of him, but I think he has the power to make Cox come and talk to me."

"Who is this amazing guy?" Sharon asked with a puzzled look on her face.

"He was introduced to me as Mouse. His real name is Steve Fox, but everybody just calls him Mouse. He's a little bitty guy, but he seems to know everything going on in Seattle."

"I know Mouse," Sharon interrupted.

"Are you serious? You know him? How come?" This was a tale I wanted to hear.

Sharon smiled at me. "Well, the fellow who came to visit me the other day, when we had our talk…" Sharon's face was flushed with embarrassment. She continued on with her story, "George likes to gamble. Or I should say he liked to gamble. A lot!"

I gave her a puzzled look and she continued, "George got himself in trouble, big trouble and he ended up owing a lot of money to… well, I don't know exactly who he owed it to but they weren't really nice people.

"One evening Mouse was waiting in the parking lot at the hospital for George when he got off work." It didn't surprise me that Mouse would know something like where George worked or how to find him. "This Mouse person instructed George to get into his limo and they took George to a house way up north. There was a man there who had been badly wounded, shot twice. Mouse told George the man could not be taken to a hospital, and that there would be no questions asked about him. George was told to save his life and keep his mouth shut. In return for that, all of his gambling debts disappeared.

"George ended up operating on this man in a vet clinic. He told me it was the most bizarre thing medical-wise he'd ever done in his career. I guess it was close, but George did save him. Later, when the man was stable, Mouse had George brought back to the hospital parking lot and dropped off. The next day a courier brought a large manila envelope to George's office with all of his IOU slips in it, and a note from Mouse telling him he really needed to get a grip on his gambling. Each IOU was marked paid. George said he hasn't gambled since, not even on a football pool at work.

"Sometime later we were at a fundraiser together at the hospital and Mouse was there. George introduced us and when George went off to get us drinks; Mouse looks up at me and proceeds to tell me he knows George told me about the man he saved, and that I'm never to say a word to anybody about it. In a joking manner I asked who this mystery man was, and Mouse looked at me with a very serious face and told me if he said who it was, he would have to have me killed. He smiled after he said it, but I felt at the time there was a lot of truth in the statement. He asked me to promise not to mention it to anybody. I didn't. Well, except for you, but you don't count." We both laughed, but I couldn't help but wonder if somehow Mouse knew Sharon had just told me about that incident.

The more I got to know about Mouse, the more intrigued I was with him. I felt I understood more about Sakol's relationship with Mouse and why Sakol seemed to look the other way when it came to the way Mouse ran his life.

~ ~ ~ ~

I was sitting relaxed at my table, my tummy happy from my excellent dinner and I gazed out across the view of Puget Sound and the snowcapped Olympic Mountains off in the distance. My old friend and owner of the restaurant, Mac, had just cleared away the remains from the as always amazing meal along with giving me another major ass chewing regarding my semi-breakup with Sharon. I tried to tell him we were still the best of friends and were still more or less an item but he wasn't interested in the facts. He thought we belonged together and he was voicing his opinion.

I was still engrossed in the sunset nursing my beer when I became aware there was somebody standing next to my table. I looked up and next to the table was a handsome, young black man. I asked him if I could help him and he replied, "I'm Bud Cox."

I stood, wondering for a moment if I should extend my hand, then decided not to. Instead I motioned for him to sit in the vacant chair across from me. "Can I get you anything?" I asked.

"No, I'm cool." He turned the chair around backwards

and took a seat, resting his arms on the back. "Rumor has it you want to talk to me."

"Who told you where to find me?"

"You asked a lot of people about me. The little man told me where to find you. I understand you want to help me. How?"

I looked at the young man sitting across from me. He was slightly taller than I am and had at least fifty pounds on me. Fifty pounds of pure muscle. Even sitting quietly in front of me, this young man could be frightening. "Help you?" I repeated, I thought for a moment and then continued. "I guess it depends. Maybe I can, maybe I can't. I'll get straight to the point. What can you tell me about Kim Tate?"

He scowled as he snarled, "That lying cunt. What's you want with dat ho?" I noticed Bud had slipped into 'street language.'

"Why do you say she's lying?"

"She be tellin' people I tried rapin' her. That's a fucking lie. I never did no such thing."

"Her roommate tells me the rumor around school is she wasn't the first girl you tried to rape. Her roomie even said you've actually raped a couple of women."

"Shit man, listen. Look at me, do I look like I need to rape some ho just to get laid?" I regarded the young man sitting in front of me. He was dressed like so many of the young black men I see walking around with his basketball style shorts, long un-tucked oversized shirt and a couple of chains around his neck. His baseball hat had the bill pointed towards the right instead of centered on his head, but under it all, there was a look of intelligence in his eyes and I had to admit, he was a handsome young man. But so was Ted Bundy.

"I'll give you the fact you're a good looking kid, but that still doesn't explain all the rumors. Why would so many women tell all these lies about you?"

"Dude, do you know what my prospects are? Do you have any idea where I'm going? I know this comes off as a power trip, but this is also reality. If this season plays out, I'm looking at being drafted in the first round next year. Do you have any idea what kind of bread that brings?"

I ventured, "A lot?"

Bud's laugh was a snort. "Yeah, a lot. And some of those chicks think if they put out the word about me, I'll pay them off to keep their fucking mouths shut. But I don't play that game. Coach knows who I am and my teammates know who I am. You look at the cunts who be spreading those rumors? They be money grubbin' hos. And I have no idea why Kim would say that about me."

"No idea at all?" I asked.

Bud paused for a moment before he answered, "Well, she did catch me banging one of her friends, but that was just sex, man. This other chick and me go way back and she like a little black cock now and then. We're friends with benefits. Kim and this girl are pissed at each other now, but she'll come back. She always does."

"Wait a minute, Sam said you raped Kim's friend. Are you telling me that you were just having sex with her?"

"Yeah, so what?"

"Why would she tell Kim and me that you tried to rape her if you didn't? That doesn't make much sense."

"The little ho don't share real well. She wanted Kim to stay away from me."

"Did you ever try to have sex with Kim?"

"Naw. She wanted to but I didn't. That's why she saying all this shit about me."

I had to admit, there was something engaging about this young man. He seemed to realize who he was and the power he had because of the money that one day would be his. I might not like his attitude about women, but I was sure he probably had his pick of many of the young ladies on campus. Perhaps he was right and the rumors about him were not true. But I had seen Gladys' fear when she told me her story, and I put far more faith in Sharon's abilities to detect the truth about what had happened between Cox and Kim Tate.

"Bud, I appreciate you looking me up. I'll agree with what you say, someday you'll be a very wealthy man and money seems to bring out a lot of bad in people." I looked the young man in the eyes as I continued, "My only comment here is this: there seems to be a lot of women who claim you either tried to rape them, or you actually have. I can understand one or two rumors, but in asking around, I've heard there are several women making these claims, and some of the women are very creditable. Are you telling me there are that many women who will lie about you just in the hope you're going to pay them off to keep them quiet?"

I waited for an answer and when he had nothing to say, I added, "I'm looking for Kim Tate." I didn't want Cox to know I had Kim safely stashed away. I felt it was best if he thought I was looking for her just the same as he was. I wanted to push the issue a little more about Kim trying to expose this young man. "I've been told Kim's trying to see what she can do about you since you raped her. I also hear you're looking for her as well and that you threatened her."

Bud stood up and glared down at me. "I'm tellin' you this, keep away from me. Stop messin' in my shit. Leave me alone, or else."

I leaned back in my chair, crossed my arms and looked up at him. I waited for a few moments and then softly told him, "The thing about making a threat, young man, is you need to be able to back it up."

"What you sayin? You think I can't put a hurt on you?" The look on his face showed he thought he had the upper hand should things become violent.

"I didn't say you're not physically able to do it. What I'm saying is, I wonder if you have the stones to do it. You know nothing about me. I know a lot about you. Some advice here for you Bud, before you make a threat, find out who you're threatening."

"Oooo… I'm scared now. Whitey gonna get me."

This punk was starting to piss me off. "Bud, you need to leave now. I'm going to find the Tate girl and since I believe you did rape her, if she wants to charge you with something, I'm going to help her." Seeing his attitude now, I knew I didn't want him to think I might know where Kim was hiding.

Bud stepped forward, and I watched as he drew back his fist. When he had first stood up, I moved myself in my chair, ready for him to make just this kind of move. I ducked with ease as his massive arm came forward. As his arm passed me, I grabbed his wrist and stood, using his momentum to slam him onto the table. My half glass of beer jumped off the table and ended up landing on the back of his neck. The table broke in half and Cox went to the floor with it. I put my foot between his shoulder blades and pulled back on his arm. "Bud, if you ever try and touch me again I'm going to make sure it's the last time you ever touch anybody. Now get up and get out of here."

I released his arm and stepped back, making sure I stayed clear of his legs in case he tried to kick back at me. He stood, holding his wet cap in his hand, beer dripping off his face. The look in his eyes told me I had just made an enemy for life. Bud glared at me, his anger had robbed him of the ability to talk. Finally he turned and stormed out of the restaurant. I noticed Mac standing off to one side with a baseball bat in his hands. I smiled at him and commented, "I don't think that will be necessary. But thanks for the thought."

Mac growled at me something about he wasn't looking out for me, but making sure none of the other customers were hurt. "Gee, thanks for your deep concern," I countered.

I paid my tab and just before I walked out the door, Mac

came up to me. As he extended his hand, he smiled at me and said, "I understand about you and Sharon, but I also know she cares about you and I know how you feel about her. Take care of her." When he turned to walk away, his face was red and I could tell how difficult it was for him to allow so much of his emotion to show. Mac was not the kind of man who wore his feelings on his sleeve. I called after him, "Thanks Mac, see ya around." I heard him grumble something but I couldn't make it out. I had been dismissed.

My truck was parked a couple of blocks away in a parking garage and I strolled down the sidewalk looking into the various stores I passed by. When I got to the garage, I pushed the button for the elevator and waited. The elevator finally arrived, the doors opened and when I pushed the button for my floor, it started to wheeze and strain to go up the shaft. The elevator was not in the best of shape.

When it stopped I got out and as I walked out of the enclosed elevator lobby I sensed something behind me. Before I could turn around my world went black.

~ ~ ~ ~

The first thing I realized was the pain. A pain in my head like nothing I had ever experienced. I tried to move but that just made my head hurt even more. I opened one eye and looked out over the parking garage. Somehow I was now lying next to my truck and I knew I wasn't that close when I got out of the elevator and was struck. I tried moving my head again a little but the pain made me shut my eye. It seemed to throb with each beat of my heart. I waited for it to subside before I tried to open my eye again.

The concrete floor was cold and I was starting to shiver. I decided I wanted to sit up, no matter how much it hurt. As I started to push down, I noticed I had a pistol in one hand.

Glancing down at it, I saw it was the same kind I kept hidden under the passenger seat in my truck. I placed the pistol on the ground, and as I pushed myself up to a sitting position I felt pieces of broken glass under my hand. My head throbbed, but I thought it wasn't as bad as before. I shut my eyes for a moment to let the pain diminish.

When I opened my eyes again I looked around. Lying a few feet away from me was a body. From the bare legs I could tell it was a black man. I looked and then I saw the cap lying next to the head. It was Bud Cox's hat. This was Bud Cox lying next to me on the ground. Oh shit! I crawled over to him and placed my fingers against the side of his neck. The body was cool to the touch and I could feel there was no heartbeat. Bud was dead. If a third of the things I had heard about him were true when it came to his treatment of women, I could think of a lot of women who wouldn't mourn his passing. I leaned back against the door of my truck and as I did, I became aware of a lot of broken glass on the ground. It was like a light bulb went on in my head. Somebody had broken into my truck, gotten out my gun and had shot Cox. As I sat there looking at the body, I remembered when I woke up the gun had been in my hand… OH SHIT, my fingerprints were on the gun now.

As I sat there in a daze, I heard footsteps coming across the garage. When I looked up I saw two Seattle police officers standing in front of me. One of them had his weapon in his hand. The one without the gun spoke, "Get up."

"I don't know if I can."

"Why not?"

"Somebody hit me on the back of the head and I'm still not tracking very well."

The office with the pistol saw the gun on the ground and pointed it out to his partner. The partner then went to the body and knelt next to it. He checked for a pulse and when he saw who it was, he jumped back. "Sweet Mary—Chuck, do you know who this is?"

The officer with his pistol drawn looked at his partner with disbelief. "How would I know who that is? Are you going to tell me?"

"Dude, it's that running back over at the U. Cox I think his name is. Bud Cox?"

Keeping his gun trained on me, the officer stepped over to the body so he could see the face. When he saw who it was he looked back at me. "Why did you shoot him? And in the back?"

"I didn't. Somebody hit me from behind and when I woke up, I found him dead and my truck was broken into."

The officer without his gun drawn lifted his radio from his belt and called in to the station. He told the person who answered they had a dead body and who the person was. It seemed like the call had barely ended and the entire parking garage was filled with police. I was slammed with questions and nobody seemed to care I had a screaming headache. Things didn't look good, I was found with a gun… my gun, which turned out to be the murder weapon. Things didn't look good at all.

With every telling of my story, I kept asking to have either Jeff or Sakol brought in. It seemed like my requests were ignored. Finally I was put in the back of a squad car and taken down to the station. After I was booked I was allowed my one phone call, which I made to my lawyer's office. Wouldn't you know it, nobody answered at Richard and Albert's law office. Just great! I left a message and told them where I was and what the issue was.

Before I hung up I added, "Please hurry. I really don't want to be here."

CHAPTER 14
JAIL

As I lay on the bunk in my cell, mentally I was bemoaning how short and small the bed was. I kept hoping somebody would come and rescue me from this miserable little hellhole. Finally, I heard the electronically controlled steel door at the end of the corridor scrape open. Hoping and wondering if somebody was finally coming to bail me out, I sat up on my bunk. I heard the scratch of a radio transmission and then a voice, "You said Preston, right?" There was a distorted reply and the person in the hallway responded, "Yeah, we're getting him now. He'll be there in a minute."

I didn't know what was going to happen, but I couldn't help but wonder if the colonel and his buddy were waiting for me in some little room down the hall. I hoped not, but by this time I was really getting discouraged. Finally, a tall, gaunt, sallow man stood in front of my cell. He paused before putting a key in the lock.

I was already standing in front of the cell door when a deep and low voice asked, "Matt Preston?" It was a stupid question since I was the only one in the cell.

"Yeah, that's me." The guard looked at me with pale blue watery eyes for a moment.

"Step back, please step away from the gate." I did, and he slipped the key into the lock. As he turned the key he said, "You have a visitor." Once I was standing in the corridor he locked the cell door behind me while another guard waited a few doors down for us. Once the cell door was locked, the two guards walked on each side of me, escorting me to where, I had no idea.

We passed through several security doors, and we waited for each door to close behind us before we moved on to pass though the next one. Eventually we stood before a dingy gray door, which the tall guard opened. He motioned for me to enter and I did. The room was bare except for an old scarred desk and two old wooden chairs. Sitting in one of the chairs was a very attractive woman who looked to be in either her late thirties or early forties. One guard addressed her, "Here he is, Ms. Sellers." the contempt was evident in the jailer's voice as he motioned towards me. "Just holler when you're done," he instructed the woman.

The woman stood, and I saw she was tall, slim and her attractive outfit looked expensive and fit her well. She had a great smile. "Thanks, Frank. I'll do that." She held out her hand. As I took it she said, "My name is Krista Sellers. Albert Bradson asked me to look into your case." She motioned for me to sit in the chair across from her.

I sat down. "Nice to meet you, Ms. Sellers." I paused, wondering if I wanted to perhaps accidently alienate this woman with my questions. "I don't wish to be rude Ms. Sellers, but where's Albert?" I wanted to know why Albert wasn't here, either alone or along with this lovely woman. After all, I certainly paid them a large enough retainer to rate the top dog, and I was also wondering why I'd been left so long in that stupid cell.

Ms. Sellers was wearing glasses and as she considered my questions, she took them off, setting them on the table in front of her. She studied me for several moments before she spoke. "I'm told that Albert has been asked not to handle this case. I've been assigned instead."

Perhaps I was a bit rude in the blunt way I asked, "Why?" Considering the length of time I'd been with Albert's firm and the amounts of money I'd spent as well, I was getting a little miffed at what I perceived as being passed along to somebody I didn't even know. I wanted Albert. I wanted Albert to be my gunfighter. I wanted his reputation in my corner—not somebody I'd never heard of before.

Ms. Sellers leaned back in her chair and picked up her glasses. She fiddled with them briefly then folded her arms across her chest and gave a deep sigh. "Mr. Preston, you present a problem to the firm. You've been a good client for many years, but as I understand it, your case is not one the firm wishes to be involved in as far as being the counsel of record. I actually handle cases for Mr. Bradson and for Mr. Silversmith that they feel the need to stay arm's length from. Neither Mr. Bradson nor Mr. Silversmith handles murder cases. But this is my specialty. I think you will find my representation of you will be to your satisfaction. Of course, if you do not wish for me to represent you, I'll leave, and we can find somebody more to your liking."

I stared at her. I was miffed by what I considered being passed along, but I also knew if Albert couldn't take my case, he would send in the best gunfighter he knew. I just had to put away my feelings about being represented by this attractive woman. I needed to view her as I would view either Albert or Silversmith. I guess I understood why Albert might not want to have his name associated with murder trials, but to be candid, I also thought we went back far enough that he just might make an exception in my case. But if Albert had sent this woman, then I should trust his judgment and accept her as my legal representative.

As I thought over my options, I looked the lady over. She really was exceptionally good-looking. Her long blond hair was piled on her head in a casual way and her lovely blue eyes looked bright and full of curiosity. She had a great smile, and from what I could tell of her body she looked slim—almost to the point of being too thin. I cleared my throat and spoke, "Ah, I'd be lying if I told you I was happy Albert's not sitting here. Nothing personal against you." She smiled. "If Albert feels you can best represent me, then it's fine with me. My main question is, how soon can you get me out of here?"

"Well, you're to be arraigned tomorrow. To be honest, I doubt if I can get you out on bail. The prosecutor's office is going for first-degree murder."

I was too surprised to stay cool. "What?" I shouted.

"Take it easy, calm down!" Krista held her hands up in front of her body. "You have to look at it from their perspective. You were found with the gun and powder residue on your hand. There were two bullets missing from the gun, and there were two bullets in the victim. You were seen arguing with the victim less an hour before the murder—seen by four people who all agree you were acting very aggressive towards the victim. The prosecutor feels he has a slam dunk."

"And what do you think?" I asked her. I looked her directly in the eyes.

"I'm here to represent you," she replied.

"That didn't answer my question. Do you think I did it?" I didn't look away. I was going to wait her out.

She looked down at the table for a moment, collecting her thoughts. Eventually she started, "Mr. Preston, it doesn't matter what I think. I'm not here to judge you. I'm here willing to listen to your side of the story. If you say you didn't do it, it would help me to know what you did do. What happened?"

I wasn't happy with her response. Albert would have believed me if I had told him I didn't shoot the Cox kid, even if I thought he had it coming. Since it seemed Krista was my best bet to get out of my current jam, I decided to be as forthcoming as I could be. "I need to give you a little of the backstory here." She nodded and I began. "Several of my friends meet from time to time, and we play poker. One of the more frequent players is Bill Tate—"

She interrupted, "Bill Tate? You mean *the* Bill Tate? Bill 'Tubs' Tate, the former basketball star?"

"Yes."

I saw her relax for a second back on her chair as she murmured, "That's a poker game I would love to sit in on." The wistful look on her face was fleeting and she quickly pulled herself together. "Please go on. I'm sorry to interrupt you."

"Well, last game Bill pulled me aside and told me his daughter was sorta missing."

"I'm sorry to keep interrupting you, but what do you mean by 'sorta missing?'"

"He told me his daughter hadn't spoken to either of her parents in several days and she had also dropped out of the U. She wasn't returning calls to either her mother or Bill, and he asked me to see if I could find her."

"Why would he ask you to do something like that? Are you a private investigator?"

"No, but I've done things in my life… ah, well, that are not very mainstream, and I can do things and find out things people in law enforcement can't do or find out." I didn't want to go into too much detail about my past and why Bill had asked me to step in, but I didn't want to leave my attorney completely in the dark.

She sat quietly looking at me for several moments again. She started to play with the glasses sitting in front of her and when she finally spoke, her words were crafted very carefully. "Mr. Preston, you know that whatever you tell me here is protected by attorney-client privilege. That means that whatever you tell me about your past stays here, in this room, unless you and I decide together to share that information. In other words, you can confide in me." She stopped and took a breath. "I hope you don't think I'm being condescending here, I just want you to understand the situation." Krista picked up her glasses and put them on. "So, what exactly have you done in your life that is considered 'not very mainstream?'"

Now it was my turn to sit quietly. I understood why she gave me the little speech about being able to confide in her. I knew she wasn't trying to be condescending in any way so I decided I needed to confide in her as much as possible. I thought if I didn't explain myself properly, she might find the information some other way, and then she'd never trust me. "Whatever I tell you is just between us, right?" She nodded her head. "Okay. When I was in the service I was in a very secret unit in Viet Nam. Some call it 'black-ops' or 'Delta Force.' The truth is, I'm still not supposed to discuss a lot of what I did over there. For what it's worth, I, or should I say my unit, was in places our government to this day still denies we were at. Some of the guys in our poker game know I did some weird shit in the service. And not too long ago I was involved with the Seattle Police in catching a hired killer up on Ross Island."

Her eyes got bigger and she leaned back in her chair. "That was you?"

"Yeah. What do you know about that?" Surprise in my voice.

"I'm dating a guy from the sheriff's department up on Ross. He told me kind of what happened up there. Did you really shoot a man between the eyes—a guy with an empty gun?"

I know you're not supposed to lie to your lawyer, but I still believed the right thing to do was keep up the story I had started when I was questioned in the hospital after I shot Hollis up in that tower. "It came down to he shot at me and missed, and my bullet didn't miss. It was self-defense."

There was a moment of silence and then she asked, "Who was up in the tower with you two?"

"It was just the two of us."

Once more Krista looked me directly in the eyes. "So it's your word against… well, it's just your word then? Right?"

I made sure my eyes did not leave her face. "Yeah, I guess he was in a lot of pain and it made him miss. I was luckier and my bullet didn't."

"Mr. Preston…"

The tension in the room had grown and I tried to make light of the moment. "Please call me Matt. If you're going to represent me, can we go with Matt?"

"Okay, Matt." She smiled. "And you should feel free to call me Krista." Her voice became more serious. "Please don't take this the wrong way. Is there's any way anybody can prove things didn't happen the way you say they did up in that lighthouse?"

I hoped my answer wasn't too fast. "Nope, cause that's the truth. But your questions make me wonder just whose side you're on."

Krista looked at me for a moment. "If I have to take this to court, I need to know if there is anything out there that can bite me in the ass."

"What can be proven is the person I shot and killed up in that lighthouse was a very bad person. I guess the question now is do you want me for a client?"

She gave me her killer smile. "Okay. Back to Bill Tate. What's his daughter's name?"

"Kim. Kim Tate."

"Mr. Tate asked you to see if you could locate his daughter. Did you?"

"Yes. She was hiding."

"Did you find out why she was hiding?"

"She had been threatened. She dated a guy who she says raped her. Depending on who I talked to, she told some people it was an attempted rape and to others she said actually happened. Kim told me and a nurse she was raped." Krista frowned. "Kim decided to try and do something about it by going to the school board of regents. The problem is, or was, the guy's Bud Cox."

"Sorry to interrupt again, when you say Bud Cox, do you mean the star running back over at the U? The kid who was shot?"

"Yeah."

Krista closed her eyes for a moment. I got the feeling she finally understood why Albert had dumped this case in her lap. She knew why the firm didn't want to be anywhere near to the killing of somebody as famous as Cox. Eventually she opened her eyes and smiled at me, though I felt the smile was a bit forced. "Please continue, Matt."

"Kim told me when Cox found out she was trying to do something about the attempted rape, or rape, Cox or one of his buddies, called her and told her if she didn't drop things, she was going to be in a world of hurt, as they put it. I found where she was hiding. She told me all of this and I moved her to a better hiding place. For one thing, I was concerned with her mental well being since she told me she was actually raped."

"Where did you move her to?"

"I have a very good friend who is the head ER nurse at one of the hospitals up on Pill Hill. I own a houseboat she rents from me and I felt it was a safe place, as well as having my nurse friend there to talk to Kim about it."

"Okay, I understand. Then what did you do?"

"I went looking for Cox, and I found him. Or should I say, he found me at the restaurant where I was having dinner. We argued and he left. Later in the parking lot, he's dead, I'm in a daze, and the police find me with the gun. I'm telling you, I didn't shoot him. Somebody hit me on the back of my head as I was walking to my truck, and when I woke up I had the gun in my hand and Cox's body was lying next to me. I did not shoot him."

"When you were tested, they found powder residue on your hand. How do you think you got that?"

"I don't know."

"It appears the gun that was used to kill him was registered to you. Do you always carry a weapon?"

"I have a license to carry. I usually keep a pistol in my truck."

"Why?"

I paused. That was a good question. Why did I carry a gun with me? I had one stashed at my apartment, too. I always thought that because of my time in the service, I felt more comfortable knowing there was one handy. "To be honest, I can't really give you a good reason. I just feel more comfortable having one."

"The gun the police found you with, was that the same one you used up on Ross Island?"

For some reason that question made my blood run cold. I wanted Ross Island to go away. But it seemed like every time I turned around, it was coming back into my life. I knew I didn't regret what I did to Hollis, but I sure wished I had used a different gun than the one in my truck. I nodded at her question.

Krista took off her glasses again and placed them on the stack of papers once more. The way she leaned back in her chair, I could tell she was working her way up to asking me her question. She took a deep breath and then slowly let it out. "Matt, I don't want you to take this the wrong way.

But you're on the record as admitting to the killing of one man. And now you've been accused of killing another man, and with the same gun. Do you see why someone might be inclined to write you off as just a violent man?"

"Well, they'd be wrong. I know a lot of ways to end a person's life, but I don't use them. I know I have the ability to protect myself, but I don't go around looking for fights. Actually I'm a very quiet person."

"A quiet person who goes around shooting defenseless people up in old lighthouse towers?"

"It's not like he was unarmed. How do you think I ended up with a bullet in my thigh?"

"Let's see..." Krista put her glasses on, started flipping through the papers in front of her and then found what she was looking for. She looked at me over the top of her glasses. "The man in the tower had gunshot wounds to both of his feet, his chest, and he had a bullet between his eyes. That's not really the act of a quiet person, Mr. Preston." I had moved backwards. I was now Mr. instead of Matt.

"The reason I bring all of this up is because the prosecutor is going to bring it up as well." She held up her fist and as she made a point, Krista would lift one finger. "The prosecutor will try and show you have a history of violent behavior. He will then bring up how you found the young man who allegedly tried to rape Kim Tate. Two bullets are missing from the gun you had in your truck, where the young man was killed. You're found next to his dead body, with a gun. You have powder residue on your hand. Several people saw the two of you argue to the point where the cops say the owner of the restaurant had to break up a fight between the two of you." By now she had all her fingers in the air. "You have to admit things do not look good as far as your defense is concerned."

This was not going well for me. I was caught in quicksand and the more I tried to move, the faster I was being sucked in. I knew this woman was here to help me, but it seemed like she was helping build the case against me. "Ms. Sellers, I'm telling you I did not shoot Bud Cox. I was angry with him, yes. I'll not deny that.

"As for Mac breaking up the fight, he only picked up a baseball bat in case the disagreement got out of hand. He did not break up any fight. Yes, I told Cox to stay away from Kim Tate. But I didn't shoot him. Somebody else shot Cox, somebody who broke into my truck and used my gun."

Krista sat for a long time now, seemingly focused on a spot high on the wall behind me. When she took off her glasses again she sighed and then placed them on the stack of papers, looked at me and sighed again. "Tomorrow, at arraignment, we'll plead not guilty. I assume that's okay with you."

"Of course!" I almost shouted. I knew I didn't shoot the creep, but the problem was, I couldn't prove it. And the worst part was sitting in jail was not going to help me prove I didn't do it. "Will you be able to get me out on bail?"

"To be honest, I doubt it. I'll try, but I doubt it."

"That's what I was afraid of." I silently swore to myself, if I ever got out of this situation I was going to have a real chat with Bill Tate. I also promised myself I would never be seduced into helping anybody again… even if they were a world famous basketball star.

CHAPTER 15
SAKOL

I knew my time with Krista was over when she stood and called for Frank, the guard. I had to admit I didn't feel very good about the way things were turning out. It was nothing Krista had said, it was just the way the conversation had gone. I didn't feel very confident I was ever going to see the outside world again. I was afraid that even if Krista was the best lawyer ever, her chances of getting me off were no better than my chances of spending a week on a Hawaiian Island with a supermodel… which were way below zero. I had gotten myself in deep trouble and Krista had a real uphill fight to get me out. I tried not to show her how depressed I was with the way our interview had gone, but I sensed she knew I was really in the dumps. When she stretched out her hand to shake mine goodbye, she took my hand in both of hers and smiled. "I won't tell you not to worry, but I believe you. I will do my very best to get you off because I do believe you are innocent. I really think it will all work out in the end." Her telling me she believed me meant a lot.

When the door to our little room was opened, I saw two guards standing there. Much to my surprise, one guard appeared to be accompanying Sakol. Krista smiled at my old friend and exclaimed, "Sakol, good afternoon. It's been a long time. How have you been?"

Sakol smiled at the warm greeting, his round face glowing. "Hello Ms. Seller. Nice see you again."

Krista took his hand as she asked, "Why are you here?"

"Matt friend. Want talk." Sakol bowed towards the barrister.

She turned and looked at me. "Do you want me to stay? You know whatever you tell him can be used against you at your trial."

Without going into a lot of detail about Sakol and myself, I just told her, "There's nothing I can't or won't say in front of Sakol. We go a long way back."

Krista didn't look very happy that she was being dismissed, but she smiled, held out her hand to me again and said, "Okay, then, I'll see you tomorrow at the courthouse. I'll be there thirty minutes beforehand to go over a few things with you."

I smiled, and she left. I motioned to Sakol to take a seat as I said, "Before we start, is somebody taking care of Bean?"

"Sharon has dog with her. No worry."

"Okay. Now, what brings you to my office?"

He smiled at my feeble joke. "Just left truck. First, hold up hands."

I looked at him strangely but complied. He motioned for me to turn my hands around so he could see both sides. He smiled at me and started talking, "Two things not right—"

I interrupted, "Shit, Sakol, there are more than just two things that aren't right."

He held up his hand to silence me. "Okay. Two things with truck not right."

"Like?" Getting information out of Sakol was like pulling teeth.

"Find blood on passenger door and blood on passenger seat. It not yours, not Cox. What you know about it?"

"Sakol, I know about the Charlie Chan thing you do. For right now can we drop it?"

Sakol smiled up at me with a sheepish grin. "Sorry about that. It's become so much a part of me I forget I'm doing it. My wife won't allow me to talk like that at home."

Married! Sakol married? I know we had never really talked about his life away from his job, but this was the first time he had even mentioned he was married. I knew the dancers at Robbie's adored him and his cute way of talking, but I just thought he was a bachelor and lived the life. Now I find out he's married. Damn! I shuddered to think what I might find out about him next.

Sakol's face turned serious. "Do you have any idea where the blood in your truck came from? There's part of a palm print, a thumb and two fingers on the seat. It looks like it was the left hand. I see that you don't have any cuts on either of your hands. Also there's blood several places on the windowsill. It appears whoever broke into your truck cut themselves on the glass."

"No, sorry, I have no idea about the blood. I assume you ran it thought your databanks and came up with nothing?"

"Yep. We just know it is not yours or Cox's."

We sat for a moment, both of us lost in our thoughts. I had an idea and I asked, "I've seen a video monitor at the cashier's stand at the garage. Have you checked the videos?"

Sakol replied, "Yes. We checked. The problem is there are only two cameras and both of them are aimed on the booth to catch people who try to rob the attendant. There's nothing on the floor where you parked."

I hung my head. This was not going well at all. "The blood on the door?"

"Yes?"

"Doesn't that count for anything? I mean, obviously somebody broke into the truck. All of the glass on the ground and all. Why would I break into my own truck? Also, strange blood in my truck. Isn't it obvious someone broke into my truck and stole my pistol?"

Sakol held out his hands, palms up. "I agree with you Matt. But what that means in a court of law has to be decided in court, not by you and me. The simple fact is you had gunpowder residue on your hand when they checked you. The bullets were fired from your gun."

"What about the medical report that shows I had been struck in the back of the head. What about that?"

"Again Matt, that has to be decided in court. That's if the DA feels he has enough to take it to court. All I can say is Jeff and I are trying our best to see what we can do. Neither of us believes you had anything to do with the shooting. But it isn't up to us to make that decision."

"I understand. And for what it's worth, I appreciate you being on my side." Sakol smiled at me and it did make me feel better to know I had the two of them in my corner.

~ ~ ~ ~

There's not a lot to do when you're in jail besides lie there and think. And trying to keep your mind away from all the bad places it can go when you're sitting in a jail cell is very difficult. Once more I was on the bunk in my cell when I heard the now familiar sound of the electronically controlled steel door at the end of the corridor scraping open. For a brief second I wondered if putting some WD-40 on it might help, but I wasn't in jail to help them fix their noisy doors.

It was difficult to tell how much time had passed since I had seen Krista. I didn't have a watch and I couldn't see outside. Hearing the door open, I wondered if somebody was coming to visit me and I sat up on my bunk. I heard the familiar scratch of radio transmission and then the guard's voice. "Preston? Yeah, we're getting him now. He'll be there in a minute." Finally the same tall, gaunt, sallow guard was standing in front of my cell. He paused before putting a key in the lock.

"Matt Preston?" Since he knew who I was it took everything I had not to make some flippant comment. But I was determined to stay on the good side of the turnkey so I just held my peace. I walked up and stood in front of the cell door.

I smiled at the thin stooped old man. "Here sir," I said. He again asked me to step back and I complied. Once I was out of my cell, we turned opposite way of the way we'd gone last time. I just assumed we were headed off to court. When we finally entered a room, I saw Sakol standing there waiting for me.

"Sakol!" I exclaimed. I don't think I was ever so happy to see his familiar face. "What's this all about?"

Sakol ignored me for a moment and spoke to the guard. "Thanks, Frank. I'll let you know when we're finished with him." The thin guard grunted and shuffled off. Sakol looked at me and smiled. "Come." I followed.

We wandered down a couple of corridors and then Sakol stopped and opened up a door for me. We entered and sitting at one of the desks was Jeff. As I embraced him, unexpectedly I found tears in my eyes. I wasn't used to being in jail and I found my emotions were not as in check as I would've liked. Jeff squinted at me and in a gruff voice said, "I'm still pissed at you for hanging up on me. You have a habit of doing that. Someday I'm going to get really pissed and you're going to regret it."

"I apologize. Sometimes you don't want to listen to me and I just—well, I just hang up. I know I shouldn't. Sorry about that. Forgiven?"

"Well, kind of."

I figured that was a better answer than 'no.' I looked around the little room and noticed a TV sitting on a desk, the picture flickering. Next to the TV there was a video machine. Jeff took the lead. "This is the tape from the parking garage. We thought you would know the players in this cluster better than anybody else. We want you to take a look at part of this tape." Sakol leaned over and punched a button on the VCR. The TV screen flickered a couple of times and then cleared up, and I was looking at a split image of the cash booth at the parking garage.

Sakol explained, "The time span of this video is from when you had your argument with Cox until the police showed up and arrested you."

Jeff pointed at the left half of the screen. "The video is speeded up and this is the side we want you to watch." The video ran and because of the speed, the cars seemed to jump past the cashier's stand. Suddenly Jeff exclaimed, "There, did you see it?"

I shook my head no. Jeff reversed the tape a few frames. This time it was running in normal speed and Jeff pointed to the screen. "There! Did you see it?"

I thought I saw a shadow in the background. I asked them to play it again. We went back and forth several times, sometimes normal speed and sometimes running as slow as possible. I was intently watching the shadows moving in the background. I pointed out what I thought was the bill of a ball cap on the shadow's head. For one brief moment the shadow looked towards the cameras and even though you couldn't see the face, the fact that the bill of the cap was set off to one side was clear. I pointed to the picture and told them, "That was the way Cox wore his hat. The bill was cocked off to one side when I saw him in the restaurant."

"We wondered if that was Cox," Sakol said. "At least we have an idea when he snuck into the garage. I'm wondering if he didn't sneak in to try and get even with you. He was hiding to jump you, but it appears somebody jumped him first?" The way Sakol's voice lifted it came out like a question.

As we talked, the video continued to run. I watched as the police car went past the booth and then several more. Just as Jeff leaned over to turn the VCR off, a white car pulled up to the booth. When the driver looked over, I recognized the face at once. It was Ambruster. I spoke so loudly and quickly I startled both of them. "Stop! Look at that."

Both of them looked at the screen and then back at me. "Who is that?" Jeff asked me.

"That is Kim Tate's nanny slash bodyguard slash father." We continued to watch as Ambruster paid his parking fee. Once he dropped a bill and when he bent over to pick it up, I saw his left hand, wrapped in a towel. "Back it up, back it up…" I urged.

This time both of them saw the hand wrapped in something white. They looked at each other and Jeff nodded at Sakol. "Go and check it out," he commanded.

"What about me?" I asked.

"Sorry Matt, it's back to lockup for you. But as soon as I find out what's up with this dude, I'll get right back to you."

I wasn't happy with the idea of going back to a cell, but my chances of getting out looked better than before.

~ ~ ~ ~

Once more I was bonding with the bunk in my cell when I heard the way too familiar sound of the electronically controlled steel door at the end of the corridor scraping open. Again, I wondered if putting some WD-40 on it might help the noise and then laughed at myself. I had the same thought every time I heard the steel door open. If it bothered me that much, I wondered how the guards could stand hearing it day after day.

This time there wasn't the familiar scratch of radio transmission, or even the guards talking. I was standing at the door by the time the tall, emaciated guard was in front of my cell. I knew the drill and stepped back as he paused before putting a key in the lock. Once the door was open, he said, "Make sure you get all your stuff. You won't be back." I didn't know what was up, but I was overjoyed to hear that.

"What's going on, Frank?"

"Not my place to tell you, young fellow."

"Can you give me a hint?"

"Cool your heels, son. My job is to fetch you and return you. This time it's just to fetch. Now be still." We walked in silence, waiting at each door as it opened and then clanged shut behind us. Frank took us to a new room. He opened the door and I stepped into a nicely furnished space. Krista was sitting at the table as were Jeff and Sakol. Sakol looked over at the guard. "Thanks Frank." Frank turned and left the room.

Jeff motioned for me to sit. After I was comfortable, Sakol started talking. "I went out to Mrs. Tate's home. When I got there, I found Ambruster. He's at Harborview Hospital right now. He tried to commit suicide but Samara found him just before I got there and the medics were already on the way. His left hand was cut and his blood is being cross-checked against the blood found on your truck right now.

"I can tell you this now. We never thought you shot Cox. Also, the handprint on the seat was way too small to have been yours, but Ambruster's hand looks like it's just about right. We found a suicide note. Basically the note says Ambruster saw that Cox was the one who hit you on the head. Ambruster had already broken into your truck and stolen your gun since he was planning on killing Cox with it. He overheard you telling Mrs. Tate you kept a gun in your truck, and his plan was to use it when he thought you might have an alibi.

"After Ambruster saw Cox hit you and before Cox could do anything more to you, Ambruster shot him. It was a spur-of–the-moment idea when he pulled your unconscious body over to the truck and then put the gun in your hand, aimed the gun at Cox and pulled the trigger. Since there's no way to tell if the powder residue was from one shot or two, it looked like you had shot Cox.

"Ambruster has been looking for a way to murder Cox ever since Kim told him about the rape. He loved that girl like she was his own. Later he felt badly about framing you and he decided the only way out was to commit suicide and leave a note which would get you off the hook."

I leaned back in my chair and took a deep breath. "So, does that mean I'm free now?"

"More or less." Jeff replied. "We still need to see that the blood on your seat matches Ambruster's. We also want to see if there is any residue on his hands from your gun, but yes, you're free to go."

I looked at Krista. "What about you?"

"What about me?"

"Are we clean? Do we have to go to court?"

"Nope. Looks like all of the charges have been dropped, or at least they will be shortly."

I looked back at Jeff and Sakol. "Does Kim know yet?"

"I don't know, Samara read the note before I got there, so maybe she's told Kim. Why?" Sakol asked me.

"I know how Kim felt about Ambruster. It's really going to be tough on her—knowing what he did for her. I'm sure the rape was difficult enough, but now having Ambruster do-ing something like that for her. I really feel badly for her."

"Is she with Sharon?" Jeff asked.

"Yeah, they're together at the houseboat. I guess if I'm free to go, I'll go over there and check on them."

CHAPTER 16

HANNEY'S HIDEAWAY

Tonight I was celebrating my freedom from jail and all the problems that had gone along with my incarceration with Gladys. I could think of no place better to be, nor anybody I would rather be with. We were having dinner at Hanney's Hideaway and this was her first time. Aside from being ecstatic that I was a free man, I was also excited to be able to show her what might be my most favorite of all restaurants.

It's just north of Seattle and to be honest, I hate to even tell anybody about it. So far it's been a well-kept secret and those of us who know about it hate to share. Sorry, that's just the way it is. Even though there are restaurants constantly going out business, this place is always packed. They don't advertise, it's all by word of mouth that people even know about them. Even so, it's still highly advisable to have reservations before you show up.

The restaurant is an old roadhouse from the twenties that's been completely renovated. The place is called Hanney's Hideaway and it's a total throwback, a restaurant out of the past. The interior matches the exterior, and it feels like a classic top-of-the-line chophouse or steakhouse. White tablecloths with heavy starched napkins, well-padded booths with small candles on the tables, and individual spotlights over each table making small intimate pools of light. If you want seduction on the grandest scale, Hanney's is the place to go.

In addition to the ambiance, Hanney's has the most delicious food. That's if your tastes run to the best Italian dishes west of New York, or prime steaks, a huge baked potato with all of the heart attack condiments and a great Caesar salad that's actually prepared at your table. I know it all sounds decadent, but once in a while you have to treat yourself. Life is way too short not to enjoy yourself from time to time.

And then there are the drinks they serve. Free poured in heavy glasses, just the way you would want, a drink to make the soul glad. In addition, there are wines from obscure vineyards in remote places of Italy, or beers from top Italian brewers.

If you were to meet the owners, you'd never believe the restaurant could ever succeed. Franka and Tony are from New Jersey and have the attitude. Franka will show you to your seat, toss the menus on the table and in her best Jersey accent say, "I'll be back. Cool ya heels." When she delivers your drink she picks up the menu. God forbid you should ever say something like "Wait, I haven't ordered yet." That comment will get you, "Are you too stupid to remember what youze wants till I gets back? Sheeze." And off she goes spreading more cheer to her customers. I know it sounds weird, but it's all part of the charm of the place. Franka doesn't treat strangers that way, you have to be special to bask in her aura. You have to experience the place to fully appreciate what I'm telling you.

Your steak is a generous cut of the kind of meat you ordered, and it's done to perfection. You only have to order once and Franka remembers exactly how you like it. If Italian food is your desire, each dish is better than the last, and the hardest part of eating there is to not pick up the plate and lick it. Tony has to have those hands insured by Lloyds of London. His dishes really are that good. Not once have I had a dinner there that wasn't one of the best meals I've ever had.

Franka not only remembers that I like Scotch, but the brand I prefer, and the way I like it served. Hanney's is truly an eating encounter that must be experienced once in your life, if you can get reservations.

I've mentioned there are several restaurants I really enjoy, so saying this one was more special than the others is really saying something. Franka showed us to a table I had reserved that overlooked the Sound and the Olympic mountains off in the distance. The setting was perfect and as Franka turned to leave, she addressed Gladys, "So, what is it, youse like hard up for a date or sumpin? Whatcha doin with da bum?"

Gladys, bless her soul, picked right up on what to say. "Naw, it's my night to do something for the disadvantaged. I'm considering this a mercy date, like a charity date if you will. One date with him gets me two dates with some rich guys."

Franka snickered and patted Gladys on her shoulder. "You have a bigger heart than I do." Turning to me, Franka said, "You done good with this one. She's all right!" With that, Franka was off to the next table. A short time later she came back and asked Gladys, "Do you like Bloody Marys?" Gladys nodded yes and then started to say something when Franka interrupted, "Honey, you gets it the ways they come. Ya love it. Now bees still." I knew better than to say a word.

When the drinks arrived, mine was exactly as I liked it and Gladys' drink was covered on top with various edibles to eat as she drank. She laughed at the way it was present-ed. "I've lived my whole life in the greater Seattle area and I've never even heard of this place. It's like out of the past. I expect to see The Rat Pack come strolling through the front door any minute."

I smiled at her, it was exactly how I felt about the place. "Sakol was the one who told me about it. He heard about it from Mouse. I think Mouse is a silent partner, but I'm not sure." As if that was his cue, I looked up to see Mouse standing at the end of our table, looking resplendent as always.

"Not sure about what?" he laughed. Turning to Gladys, he took her hand and kissed it. "You look lovely, my dear." Mouse tipped his head towards me and said, "Much too good for this bum."

"Yeah, well usually I leave him out in the truck, but tonight I decided I'd feed him. He has fairly good manners and he does clean up well." I was getting a little tired of being spoken about as if I wasn't present.

I spoke up, "I am pleased I can be fodder for the two of you and your jokes. Nice to see you again, Mouse. How are things?" Mouse was dressed to the nines. His double-breasted suit with vest looked right at home in the restaurant. The way he was dressed made me think of a character from "The Godfather." But I knew the difference between those characters that were respected out of fear, while Mouse, on the other hand, earned his.

He smiled at me. "Doing well, thank you." He paused and then continued, "I think I may owe you an apology. I had doubts about the Cox kid and I wondered at the time if it was wise for me to have told him to go and find you." Mouse spread hands out, asking for forgiveness. "For once I was really wrong about somebody. I heard the rumors and yet when I spoke to the kid, he was so engaging. It was difficult for me to see the, ah, shall we say, his evil side?"

Gladys interjected, "I wish you had talked to me. I saw firsthand some of the crap he pulled. I sat in the ER with one of his victims. I never met the kid, but I had heard what a nice young man he seemed to be. But something up there just wasn't right." Gladys pointed at her head. "He was a bad apple who couldn't control his demons. I'm sorry he's dead, but I can't say I am surprised, considering how many lives he destroyed."

Mouse said, "I'm sorry you had the problems you did. I'm pleased you came out in one piece. I would imagine you had a few anxious moments with the police and all."

"I'll admit it wasn't looking good for me." I had to laugh when I looked back at the past couple of days. "But I do appreciate you stopping by the table and talking to me about things. I never blamed you for any of the difficulty I was in. Things just turned out the way they did. I hate to see him dead too, but I'm sure a lot of women are glad to see him gone."

I could see he hadn't gotten to the reason he'd stopped by our table. This was the first time I'd seen Mouse having difficulty in expressing his thoughts. I tried to help, "What is it? You seem like you have something to say. Would you like for me to go outside with you so we can talk alone?"

Mouse smiled at me and said, "No, I just wanted to phrase this correctly. I warned you before about the two men who are following you.

"After our last chat, I put out my feelers and I've been trying to get some information about them. Matt, for the first time in my life, I've had a lot of doors slammed in my face. People who owe me big favors are running scared and won't return my calls or talk to me. Because I know the tall one, I can assure you he is a very dangerous man.

"When I asked questions, I was told I would get just one warning to leave things alone... and I've had that warning." I could see the concern written on his face. Whoever these men were, they had Mouse's attention and he was handling them with a lot of care.

He cleared his throat, and continued, "As for the little fat guy, I don't think he's who he says he is. Things my sources tell me about him don't add up. Anyway, either Price or Hollis had something the two of them are frantic to get. Part of what they want is information that I am told would still be damaging. Even today it would create a lot of stink, maybe even cost some lives. Matt, I'm telling you as a friend, stay away from them. They're dangerous."

I replied, "Mouse, I would love to heed your warnings and stay away from them, but it seems like every time I turn around, there they are. You already know you surprise me with your awareness of what's happening around town, but these two scare me with all of their knowledge. I appreciate your warning, I just wish there was something I could do to keep them out of my life. They keep asking me questions about things I know nothing about. They keep bringing up something called Crescent." At the mention of that word, Mouse quickly glanced around the room to see if anybody was listening.

Mouse leaned forward and put his hand on my sleeve. "Matt, listen to me. Listen to me very carefully. Never, I mean this now, NEVER mention that word again in connection with your past. I cannot stress this enough." His voice was low and his words seemed sinister.

"What do you know about this, Mouse? Come on, please tell me. I'm in the dark here."

Mouse shook his head. "Sorry Matt, the less you know, the better off you are. Stay away from those two men and keep quiet about," he paused, thinking of the way he wanted to word it, "well, just keep quiet. Period. Understand?"

"Thanks. I know your intentions are good, but for some reason our two friends just won't leave me alone. But I will heed your advice as much as I can. I'll stay away from them if they stay away from me." Mouse shook my hand, smiled at Gladys and took his leave.

After our salads were in front of us, Gladys looked at me and leaned over. "What men is Mouse talking about? Are you in some sort of trouble?"

I shook my head, "Naw, it's just some sort of a mis-understanding. There are a couple of guys who have been following me and I really don't know why."

"What is this crescent thing you said to Mouse? He seemed really upset about it."

I was not going to allow her to put a damper on my evening. "Sweetheart, this is a celebration. I'm a free man and I am with the most beautiful, sexy woman in the restaurant. What you ask are subjects for another time and a different place."

Gladys reached out and took one of my hands and kissed it. "Thanks for bringing me here. Like I said, I'd never heard of this place, but I think you were correct, I'll bet Mouse owns part of this restaurant. Actually, as I understand it, he owns bits and pieces of a lot of businesses in Seattle. Have you ever seen his girlfriend?"

"I didn't even know he had one." Another surprise. I never saw him as somebody with a girlfriend. "Tell me about her."

"I know she's Asian and her name is Jade."

I interrupted, "I have met her. I thought she was like a servant or something."

"There's a long involved story, but basically she's pay-ment to Mouse for a debt of honor. She's so in love with him and he thinks she's just saying that because of the debt thing. I know he's in love with her as well. I hope somehow it all works out."

I laughed. "How can you pay a debt with a person? That's so barbaric." I reached over and pulled her hand back to me. "By the way, you're quite the romantic."

She blushed a little and bowed her head. When she looked back at me she had a cute grin on her face. "Mouse is a long story. Someday I'll tell you about it. As for being a romantic, guilty! I know, considering what I do for a living, most people would expect me to be jaded, but I do like romance and a happy ending. And I'll tell you a secret, Mr. Preston, for all your bluff and gruff, you are a softy and just as much a romantic as I am. You've treated me like a lady from the moment we met. You are a special man, sir." Gladys turned my hand over and kissed my palm again. "Thanks for being so sweet to me."

We gazed out the window and watched as the sun slipped slowly behind the Olympics, turning the clouds various hues of red, orange and gold. It was a spectacular sunset. Our steaks arrived and they looked perfect. I was at peace with the world and the evening had gone very well so far. I was so grateful for everything.

We both dug in and didn't say more than a couple of words during the meal. Much later we were finished and I pushed my plate away. Both of us had left food on our plates, the meal just too much to finish. As Franka bussed our table, she sat two cups of their special coffee on the table and smiling at Gladys, said, "It's on the house, part of your reward for putting up with this oaf."

"Yeah, but he really is a sweet oaf."

Franka reached out and squeezed my hand. "Yeah, I hate to admit it, but you're right, he ain't bad." In case you didn't know it, that was the best compliment one could ever expect from Franka and I was flying high.

I paid the bill and we headed out to my car. "Is there anything you'd like to do?" I asked Gladys.

She smiled and winked at me suggestively. "Yes there is. Take me to your place. Take my clothes off real slow and then make love to me. And then tomorrow I want you to wake me by making love to me again." She kissed my cheek. "Do you think your senior body can handle that?"

"Get in," I pointed to the car, "Let's see what the old man is capable of."

I opened her door and Gladys was still laughing when I got behind the wheel. "Oh goody!" I was surprised, for all of her class there was still a nice chunk of good old nasty about her as well.

That evening I did my best to show her just what an old man was capable of.

And even better, how things work the next morning as well.

CHAPTER 17
RETURN TO ROSS ISLAND

Today was going to be a day of celebration for me, and for Beanie it was her first trip to a beach. I was celebrating my freedom and the fact that I was totally off the hook as far as Cox's death was concerned.

The newspapers were having a field day with the Cox murder once the news regarding the rapes got out. The juicy details about Ambruster hunting Cox down and killing him were daily fodder. I did think one paper went a bit overboard with the headline, 'The Butler Really Did It.' Ambruster was a lot more than a butler to Samara and Kim.

Ambruster was recovering and there was a lot of legal maneuvering over what the charges would be. I'd lost count of the number of women who were coming forth and relating tales about that rat bastard Cox. The newspapers had vilified him and the University was doing all it could to distance itself from the whole ugly mess. The media was making Ambruster out to be a saint. Krista Sellers had agreed to handle his case and he was getting the best representation he could ever want. If there was any way for him to get off, I was positive Krista was going to find it. Between the positive press and a stellar attorney, Ambruster was in great hands.

I was headed for my favorite beach on Whidbey Island. I remembered the first time I had taken BJ there and how much she had enjoyed running up and down the beach as fast as she could. Whenever I took BJ to the beach, she would be so exhausted I'd have to pick her up and set her in the truck. I had made the mistake one time of just putting her on the floor and then I had to stop and pick her up and put her on the seat, she was too exhausted to climb up without help. For the rest of the trip home, she didn't move a muscle. The next day every time she moved she groaned. Her first trip to the beach had been perfect.

Beanie had been on a ferry before, but she had never explored a shoreline. After we got off the ferry, we drove up the island to a small road where I can park the truck near the water. Once we hit the beach and I released Bean, she was gone. For a while all I saw was a small brown speck off in the distance, and then she came running back as fast as her little legs would go. She raced around me a couple of times, barked twice and then off she went running down the beach the other way. I chose today since the tide would be out further than any other day for the next four weeks.

As we rounded the promontory, I was greeted by a totally empty bay. The tide was completely out, revealing a huge expanse of beach. There were a few tidal pools, but for the most part, the bay was now just tidal flats. Bean saw a flock of seagulls walking out on a sandy spit and she took off at a dead run, barking as she went. The birds seemed to know just how close they could let her get to them before they went wheeling off into the air, their cries sounding like they were laughing at her, teasing her because she couldn't catch them. For the next half hour, Bean chased them, only to have them fly off at the last moment every time she got close.

I found a log and sat down, using it as a backrest. I've always enjoyed the beach, but today it was extra special. I was savoring every little morsel of the experience. This was so much better than sitting in a jail cell wondering what was going to happen to my sorry ass. The heat of the sun felt good and Bean's antics amused me. As I sat there, I must've dozed off for a moment, because the next thing I was aware of was Bean crawling into my lap, wet, sandy and stinky. I kept pushing her away and she couldn't understand why I didn't want a stinky, sandy, soaked dog curled up in my lap.

I reached into my backpack and pulled out a dish and a gallon jug of water. I was sure she was thirsty and I didn't want her trying to drink saltwater from the Sound. She lapped up the water and when she was finished, the bottom of the pan was covered in sand washed from her face as she drank. For a long time, we sat there, side by side, looking out across the empty bay. Eventually Bean got bored and started to walk out across the flats again. I decided I needed to get my lazy butt in gear as well so I stood and followed her.

As we walked across the bay, when I would come to a tide pool I'd just walk through it. Bean followed and as I walked through one that was deeper than the rest, she found it necessary to swim part of the way. When we got to the other side, she made sure she was standing right next to me when she shook off. She was determined to share. I laughed and as I tried to move away from her, she followed me.

We continued on until we got to the other side of the bay and started to round the next point. I looked back to where I had grounded our stuff. We hadn't seen anybody so far and I thought it was safe to leave our gear unguarded. As I started to turn back, I happened to glance up at the bank above where I had been sitting. The bank was made of sand and clay and was between eighty to a hundred feet high. Above where we had been sitting on the beach, I spotted a crack in the bank. I thought the crack was in the shape of a partial moon… like a *crescent moon!*

In that instant, I had a flash.

Crescent!

I can't begin to explain how the human mind works. Why something will click in the brain and start a flow of information, and the strange thing is somehow the trigger that makes everything happen is so obscure. Why would a scar on the bank start me thinking along the lines my mind started to run? I thought about when Hollis was on the run, how he could have gone anywhere he wanted. He knew he was being chased; he knew he was a wanted man. When he was at Lan's apartment, Hollis had talked to somebody on the phone. Lan had heard him tell somebody he was going to a lighthouse on an island and I had found him there. Why had he gone to that lighthouse? What was there that I had missed? I knew Hollis had grown up on the island and knew it well, but it was an island, not an easy place to escape from. Why would he go to a place he had to have known was going to be difficult to escape from?

As I trudged down the beach after Bean, my mind drifted back to that day in the tower. I tried to remember everything I'd seen as I crawled up towards the lighthouse that day. I remembered the sounds the bugs were making and the feel of the sand on my hands as I crawled towards the tower. I remembered the scent of the bushes and how I had felt seeing Sakol lying wounded on the ground. I remembered how sad I was that he might be dead, and how happy I was when I saw him move and heard him groan.

In my mind I once again ran towards the lighthouse, waiting for the feeling of a bullet tearing into my body. I remembered how when I had moved into the cold round dirty tower, there was a difference in temperature between outside and inside of the structure. I looked down and I noticed I actually had goosebumps.

I recalled what the sound was like when I heard Hollis above me. My mind went carefully over each detail: the feeling of the damp wall of the lighthouse on my hand and moving up the stairs so carefully. Then I remembered how I had slipped and fallen and how lucky I had been that my arm was extended up towards the top of the tower. I still shuddered as I recalled looking up and seeing Hollis pointing a gun down at me. Again I heard report and I felt the hot pain in my thigh. My hand actually went down to the scar and it felt as if I had just been shot again. I remembered seeing the wound blossom on his chest from my bullet and I saw him fall backwards.

I forced my mind to go back once more to climbing the tower, going up each step, carefully up and up while keeping my eyes trained on the opening above my head, never looking down until I tripped.

Tripped!

My mind stopped. Mentally I went back down a couple of steps and then tried to remember each step up. Tripped! Why? Why had I tripped? As far as I remembered, every step had been the same height, so uniform that I didn't even think about my ascent. I had been able to move up the stairs with such ease, and then BANG! I never did look at what tripped me. And on the way down out of the tower, I was passed out. From the time I lay my head on the cold floor until I woke up in the hospital bed, there was nothing.

Ross Island was just one island over from where Bean and I were, and I knew there was a little ferryboat that ran between the islands. Since we were this close, I decided to go visit Ross Island. I wanted to go up the steps in the old lighthouse one more time. This time I was going to examine each step very carefully. I called to Beanie and we headed off to pick up our stuff and head over to Ross.

There was a long line of cars waiting at the ferry when we got there, much longer than I had expected and I was surprised. A skinny little older gentleman was sitting under a tree when we pulled up. Once I was stopped, he stood, dusted off the seat of his pants and then came over to my truck. The old fella was wearing filthy tan pants and his red woolen plaid shirt had seen better days. His face was covered in gray stubble and when I put my window down I noticed he really needed a bath. Even from a few feet away he smelled bad. When he spoke he revealed spaces between his yellowed teeth. He started the conversation with, "Tide's out."

"I take it that screws up the ferry?" I asked.

He looked at me as if I wasn't playing with a full deck of cards. "Well of course." He spat out some vile looking dark yellow liquid from his mouth onto the ground. "It's way too shallow for the ferry to pull into the slip. Fucking government too cheap to fix it. Pays my taxes and they just fritter the money away. Fucking crooks."

"Any idea how long before the ferry can move?" I could see the ferry was only about fifty feet away from the dock with a few cars stuck on board.

"Bout half hour or so, I reckon." Another wad of yellow spit hit the pavement.

"Will all of us fit on the ferry going over?"

"Yeah, but not too many more." Once more with the yellow spit. I had considered letting Beanie out for a quick run, but there was no way I wanted her to get near the old man's spit.

"Well, thanks for the info."

The old fellow wasn't done with me yet. "What ya want on the island?" He pointed off towards Ross Island.

"I wanted to see the lighthouse," I told him. I wasn't too keen on sharing my reasons for visiting.

"It's closed ya know?"

"Yeah, I know, I just want to walk around and look at things."

"Durn fool, ain't nothin' to look fur. Fort's gone. Light-house is almost falled down too. What'cha wants over der?"

"I just want to look around."

"Waste of time if 'n ya asked me. Tower ain't safe neither." Some more yellow spit hit the ground. I was surprised there was that much room in the old guy's mouth.

"Well, I had some time to kill and I always wanted to see the island."

"Waste of time…" The old man had started to move away, calling back over his shoulder, "Durn young people today, don't listen to a thing, just fritter away their time. Harrumph!" A new car had pulled up behind me and the old fella had somebody new to explain the reason we were waiting.

It didn't take much more than the promised half hour. I felt sorry for those stuck on the boat. None of the drivers seemed very happy as they drove over the gangway and away down the island. It must have been very frustrating to have to just sit a few feet from the dock and not be able to do anything about it.

Soon it was our time to pull onto the little boat, and the old man who had explained why we had to wait was still standing on the dock talking to those who now had to wait for the ferry to return.

The ride over was short and I could see even if the ferry had been able to discharge the cars on the other side, it would have been impossible for it to get into the dock on the Ross Island side. We were just able to pull into the dock and I felt it as the keel bumped up onto the sand.

It was eerie pulling into the parking lot at the fort. I tried to keep the memories out of my head, but it was difficult. Somebody had put up a chain across the parking lot, so I had to park the truck on the road and walk back to the lighthouse. I didn't know what to expect so I decided to leave Beanie in the truck.

This time I didn't need to crawl through the bushes; there was no need to keep myself hidden. As I passed the place where I had seen Sakol lying that day, I thought I saw a dark spot that could have been blood. I tried to keep my mind off those thoughts. I stepped into the cool tower and looked up. I half expected to see Hollis look down at me.

I started to walk up the stairs circling the inside wall. When I came to each step I looked carefully at it. Did it seem any different than the step before or after? Slowly, step by step, I climbed. A few steps from the top I spotted the step that actually looked a bit different. The step was just a little higher than the steps before and after it. I got down on my knees and looked at it carefully. A person could have passed over that step without ever noticing the slight difference. The only reason I found it was that I knew what I was looking for. My body had been so in tune with the building the day I was stalking Hollis, my feet could tell the difference. I had expected the step to be the same height as the last one and the slight difference had caused me to trip.

I tried to move the step, but it seemed to be firmly set in place. I knocked on it with my knuckle, but I couldn't really tap hard enough to tell if it was hollow under the riser. The only thing I got out of knocking on the stone was a sore knuckle. I had a toolbox down in the truck and I went back to get a hammer and a cold chisel.

When I got back to the step, I took the hammer and rapped on the stone. I tried tapping on the step before and after and I thought it sounded different. It sounded hollow. But the tread was so thick, and being stone, it was difficult to really tell. Taking the cold chisel, I started working on one corner of the tread. I gently tapped back and forth across the lip of the step. Slowly the tread moved a little. Just as I was about to try and pry the step up, I heard voices coming and I quickly pushed it back into place. I stood up and stepped on the tread to try and make it look normal.

I went ahead and climbed the rest of the way to the top, hiding my tools behind a piece of cement sticking out of the wall. When I looked towards the spot where Hollis had died, there were several dark stains. Even though it had been either kill or be killed, I felt bad it had ended the way it did. At the time, I had hated Hollis with a passion, a hatred I don't think I'd ever before experienced, but I still regretted taking another person's life. I think anybody who can take a life and not have a little regret must have something missing in their personality. Back in Nam, when I was positive I had killed someone, even though they were the enemy, I always felt some sorrow.

The voices turned out to be four boys who were wandering around the fort and the lighthouse. When they got to the top they pointed out the dark spots and one of the boys asked me, "Hey mister, do ya know what them dark spots are?"

I decided to play dumb. I didn't want them to know anything about me. "No. Weather stains?"

"Naw, that's blood."

"Really?"

"Yeah, did you hear about the guy getting killed up here? And a bunch of other people got shot here too."

The boys were way too excited about people getting killed for my taste. I guess at that age they didn't understand what death really means. What with today's video games, you can kill monsters and bad guys and all you have to do is hit the reset button and everybody comes back to life and you get to do it all over again. The sad thing is life doesn't come with a reset button. When you take a life, that game is over. I was sure none of these boys wanted to listen to an old guy tell them people dying was not a cool thing, so I just kept my mouth shut.

I decided the boys were going to be in the tower for a while so I went back down to the truck and let Beanie out. For the next few minutes I watched as she ran and I waited for the boys to leave. It seemed like the boys took forever to come back out of the lighthouse. Finally, they left and I made my way back into the tower. Beanie came with me but stopped at the bottom of the stairs. She stood and looked up at the stairs and I could see she was not going to follow me up.

I slipped up the stairs and retrieved my hidden tools. I went back down to the loose step and started to work it away from the stair riser. Once it was loose in my hand, I was able to pull the stone away.

There was a small hollow under the stone. The space looked old, as if somebody had chipped away the concrete under the tread a long time ago, and now it was being used as a small secret place to hide something.

My hands were trembling as I reached down to pick up the contents of the small cavity. I could feel my heart racing and the hair on my arms stood up. I could see a little box and under that was a badly deteriorated leather pouch, both of them stuffed into the small hollow. I carefully lifted up the box so I could get a better look at the pouch. On the front cover of the pouch I could just make out a mark embossed in the leather.

It was a sliver of…?

The embossed pattern was shaped like a crescent!

My hands were trembling so badly I dropped the chisel.

CHAPTER 18
CODE NAME: CRESCENT

I can't begin to describe how much I wanted to open the box and the pouch in front of me. But I knew kneeling there on the stairs was not the best place to do it. I was concerned the boys might return or somebody new might show up. I wasn't comfortable staying too long in the tower. I pulled the box and the pouch from their hiding place and then slipped the step back into the notch I had pried it from. As I tapped the tread back into place I noticed a small indentation on the edge of the tread closest to the wall. I wiped the indentation off with my hand as it was covered with dirt and grime deposited there over time. Had I not been down on my hands and knees I would never have seen it. There, on the edge of the stone, was a crescent, a small sliver of moon carved into the rock. Who had carved the crescent into the stone? But even more important, who had hidden the two items in the riser? I thought it might be Hollis since he wanted to come and visit the tower before he died, but that was just a guess on my part. What I also found strange was the evident age of the crescent mark on the stair; it would have meant Hollis had put the box and pouch up in the lighthouse a long time ago, or at least the hollow space had been created a very long time ago. There was too much dirt and grime imbedded in the mark for it to have been during the time Hollis was on the run. No, this was something that had been created a long time ago. More mysteries to ponder at a later time.

I tapped on the top of the tread a couple of times to settle it into place and once it was in, you couldn't tell it had ever been out. I wondered if Colonel McNaulty had been up and down the staircase. Had he stepped over this step and missed the small difference? Since it was obvious the step had not been moved for a long time, I was sure McNaulty hadn't found the secret place. Also, I was positive if he had found the hiding place, it would have been empty.

When I got to the bottom of the stairs, Beanie was there waiting. She danced between my legs and we headed to the truck. I thought for a moment about where I might hide the things I had just found and decided to hide them in a storage compartment behind my seat, and we headed back for home. I wasn't going to open either of them until it was someplace I felt was safe, or at least a lot safer than sitting in my truck out in the open.

Beanie and I caught the ferry back to Seattle. I hadn't been followed for a couple of days, but I was still leery of it happening again. I thought the best place to examine my find was at my hideout, my man cave where I keep my car collection stored. I had no idea if the van that had been following me a few days ago was still around or if they had perhaps switched vehicles. I decided I needed to find a different car, a car they would have no way of knowing was mine. The cars I had in storage were all too memorable. What I needed was something that people were used to seeing every day. Suddenly Scott, my poker buddy and close friend, came to mind. One of his cars is an old Lincoln Town Car. The kind you see every day taking people to and from the airport and delivering people all over Seattle. I knew the windows on his car were tinted and people wouldn't notice it. I called Scott.

"Matt, what's up?" Since this was Scott's greeting, I figured he must have recognized my number off his incoming screen.

I cut straight to the chase. "Scott, can I borrow the Town Car?"

"Are you serious? The man who has every car anybody could possibly want? Do you really want to borrow that piece of shit?" He laughed out loud as he teased me.

I was perhaps a bit short with him as I replied, "I'll explain later, can I borrow it?"

"Yeah, it's here in the garage. There's a key in the glove box." Many of Ford's products have a keypad on the driver's door. If you know the five-digit code, you can open the door. Scott gave me the code to open the car and I thanked him. I already knew the access code to his condo garage.

I lucked out and there was a space right next to his Lincoln. Since Scott owns the building, I wasn't worried about taking somebody's parking spot. I moved Beanie to the car and then checked to see if I was being watched. When I was positive it was safe, I moved my find into the trunk of the Lincoln. I found the keys where Scott had said they would be and I left the garage from the other entrance.

I watched my mirror a lot as I weaved my way through downtown. A few blocks before my building I turned down an alley and drove to the end. I waited several minutes and when nobody pulled in behind me, I decided it was safe to go up to my man cave. Thanks to Pop's foresight by purchasing properties scattered around town, I own a row of three buildings. I could park in the garage of one building and then walk down the alley and sneak in the back door of the building I wanted. I took the elevator up to my floor and found a backpack I'd left in the small office. I returned to the Lincoln and retrieved the box and the pouch. Holding Beanie under one arm with the backpack slung over my other shoulder, we went to my garage on the top floor of my building.

I have a bed for Bean to curl up in and I put her down on it. I cleared off a spot on one of the workbenches and turned on the light over it. I stood for a moment and looked at the two items lying in front of me. I couldn't believe I'd found them. I also wondered if I should consider myself lucky or unlucky. The old leather pouch was crumbling and I hated to even move it. I had no idea about any of the places it had been in the past, but I the tower hadn't been good for it. It was no wonder it was so deteriorated. I carefully sat the pouch aside and picked up the box.

The box had once been lacquered black but now age and weathering had blistered it in several places. The hinges on the back were crusty and it had an old rusty lock set into the face. I turned the box over in my hands several times and shook it for good measure. The box was fairly heavy for its size and when I shook it there were no sounds.

I looked around my workbench and in the tool chest. I picked out a tool I thought I could pick the lock with, but I didn't have any success. I decided it didn't matter if I destroyed it so I got a drill and bit and drilled out the center of the lock.

I set the drill to one side, took a deep breath, and carefully lifted the lid. The inside was lined with deep blue velvet and there was a block of wood fitted to sit tightly. There was the wood was notched and nestled inside the notch was what I guessed to be a key. I'd never seen anything quite like it. The key was much bigger than any standard key, it was as long as my hand. The part where the teeth should have been was just a round piece of metal, like a long skinny barrel. I picked up a magnifying glass and looking at it closer I could see little notches around the barrel.

This was like no key I had ever seen before. I looked through the rest of the box and there was nothing else inside, just the block of wood covered in velvet and notched to hold the key tightly in place. I was disappointed.

I wondered aloud, "Where does the key go? What lock does it fit?" There was no indication on either the key or the box. I put the key back in the block of wood and closed the cover.

I carefully picked up the pouch and when I opened the flap, it came off in my hands. As gently as I could I placed it on the bench but even as careful as I was, as I set it down it crumbled into two large pieces and several smaller ones. Part of the sides sloughed away, revealing a book wrapped in some sort of wax paper. It was like the book had been sealed inside a heavy wax bag.

Picking up the book and setting it aside, I pushed away the remains of the old deteriorated leather pouch. I found a sharp knife and I carefully started to cut open the paper. I was surprised at the condition of the book. It was in relatively good shape, all things considered. Once free of the envelope, as carefully as I could, I slowly opened the cover. The first page read *DIARY* and below that was written, *Hayward Hollis*.

Oh shit!

I set the book down with trembling hands and thought for a moment. Did I really want to know what was in the book? Was this something I really wanted to read? Walter's warning echoed in my mind.

I was guessing information about the key might be contained in the diary. But I was also sure there were a lot more interesting things written in that diary than what the key was all about. I decided I needed to think about this for a while. I knew if McNaulty got ahold of me and found out I had the diary, there was no way I was going to convince him I hadn't read it. But for my own peace of mind, I just didn't know if I wanted to read some of the stuff Hollis had been involved in.

The only person I could discuss my findings with was Walter. He might not want to read it either, but at least he would understand my problems with knowing the contents of the diary.

My next challenge was to find a hiding place. I had never had to hide anything in my buildings before. I discarded the idea of putting it in any of the cars. If anybody ever found out I had the diary, the first place they would look would be in the cars. After my mental exercise of trying to hide something in my workshop, I decided there was no place I was comfortable hiding them. I would take them with me and see if I could find a better spot. The one thing I did need to do was get a letter to Walter as soon as possible and tell him I was coming over again.

Suddenly it dawned on me, each of my apartments has a storage unit. The person who rented Sharon's place didn't use theirs. There were still some things Sharon had left and I had a key. Her locker was the safest place I could come up with until I could get over to see Walter and discuss what to do with my find. I wanted to go see him and I didn't want to wait for mail to get to him and let him know I was coming. I was going to go over and take my chances I could find the cabin. It was just too dangerous to wait much longer.

The next day I'd be off to the peninsula to talk about Crescent with Walter. I knew that the two items I had were dangerous, but I also had to dispose of them in such a manner that I didn't get screwed. Finding them had put me on a tightrope, and I had no choice but to get to the other side. I thought *Walter, don't fail me now!"*

CHAPTER 19
WALTER II

I decided the best thing to do was to leave Bean with Sharon since this was going to be a quick trip over and back. I didn't want her slowing me down. I was still using Scott's Lincoln and so far I hadn't seen anybody parking out in front of my apartment I didn't recognize. I was aware there still could have been somebody watching me, but right now I had some chance to move around without the colonel and flyboy watching me.

For the first time in a long time I was impatient at how long the ferry was taking. Normally I can relax and enjoy the trip over, but today I was in no mood to take in the beauty. I wanted to get to Walter's as quickly as possible. I went topside and purchased a cup of overpriced coffee and stood at the rail watching the water go by.

After what seemed like the longest ferry ride of my life, we docked and I was headed off for the mountains. I parked the car in the gravel lot and headed down the trail. I made a couple of wrong turns but I quickly realized my mistake and returned to the right trail.

I had moved so quickly, I was surprised when I came around the big rock behind his cabin. As I approached, I called out. When I stepped around to the front deck Walter came out of the house, naked. "Holy shit, please put on some clothes," I told him.

Walter laughed, "Why? This is my place," and he turned around. As he walked into the cabin I heard him call out to Thien, "Put on some clothes, we have a guest."

I heard her answer, "Who is it dear?"

Walter answered, "I think it's a lost door-to-door salesman. The guy's offended I'm naked in my own home."

I called out as loudly as I could, "Hey, leave your clothes off. I don't care if you want to run around with a pink ribbon tied around your twanger. Just get out here! I need to talk to you." When Walter finally came out of the house he didn't have on much more than when I first saw him. He motioned for me to come up on the deck and pointed at a chair. "Sit. What can I get you to drink?"

"Water, please." Walter turned and asked Thien to bring out some water for me, and pulled up another chair and sat down. When Thien brought out my water she had on an outfit exactly like Walter's. She didn't seem to be the least bit self-conscious about being almost naked in front of me. I stood when she came out and she handed me the glass, and then wrapped her arms about me and gave me a big hug. I bent over for her and as she kissed me on the cheek she remarked, "What an unexpected treat. It's nice to see you."

"Okay. Now what brings you out to my lair?" Walter inquired. I handed him the bag with the things I'd found in the lighthouse. "What's this?"

"I found them in the lighthouse on Ross Island. They were under a step that had a small crescent carved in it."

Walter quickly extended the bag back to me. "No. I don't want to see what's in there. Drink your water and then go back to Seattle. I don't want to get involved."

Walter had started to push himself out of his chair and I leaned over and placed my hand on his arm. "Walter, over the years we've become fairly good friends. You saved my ass back in Nam and I like to think I kind of saved your ass back in Seattle." Walter leveled a gaze at me. "I can think of nobody I trust as much as you when it comes to our time back in country. I value your judgment. A lot!" Walter grunted and I continued, "I need your advice. Please at least look at what I have. Please?" I pleaded.

Walter reached over and picked up the bag and opened it. First he took out the box. He held it up and looked over each face very carefully. "It looks very old, see all the blisters in the paint?" He opened it and examined the inside just as carefully as he had the outside. When he picked up the key he looked at me. "This is a storage box key from a high-security lockbox, like in a big bank. I've seen one before. I wonder what it's doing in this box? I don't know of any banks in the US that have anything like this. This comes from what I call a 'don't ask, don't tell' kind of bank."

"Could it be the key to the box where the gold from Crescent might be kept?"

Walter continued to turn the key over in his hand. Finally, he slipped it back in its place in the velvet box. He looked over at me and shrugged his shoulders. "Could be." He reached back in the plastic bag and drew out the diary. As he shook the book out of its envelope and saw what it was, his tanned face turned white. He opened the cover and immediately snapped it closed. "Jesus!" he exclaimed. "This is Hollis' diary." Walter shut his eyes as he continued, "I wasn't just dreaming it. In a way I'm glad to see it and know I was sane, but I also have to tell you this scares the shit out of me. Matt, have you read this?"

"No. I wanted to see you first. I need your advice. If the flyboy and the colonel know I have these, I am afraid they'll think I read the diary. I wanted to—you have no idea how much I want to read it. But if they think I've read it I'm afraid they'll kill me. I also need to know what you think." I waited until Walter was looking directly at me. Pleadingly I asked, "I need your advice."

Walter leaned back in his chair and closed his eyes once.. Suddenly he stood and walked to the edge of his large porch. For a long time, he stared off into the distance. Eventually he turned back and returned to his seat. I could see he was wrestling with the problem.

Walter cleared his throat and started, "My first reaction is still to tell you take them and go away. But, we *are* friends and I can tell you need a friend right now. One thought is for you to take these back to the tower, put them under the step and forget you ever found them. However, that's not going to make flyboy and our colonel go away. Since neither of them is going to believe you haven't read the diary, I guess if you want you can read it."

Walter leaned forward. "My advice is still not to read it. If that diary goes into detail about his missions, I doubt you want to know what went down." I understood what he meant.

Walter looked off into space for a while, took a deep breath and then let it out. His voice took on a dreamy quality as he spoke, "I'll be honest, I'd love to read the diary as well. But I've spent too many evenings out here or in bed with Thien holding me. I'm not going to purposely take myself back there. Most of the time I'm in a good place. Thien is very protective of me and I think she would be really upset if I read it. She works hard at keeping me sane."

I don't know if she was listening, but when Walter said her name, Thien came outside. She pulled up a chair and sat between us. "I heard my name," she said.

Walter leaned over and put his hand on top of hers. "I was just telling Matt about the difficulty I had putting away what I did over in your country. I don't know if I ever could have managed it without you, but you know that." Thien smiled at Walter, the love and affection written on her face. "Matt brought Hollis' diary—you remember me telling you about Price and Hollis." I actually saw fear in her eyes. "I was telling Matt I was interested in reading the diary, but I don't know if I want to deal with what that might do to me."

Thien reached out and rested her hand on top of Walter's forearm. "I do not want you to read that. Those nights when you wept in my arms were as difficult for me as they were for you. I love you. If I thought it would help, I would take that damn book and burn it." Thien's voice was filled with anger. "You are a good man. Yes, you did some bad things. So did Matt. But that is not who you are now. If you read that book, both of you are going to relive what you did. Is that necessary? And you Matt, if Walter reads the diary, he has me here to help him deal with any bad effects it might cause him. Who do you have?"

She had me there. I don't know exactly where I stand with Sharon or how she would feel if I showed up some night with my problems. As much as I cared for Gladys, I don't know how she would react. I had never told her much about Nam or what I had done over there. I had felt comfortable with Sharon when I had shared my problems, but I was nowhere near that point with Gladys and I really didn't know if I would ever get to that point.

"Okay Thien, you've talked me out of reading the diary. How do I get rid of these things and come out alive on the other end? I am positive both of my 'friends' will think I read the damn thing and since I don't know what's in there, it might be something they think they need to get rid of me for." All of us sat there for a while thinking.

Finally, Thien smiled and looked at us. "I have an idea. Go and have a copy made of the book. All of it. Take it to the lawyer that helped Walter when he got in trouble back in Seattle."

"You mean…"

"Yes. Tell them if anything happens to either you or Walter, if either of you even stubs your toe then he is to read the diary and then decide who he needs to take it to in order to deal with whatever is in it Do you trust your lawyer friends?"

"Actually that's not a bad plan. I'm going to have Richard's people do the copy. That way there's nothing to fear about something getting leaked." I looked over at Walter. "What do you think of the idea?"

"I know when I was arrested I thought I was going to spend a long, long time in prison. I couldn't believe what they did for me, and you too, Matt. I trust them. I trust you. I think that's a great idea. You can turn it over to the colonel and you're covered. All you have to do is make sure neither the colonel nor the flyboy gets his hands on you first. Once the diary is in your lawyer's hands there's nothing your two buddies can do." Walter looked over at Thien and asked, "But why should Matt say anything about me?"

Thien leaned back in her chair. "Neither of you really knows how much the two of them know. She gestured at Walter. "Make sure you cut a deal for both of you. Set it up so both of you are protected. Okay?"

Walter and I sat for a long time just staring out across the valley and the mountains in the distance. I wanted to know where the key went. I wondered if there was a way to give them the diary but hold on to the key until I knew more about what was going on. The more I thought about that idea, the more I realized that was a stupid plan. The last thing I wanted was those two pissed at me. If I was going to make a trade, I needed to make it for everything.

Sitting on the ferry in Scott's Lincoln I called Silversmith's office. Once I had Richard on the phone I made an appointment with him. The best he could do was the day after tomorrow at eleven. I wasn't too happy with the wait, I really wanted to get rid of the stuff. I asked him if there was any way to see me the next day and he gave what I felt was a very evasive answer. "I'm sorry Matt, but I ah… well… tomorrow just isn't going to work. But you have all of my attention at eleven the day after tomorrow. Gotta go. Bye." And he hung up. Strange phone call.

But with any luck, my problems with the diary and the key would be over in a couple of days. I could only hope. All I had to do was keep out of sight. I mean that couldn't be too difficult, could it?

CHAPTER 20
AN EXPLANATION

The next morning my cell phone buzzed in my pocket while I was outside with Bean, and when I fished it out I saw the caller was Mouse. I answered, "Good morning. Normally I'd ask what's up but you're are a bit too refined for that kind of greeting." He laughed and I continued, "So, to what do I owe the honor of this phone call?"

"Matt, you always seem to put a smile on my face. Good morning to you. I was wondering if you would attend a little soiree I'm having tomorrow evening?"

"Are you serious? Sir, I would be glad to."

Mouse's tone had a touch of humor as he told me, "Matt, if you don't knock off that *sir* shit, I'll retract my invitation. Calling me sir is like installing an elevator in an outhouse!"

"Please don't do that si... ah… Mouse. You know, that really doesn't sound right either."

"Okay Matt, tell you what we'll do. I give you permission to call me by my first name. Do you happen to know what it is?"

"Yes Steve, I do."

Silence. Total silence and finally I asked, "Are you still there?"

Mouse started to laugh. Not just a chuckle but a deep rich laugh. After a few moments he finally got control of himself and he asked me, "How the hell did you know that?"

I saw no reason not to tell the truth. "Sakol told me in your office the first time I was there. Am I right??"

"That son of a bitch. We were never going to tell on each other. Okay, let's fight fire with fire. Do you know what Sakol is? I mean do you know if that is a nickname or if it's his first or his last name?"

"No idea," I replied.

"Sakol is his first name and his last is Hasaphongse. Oh, and make sure he knows I was the one who told you." His laughter was infectious.

"Really?"

"Really and I believe that not even Jeff knows that." I found myself laughing and getting in the spirit.

"Okay, ah, Steve, when and where is your soiree?"

"Do you know the Columbia Tower building?" DUH? Only the tallest building in Seattle.

"Yes si... ah Steve."

He laughed again and told me to be at the elevators at seven PM sharp and to bring a date. I was tempted to say something about how the last time I was there I had a limo pick me up and deliver me, but I thought better of it. Just as we were hanging up, I heard him calling, "Matt! Matt, are you still there?"

"Yes sir!" It just slipped out.

"Matt, if you want, and you think you can handle it, you may bring both of your ladies." And as he hung up the phone, I could hear him laughing.

By now Bean was pawing at my shoe to go in and have breakfast, and I wanted a cup of coffee. When I was finished feeding Bean and had poured myself a cup, I wandered up to the front of my apartment and curled up in my favorite chair. Now I was stuck with the decision of whom I wanted to take. The truth be known I wanted to take both of them. But I knew better than that. I called Sharon first and got her voicemail. I left her a message and by the time I had gone to the bathroom, my phone rang. It was Sharon.

"Hi kid."

"Hi babe. I see you called and I missed you. What's up?"

"Mouse just called me and asked me to a party tomorrow evening and I wanted to see if you were interested."

"Oh shit! I have duty tomorrow evening. I'm sorry. That's a party I would love to attend. Make sure you invite me to the next one. Okay?"

"It's a deal. I'm sorry."

I dialed Gladys. Since I knew she liked to work days I wasn't too surprised when she didn't answer the phone. I left her a message to call me. Since I didn't want to accidentally run into McNaulty and Mr. Pillsbury, I needed something low profile to do. It had been a long time since I'd worked on any of my car projects, so I headed out for my man cave. Normally I leave my car in the alley but this time I thought it was best if I used the dilapidated old car elevator that services the back of my building.

Art, the old fellow who helps me, was overjoyed to see me. He showed me some of the new pieces he had for our MGBs and we got busy. Over the years I've bought so many Bs I'm not even sure how many I have. Some were complete and some were rusted relics. My goal was to restore as many as I could. So far I have three of them in perfect condition. I knew I would never see all of the money I had invested in them; it was a labor of love. They were a direct link with my boyhood.

My parents had a summer home on one of the islands in the San Juan group and one winter I found—yes found—out in the woods an old MG that somebody had abandoned.

The plate that had the VIN on it was removed and I always thought somebody had stolen a good MGB and swapped the good tag with the bad tag on the stolen vehicle. Whatever the case, I now had a free MGB. While it was true that the motor and the VIN plate were missing, all of the rest of the car was there.

With a friend I was able to get the car to a garage, and then I started searching wrecking lots and the newspapers for an MGB that still had a good motor. One glorious day a dealership down south called and said that the previous night one of their salesmen had totaled his dealer car. As far as they could tell, the motor was in perfect shape. With great haste I drove down to look at the wreck. The motor did look like it was undamaged and even better, one of the seats was in pristine condition. I made a deal with the insurance company and now I owned two MGBs. I won't bore you with all the messy details of the marriage of the two vehicles, but after a couple of months of true sweat and tears, I turned the key and the motor started.

For the next couple of summers and winter weekends, the car was the scourge of the south end of the island. Both of the state troopers knew the car wasn't registered and I didn't have a driver's license but they never stopped me or questioned me. In return, I didn't speed, and I was a careful and most courteous driver. Those two summers with that old car captured my heart. I was now a convertible person for life.

The winter of my first year off at college somebody broke into the garage on the island where it was stored and stole it. Whoever took it blew the motor up and wrapped it around a telephone pole. There was a large amount of blood on the seats but the hospital on the island never reported seeing anybody with injuries that would correspond with the totaled car. To this day I have a special place in my heart for that old car. No heater, a radio that only played one station, one seat held together with tape and it burned oil like I owned Chevron. But it was still my favorite car of all time.

After a wonderful day of working with Art, I stopped by Gladys' apartment and found her home. She must have looked through the peephole in her door because when she opened it, all she had on was a towel wrapped around her body. I took her in my arms and as we kissed, the towel fell away and I ended up kissing a warm, damp sexy woman. When we broke off, she took me by the hand and led me to her bedroom. "You're wearing too much, take something off." She demanded. Of course, I obeyed.

Later as we lay on her bed, I told her about my phone call and the invitation from Mouse. When I asked her if she wanted to go her eyes got big and she nodded her head like a little kid. I told her I was going to wear a suit and if my old tux still fit, I might even consider wearing that. I knew I had lost her as she lay in my arms mentally going through her wardrobe. Finally, I kissed her and told her anything she wore would be just fine.

Bean crawled up on the bed and was standing on me looking down into my face. It was her signal that she wanted to go outside. I had no choice so I got up and took her for a walk. When I returned I told Gladys when I was going to pick her up the next evening, and headed home.

When I got home, the light on the answering machine was blinking. It was Mouse. "Matt. Change in plans. A limo will pick you up at six-thirty and then go pick up Gladys. The driver will call you when he's out front. See you tomorrow." I wondered, how he knew I was going to bring Gladys? That cat surprises me at every turn.

~ ~ ~ ~

Dusk was gathering and I was trying to encourage Bean to do her things so we could go in. I had my small, but nourishing, Scotch in my hand. The evening was cold, but it had the nice crisp smell of leaves and autumn. For some reason I'm built backwards. For me, September to late-November is like my summer. It's my time to get things done. I've never felt comfortable with the calendar. Have you ever wondered how it all started? Who decided that tomorrow is going to be a Tuesday on the third of some month? I guess we have to have order and all, but who picked the person who made the order? I know, put down the Scotch, you've had too much. But it was just me watching Bean do her thing and my brain running.

Finally, she finished and headed back down the walkway, never looking back as she expected me to follow her. After all, she who must be obeyed had spoken. After I gave Bean her treat, I walked through the kitchen and noticed it was time to grab my jacket and expect a phone call.

At six-thirty the house phone rang, announcing my ride. I had dug out the old tux and it still fit. As I glanced in the mirror next to the elevator door, I was pleased with what I saw. The hair had more silver than I would have liked, and my moustache had more salt and pepper in it, but my brown eyes were clear and the lines around my eyes were from smiling in my life, not from frowning. All in all, I thought I cleaned up pretty well.

Of course, Gladys was a knockout. Her dress was elegant but sexy. There was a nice show of cleavage and when she walked, there was a flash of leg from the deep slit. She really looked great!

"Why do you think Mouse invited you tonight?" she asked once we were in the car. "I mean, this is a first. For either of us."

The question brought me up short. Why *did* he invite me? We don't travel in the same circles. I may clean up well, but basically I'm still the kind of guy who wants to lick the dessert plate if the dessert is really good. I know everybody wants to do it. It's just that some do what they want and others do what people expect of them.

I don't try and hurt people, but I do want to live my own way. The best part is mostly I get to do as I please and for that I am most grateful. Out of six plus billion people in the world, out of over six billion possible existences I could have experienced, I got this one. Sorry, but screw your lotteries, I have food, a place to put my head, good people for friends. In the lottery of life, I hit the jackpot! I ain't dodging bullets. I'm not wondering when there will be a knock on my front door in the night. Life is good and I want the universe to know it.

I answered Gladys' question, "I really don't know. I hadn't thought about it. But now that you say something, yeah. We do travel in different circles. Why invite me to something tonight?"

I never figured out an answer because we had pulled up to the entrance of the Columbia Tower and the doorman was ready for us. We were escorted to the elevator and once we were inside, our escort reached in and pushed the up button. The door closed and we were whisked up to the top floor. As we rose into the air, I wondered why it was necessary for the doorman to push the up button for us since there were only two buttons on the panel, one for up and one for down. The mind boggles.

When we arrived, we were greeted by a comely young lady who was carrying a tray with crystal flutes of champagne. We plucked two of them away and then clinked glasses. Before we had finished our first sip, as if by magic, Richard Silversmith was standing in front of us. I didn't expect to see him this evening. He had said nothing about tonight when we last spoke. My antenna was quivering. Richard made a real show of looking Gladys over and then took her right hand and kissed the back of it. "You look marvelous!"

"And me?" I asked.

"Well, you don't look so bad yourself."

"Don't think you're going to kiss the back of my hand!" I exclaimed. As Richard chatted with Gladys, I looked him over. He was dressed in what was obviously a tailor-made tux. He looked great and I was jealous.

A few moments later Sandy Silversmith joined us. Her dress was a deep green thing that looked Asian and I have no idea what it was called. With her trim figure, she was stunning. Richard turned to her and asked her if she knew Gladys. After the introductions Silversmith said, "I know you know Matt."

We both laughed and she asked me how Sharon was. I told her she was fine, and that she wanted to come tonight as well but she was on duty at the hospital. I thought that should keep her wondering what my relationship was with the two women. I told her how amazing she looked and she thanked me. I really wanted to ask her what her outfit was called, but at the last second sanity kicked in and I kept my mouth shut. Shucky darn, I'm learning in my old age.

The two of them stayed by the elevators and greeted people as they stepped into the lobby and Gladys and I wandered off. So far no Mouse and I was trying to figure out where he fit into all of this. It was at his invitation we were there. He was nowhere to be seen.

Eventually we were escorted to the next room by one of the waitstaff and as we entered, I was stunned at the vast array of who's who in Seattle as well as Olympia. The mayor was chatting with the governor and his wife. The top two executives of the major television stations were discussing something while their wives had their own conversation. One of the executives of a major software company was with the chief of police and two members of the city council. I saw several people I knew from the papers and television. Off in one corner I saw David Wheeler and when he saw me he came barreling across the floor to where Gladys and I were standing. He held out his arms to her with a huge grin on his face. "Gladys," he gushed.

I was a bit taken aback by his greeting. Gladys slipped her arms around Wheel's stout figure and smiled up at him. "Hello David. Nice to see you again."

I asked, "You two know each other?" And after I asked my question I realized how stupid it sounded considering the way they had just embraced.

"Hell bells, Matt, if it wasn't for this lovely lady, my marina would have gone out of business a long time ago. She's my best customer." They both laughed.

Looking at me, Gladys explained, "David has some very good sources for parts for my old Chris Craft. I would never have been able to restore the boat to the condition it's in right now had it not been for this sweet dear man." I swear I saw Wheel turn pink.

"You know," I explained to Gladys, "You're the only person I know who's allowed to call him David. Everybody who know this galoof call him 'Wheel.'" Wheel grinned at me.

"This is a special lady. As long as she keeps spending money at my store she can call me anything she wants."

At that point a woman who was almost as tall as me stepped up and put her hand on Wheel's arm. "You left me all alone. I got lonely." Looking at the way the woman was dressed and the little girl sound of her voice, I thought that Wheel had probably rented the lady for the evening. And as I had that thought, I felt bad. That was really uncalled for and I watched the two of them wander off.

Gladys hugged my arm as she explained, "That man knows more about old wooden boats and where to find the parts I need. I don't know what I would have done without

him." To me, Wheel was just a poker player I saw every other month. Now I was seeing him in a totally different light.
Funny how you think you know somebody only to find out
they are so much more than you ever dreamed.

I spotted Krista Sellers with a very handsome gent I assumed was her police friend from Ross Island. When she
saw me she waved and promptly came over and kissed my
cheek. I introduced her to Gladys and then Krista was off to
greet somebody else. I saw Jeff and Sakol standing against
a wall with Jeff's wife and someone I assumed was Sakol's
wife. When Jeff saw me waved me over. "What's this all
about?" he asked me.

"I was just going to ask you. All I know is Mouse called
me yesterday morning and invited me and a guest."

Jeff asked me with a surprised look on his face, "You
were invited by Mouse?" I nodded. "Wow, all I got was a
call from Silversmith's office inviting me."

Sakol popped off, "Situation similar. No warning provided. Silversmith's office call wife, tell her presence is
mandatory."

The woman I assumed to be Sakol's wife gave him a
look that only married women give their spouses... a look
telling him to stop with what she considered his silly way
of speaking.

I smiled at Sakol and said, "Mr. and Mrs. Hasaphongse,
both of you look very elegant this evening."

Sakol frowned at me for a moment and then his face
lit up in a smile. "Mouse? Right?" I laughed. "Even! I will
enjoy having. Not sure how, but he soon big sorry!" All of us
laughed. Sakol's wife elbowed him to show her displeasure
that he was talking with his Charley Chan routine.

Eventually the room was full of people and Richard
stepped to the front and turned to the assembled crowd. He
held up his arms and without his saying a word, the room
grew still.

He smiled warmly. "Good evening one and all." There was a slight murmur and he frowned for a second and then smiled again. With great feeling, he addressed the crowd once more. "Excuse me, but that is unacceptable. One more time, good evening one and all." This time most of the guests responded. That brought a big smile to Richard's face and he made a slight bow.

As he pointed to the top of the stairs he began, "Some of you may know me, but I know all of you know my partner, Albert Bradson."

Albert stepped out from behind a curtain at the top of the stairs as Silversmith continued, "Ladies and gentlemen, it gives me great pleasure to be able to introduce to you the next senator from the state of Washington, Albert Bradson!" The room was totally still for a moment and then broke into a tumultuous roar. I had no idea he was running and I found myself yelling just as loudly as everybody else. I knew he'd be perfect for the job.

Eventually we were shown to tables and I was astounded to find Gladys and myself sitting at the same table as Richard and his wife, Bradson and his wife, along with the current senator and his wife. Normally I am not a man for politics. Too many politicians go into the business for themselves, rather than for the benefit of the rest of us. I won't get on a soapbox, but I knew Albert would be honest and fair. It was fun sitting at his table and watching so many of the gathered guests coming to present themselves. A few of them were blatantly trying to curry favor, and he wasn't even elected yet.

Somewhere between the salad and a very good piece of salmon, it dawned on me that I still had not seen Mouse. I thought this was Mouse's party. I leaned over and whispered to Gladys, "Wonder where Mouse is." She looked around the room and when she didn't see him, she leaned over and whispered, "Ditto!"

Between dinner and dessert, Gladys whispered in my ear, "Follow me." I stood up and pulled back her chair. She headed down a hallway to a door labeled *Ladies*. I wondered if she was crazy. We were at a high-powered dinner and she wanted to take me to the ladies' room? She held up a finger and stepped through the door. Within seconds, she had returned and was pulling me through the doorway. She pulled me to another open door and after I stepped through, she quickly shut the door and locked it.

I turned around.

Oh My GOD! We were standing in a toilet stall almost eighty stories in the air, and one full wall of the stall was glass. I was looking out on a territorial view of the city and out to the beautiful Cascade Mountains. The little room had a toilet, a sink, towels and a couple of bottles of something. But when you went potty, you sat there and looked out the window at a breathtaking view from eighty stories up. I had forgotten I was in the stall with Gladys until she asked, "What do you think? Do the guys have anything like this on your side?"

I laughed and told her it was very impressive. Gladys carefully opened the door so we could escape. She looked both ways down the hall, reached out and grabbed at my hand and as we headed back down the hall, I heard the sound of a woman's cry come through the door of another room. I heard, "Oh God, I'm coming now!" followed by a male's groan and I assumed he was also in climax. I was snickering when we stepped back into the dining room. Jeff and his wife were headed in our direction, and his wife winked at us. Gladys told her the number of the room we had just left and that it was vacant. Dee laughed and they slipped through the door.

Once we were back at our table, Gladys whispered in my ear, "I've been here twice before and it's kind of a custom that the gal will show the potty to her date, if she thinks he's cool enough. A lot of women do it and the staff just looks the other way as long as the person is discreet. I've always wanted to show my date our little rooms and tonight I was with the right person."

I didn't know what to say. I agreed it was sexy as hell and I wondered how many of the rest of the men at the party had been in the lady's toilet stalls. I felt very privileged.

Later in the evening, Richard came to me and led me into a small private dining room. I was floored to find Mouse sitting in a large executive's chair. He was dressed in a well-fitted tux and he stood immediately when I entered.

This was just too weird. Why was Mouse in here alone? Why was Richard bringing me to see Mouse? Richard said to me, "Matt, seeing what was happening tonight, I trust you understand now why I couldn't see you today?" I was sure their office had been a zoo all day long getting ready for tonight's announcement, and I could keep hidden for one more day.

"It's okay. At least I get to see you tomorrow," and I turned to leave the room.

I heard Mouse speak. "Matt, wait a second. I want to talk to you. Please sit down." He motioned towards the large chair. When I was seated, I found that the two of us were now at eye level with one another. Mouse continued, "I wanted to express one more time how sorry I was about all your problems with Cox."

"Mouse, don't worry. It's over." I started to push myself out of the chair to leave and he placed his hand on my sleeve.

I dropped back in the chair. "No, it was a bit more than that and I wanted to explain some things to you. The reason you had to wait so long in jail before anyone showed up was because I had to reason with Albert. I had to show him it was better for him, and the firm to step away from defending you.

"Since it was just a matter of a few short weeks and Richard would be announcing Bradson was running for senator, how would it look for the next senator to be defending the man who is accused of murdering the top running back in the nation?" Mouse continued, "To preserve the illusion of the world being on the up and up, other than you, nobody else knows I'm here tonight." Mouse looked at me intently for a moment. He then went on, "Matt, you asked me once about my life and how I do things. I'm helping Albert and Richard with their campaign. The problem is I cannot be seen too close to this. It would not be good to have my name associated in any way with the two of them.

"The only reason I'm telling you this is I feel I owe you something because I was the one who set the Cox boy on you. I know it wasn't your fault, but somehow, somewhere somebody should have seen how messed up the kid was. I used you and I'm sorry. I wanted you to question the kid and find out for me just what was going on. I played puppet with you and it almost got you in a lot of trouble. I want your trust. I want you to be my eyes and ears. People like you tell me things. When I see it might affect you, I warn you. But my ties go way beyond this state. I may have to ask a favor of you.

"I heard about the diary and the box." I actually tried to lean further back in the chair I was so stunned. "I hope you are well covered in this." I nodded. "I'll let you know as I learn things. But I wanted to tell you that I swear, when you were in jail, if it looked like there was going to be any problems with your defense, Albert would have stepped in and brought the full weight of Goldstein, Bradson & Silversmith on your case. We believed that Krista Sellers would provide you with as good a chance as any attorney at the firm. Matt, I'm sorry it went down that way."

I thought about this for a moment and started laughing. I could see by the look on Mouse's face it wasn't what he expected and he was puzzled by my reaction. "I can't be mad. When Tate asked me to help him I should have expected it to go sideways. Look where Bud Cox came from. Look at the violence he was committing on women. Once I realized just how many women were involved, I should have gone to Sakol and Jeff and made them do something. Actually now that I know you better, I should have made you understand what a bad apple the kid was. I don't feel used, I I should have guessed a little sooner along the way what was happening."

"What? What was anybody going to do? Matt, don't be naive!"

As I thought about it, I realized that unless they actually caught him with his pants down, so to speak, nobody would ever believe what he was doing. Once Cox was dead, women felt safe coming forward and telling their stories. Without realizing it, Ambruster had actually done the right thing. Nobody is supposed to be judge, jury and executioner, but sometimes it does seem to work out for the best.

Later as Gladys and I headed for the elevator to go down to the limo, Albert came over to say goodnight. As he grabbed my hand with his hand and placed his other hand on my arm, he asked, "Can I count on your vote? Do you still trust me?" I knew what he meant, for not defending me. Albert leaned in close to my ear and said quietly, "Did you find the ladies' room interesting?"

I think I about dropped through the floor and Gladys started to giggle. As I pulled Albert into a hug, I whispered into his ear, "I forgive you my friend for not defending me, but if you ever do that again I'm going to kill you!" When I let him go, he walked off laughing. Just as the door to the elevator was closing, he turned and pointed a finger at me with his thumb cocked back. I saw his thumb move forward and his lips say, "Bang!"

The doors closed and we went home.

Once we got home…

Well, that's a different story.

CHAPTER 21
THE EXCHANGE

Everything had gone well at Silversmith's office. The diary was copied and Richard had given me some excellent advice on how to handle the exchange. Both Albert and Richard had wanted me to do the exchange in their office, but I wanted only the colonel and flyboy involved. I told Albert if for any reason something went awry he needed to be as distant from me as possible. Reluctantly, both of them eventually agreed.

When I arranged for the pair to come to my apartment, McNaulty seemed surprised I'd called. From his reaction I guess he'd finally believed me when I'd told him for the thousandth time I knew nothing about Crescent. When I had told them that, it had been the truth.

The telephone next to the elevator signaled me somebody wanted to come up from the lobby. Since I expected the colonel and flyboy, I sent the elevator down for my two guests. I had decided the best place to make the exchange was right here in my apartment. The door opened and it was just the suit. I asked him, "Where's McNaulty?"

"He had to deal with a slight problem, but he'll be here shortly. He asked me to come here and wait, I hope it's okay with you?" Suit waited in the elevator until I asked him into my apartment.

"Yeah, sure. Can I get you something to drink?"

"Do you have any whiskey?"

"What kind?"

"Canadian?"

"Yep. Straight? Over rocks? With something?"

"Coke if you have it? Oh, and rocks."

"Hang on. I'll be right back." As I headed towards the kitchen to make his drink I realized he was following me. As I made his drink I tried to make small talk. I asked him if he still flew helicopters.

"Naw. I had enough of that in Nam," he replied. "I've no idea why I got interested in flying choppers in the Army. But, I did really well in chopper school and then I'll admit, I had fun flying in Nam. I know I was good at it but I got good at it to keep myself alive. I haven't been in a chopper since I left."

Something set off my alarm. I could feel my skin tingle and I wondered why I was so freaked out. Right then the phone next to the elevator sounded again and I went to send the elevator back down to the first floor. When it returned, the colonel stepped off dressed in slacks and a Hawaiian shirt hanging over his belt.

I motioned for the two of them to come into my living room and take a seat on the couch. I asked the colonel if he wanted a drink and he asked for water.

Before I sat down in a chair across from them, I went to a drawer and pulled out the box with the key and the diary. I set the two items down on the coffee table in front of them and then took my seat. Suit almost broke his hand reaching out for the box. The colonel picked up the diary instead and opened the cover. When he saw what it was there was an almost sadistic look on his face. He looked at me. "Did you enjoy reading it?"

Looking him straight in the eyes, I told him, "Other than looking at the first page, I haven't even looked inside the book."

"Bullshit!" the colonel retorted.

"True. I'm curious about what's in there, but I really don't want to know. However—"

"I don't believe you," he interrupted.

"Look," I tried to reason with him, "I have a good life. Now why would I want to read something that will just bring back ugly memories? Look at it this way, do you pick at a sore and pull off the scab? No! You leave it alone and let it heal. I'm healing from my time back in Nam and I see no reason to pick the scab."

The colonel stared at me for a moment. "I still don't believe you. Besides I can't take the chance. Hollis knew too much and if there's the slightest chance you read it, then you know too much. Preston, I really do not want to do this, but if you did read the diary, you'll understand and if you didn't, I'm really sorry." I watched as McNaulty pulled up his shirt and revealed a pistol. As he extracted the pistol, I held up a hand.

"Hang on, Skippy, not so fast!" McNaulty still held the pistol pointed at me. "Before you do something really stupid, I think you first need to look at the two pieces of paper on the table. I wondered if you might react this way so I took out an insurance policy."

I pointed to the two pieces of paper and they stared at them as if the papers were going to reach out and bite them. "What the fuck is that?" suit asked.

"Instead of asking, how about you read it," I said with an edge in my voice.

The colonel snatched the papers up and scanned them. He shook them at me as he snarled, "Exactly what does this mean?"

I smiled as I replied, "One of those pieces of paper, gentlemen, is a receipt from my attorney. It shows they have three copies of the diary which are now stored in three different banks around Seattle. You might luck out and find one, but I doubt if you could ever find out where all three are stored. The second sheet contains instructions for my lawyers if anything happens to me." I leaned forward and tapped the table with my finger. Once I had their attention I continued, "Anything! I mean if I get hit in a crosswalk, if I get in an accident on the freeway, if I fall in the shower... anything, gentlemen, one of the copies of that diary will be read by my lawyers and they will do with it what they think best. It might be sent to the press or, well, I leave that to your imaginations.

"From your actions so far, I would guess you do *not* want the contents of the diary to see the light of day. Is that about it, Colonel?" McNaulty slowly nodded as he realized what was happening. I continued, "Then, if you understand what I'm telling you will happen, I think you can take the diary and the key, and get out of my life."

We sat there for several minutes. I could see the colonel was wondering if I was bluffing. He looked over the two sheets of paper and again read each one very closely. His voice was a frightened whisper, "I hope you're kidding. You really don't know what you've done."

"If I've done anything wrong, it was because you backed me into a corner. I took the best way out. It would appear, McNaulty, that there are things in that diary that would present some real problems for you. Even today?" I got nothing in return. "Okay then, nothing happens to me, ever and you go away. Any more questions?"

The colonel looked up at me with a pained expression. Eventually he spoke. "But that's not fair," he complained, "We can't be with you all the time. What if there really is an accident? What happens when you die? Preston, this is not fair." I exploded, "Fair! What the hell is fair about coming into my life and ordering me around? What's fair about having you two following me everywhere I go? What's fair about you screwing around with me?" I paused and then pointed as I bore down on the Colonel, "And you, asshole. You are full of shit. I checked with a buddy of mine who works at the Pentagon. The *Pentagon*, dipshit. Ever heard of it?" McNaulty looked down. "Don't look down, look at me." I waited, "Since I was active for over five years, the day I got out of the service I was done. No reserve to serve, I was discharged and I was out. You fucking liar. Tell me some bullshit I was still active until I was an old man or something."

We all sat glaring at each other. I needed to calm down. I took a deep breath, and leaned back in my chair until I was able to continue. "Like I said, you seem so frightened of the diary I would assume there's a lot written in that book you really don't want known. I'm not even going to speculate about the contents." I took a deep breath and as forcefully as I could, I told them, "I'm telling you I haven't read it. Not one word. You'll just have to take my word on that." I paused for a second and decided I didn't have any more to say. I wanted them gone. "You two can take the book and the key and go. I want nothing to do with either of you. I think I'll go back and also add to the document that if I ever see either of you, the diary will be published."

The colonel asked, "You're telling us when we walk out of here, everything is over? Is that correct?"

"Well, that's really up to you, but to answer your question, yep."

"Where did you find all this? You told us Hollis never told you anything."

"It's a long story, but the upshot is I remembered something that happened up in the tower and when I went back, I found them."

"Has McLaughlin seen this stuff?" the colonel asked.

I wanted to keep Walter in the clear. "I told him I had them, but he never saw them. He wondered what might be in it, but he decided the same as me, we didn't want to know the contents. Oh, by the way the same conditions are set up for Walter, Thien and their son. If anything, and I do mean anything, happens to any of them, the diary will be read by the lawyers and they will do what they see fit to do. For all I know, it's nothing but a bunch of gay love letters to Price. Unless you know different?" McNaulty shook his head no. "Okay. This meeting is over. You have what you came for and you know what the repercussions could be. Now get out."

"What about the gold?" the colonel asked.

"What about it?"

"Do you expect any of it?"

"Why would I expect that?"

"Well, you found the key and all. Are you just giving up any claim?"

I couldn't help it, I laughed. It was beyond their comprehension that I wouldn't want any of the money. They couldn't fathom that I didn't give a shit about the gold. When I got my wind I tried to answer. "Gentlemen, life has been very good to me. I have no interest in the gold. I don't know where it came from and I doubt if it's really yours. But that's none of my business. You need to take the key and the diary and get out of my home. You have fucked with my life long enough."

They rose and walked to the elevator. As the door opened, flyboy stepped in and the colonel turned back to me and extended his hand. I looked down at it for a long time. Finally I said, "You have got to be kidding me. You show up at my doorstep and you turn my life upside down and then expect me to shake your hand?" I glared at him as I snarled, "You sir, have got cojones of steel. Goodbye."

The elevator door slid shut and Bean gave a short bark. I laughed and told her, "That's it, kid. You tell them what we think of their shit." She gave one more short bark and then pawed at my shoe. It was her signal for me to take her out. I felt as if a big weight had been removed from my shoulders and I decided we both needed to take a nice long walk.

And we did.

And when we got back I gave her a double treat on account of just because.

CHAPTER 22
DREAMS

I've never understood how dreams work. I knew I was asleep, yet the dream was so real. It had been a long time since I'd had dreams that vivid. I guess it was because of all the stuff Crescent had dredged up. Somehow I knew I was having a flashback and I somehow realized I had no choice but to ride it out.

I was remembering my friend Jonathan A. Orchard. Johnnie and I went way back to what I like to think of as 'the start of the good times.' We met when I was being shipped back to the States and on the flight across the Pacific we were bunkmates of a sort. After I had recovered enough from my injuries to travel, John was in the bunk next to me on the MATS transport airplane.

As I lay there sleeping and dreaming in my bed at home, I could smell the inside of the cargo plane, I could hear the roar of the engines. The dream was so real I could even feel the vibrations of the plane and the pain from my injuries. They had given us shots before we left and we had been told we wouldn't feel any pain. During the flight I hadn't, but now in my dreams, I did. My entire body seemed to ache from my injuries.

Suddenly I sat up in my bed and realized I was screaming. Bean was barking and I picked her up and held her. I guess I had scared her since she was trembling in my arms. Still holding her, I got out of bed and walked out to the front room and settled down in my favorite chair. Once I was curled up, I let the memories of that flight unfold.

John and I had been next to each other on the flight to Hawaii, and after we had been moved to our rehabilitation quarters, I was surprised to find we were next to each other again—normally officers and enlisted never end up in the same room. I found out later he'd asked we be assigned to the same room as he had enjoyed our talks during the flight so much. Also the fact that his father was a four star general seemed to have some weight in the matter as well.

Even though he was an officer and had flown a helicopter, somehow we just seemed to hit it off. Johnathan had been cursed with a really bad middle name, Apple. And yes, that is correct, his full name is Johnathan Apple Orchard. He asked to be called with John or Johnnie and never ever to use his middle name. During the flight we had exchanged a lot of info from our lives and one of the things he had mentioned was how it sucked to have such an awful middle name going through grade school and junior high. I thought to myself if the worst thing in his school life was Apple as a middle name, his life wasn't that difficult.

During the flight we also discovered we both loved to fish. He had been out to Washington state from his home back east, and had done some trolling for salmon and after he hooked up a couple of big ones, he was hooked, pardon the pun. He told me how he had always dreamed of fishing in Alaska and we made a pact to someday go to Alaska together and go fishing. Sitting in my chair I also remembered the trip when we had fulfilled our promise to each other.

The little floatplane we had to take up from Vancouver, BC hadn't instilled me with a lot of faith. I've always hated to fly and when you can stretch out your arms and touch both sides of the plane at the same time it's even worse. Johnnie said he would have rather been in a helicopter than this little puddle jumper, but that idea frightened me even more. He got a good laugh out of my discomfort during the flight.

The trip was even more than either of us could have asked for. We were on a small island at a fishing camp that was famous for its cuisine. Each meal was better than the last and the box lunch provided when you were out fishing was right up there with the rest of the meals. And then there was the fishing. We released at least three quarters of what we brought in. We kept only the very best and when we got back to the camp they would clean the fish and pack it in ice for our trip back. On the other end of the island there was a cannery and if we wanted, we could have our fish smoked, canned, then packed and shipped back to our homes.

Those two weeks were the best. One night as we were sitting on the dock at sunset, sipping Scotch and puffing on cigars, everything we had promised ourselves on the flight back from Nam came true. A couple of times Johnathan talked a little about his life and how he was still flying birds but when I asked him where, he looked over at me and laughed. "You know the old saying, if I told you, I'd have to kill you? Well in this case it's kind of true." We both laughed but I knew deep down inside he was serious. He did mention he flew for Bell Helicopter but I knew better than to ask him where, or what he did for them.

Another evening as we were sitting, watching the sun slip behind a mountain in the distance, we were talking about helicopters and he told me, "You know, it's been said they don't really fly. They just vibrate so badly the Earth rejects them." I know from my couple of trips on those birds, I wasn't too wild about sitting inside a tin can that seemed to be trying to shake itself apart. I laughed at his comment and told him I believed him.

This was a good night and we started to reminisce. I hadn't told him much about what I had done for our beloved uncle and I felt I could open up to him a little. I told him about a couple of my missions and he started to tell me a couple of his stories. As we were talking, he told, "By the way Matt, a helicopter pilot will never call them a chopper. They're either a bird, or a helicopter or something else, but never, ever did we call them a chopper. If you ever hear anybody claim they flew and they call it a chopper, they're full of shit!" I thought it was a really strange thing to say but he was adamant about it.

As I sat in my chair with Bean curled up in my lap, I could feel my blood run cold. Burt James was supposed to have been a legend. From what Walter had told me, when this dude would sit in a helicopter, his butt became part of the seat, his whole being was part of the bird. Every profession has its secret codes, and Johnnie had let me in on the code. According to him, my flyboy was as fake as a three-dollar bill.

I remembered now why hearing that little fat dumpy dude in his ill-fitting suit talk about the choppers he had flown in Nam had set my radar off. I wondered who the man was that was impersonating Burt James. I had no idea, but I thought if I wanted my misery with flyboy and his sidekick to be over beyond any shadow of a doubt, I needed to have as many questions answered as I could.

I continued to pet Bean, staring out across the water towards the canal. I may be slow, but I finally figured it out. I knew what was bothering me about the pair. I was positive now that the pilot was a fake and that made me wonder if McNaulty was a fake as well. I could hear a voice in my head. If there was any doubt about what I should do about the colonel and the fake pilot, listening to the voice inside my brain, I knew what to do.

It was time to stir the pot!

~ ~ ~ ~ ~

I called the number I had for McNaulty. After the second ring the phone was answered. "Hello."

"McNaulty?" I asked.

"Yeah, who's this?" The voice on the phone was fuzzy from sleep and I could tell I had woken him up.

"It's Preston. Listen, I thought it over and I changed my mind."

Long pause. "What do you mean, you changed your mind?" the voice snarled back at me.

"I want some of the gold. I earned it," I snarled in return.

"What? What is this shit, Preston?" McNaulty's voice was now almost a scream.

I was really enjoying his fury. "Well first off, there were all the problems with Hollis and me getting shot. Now that's worth a nice chunk of that gold all by itself. The other thing is I still have access to the diary and I really need something to help me forget about it." I figured McNaulty was just crooked enough to understand that logic.

After a lengthy wait, he continued, "So," another long pause, "how we gonna do this? How do you want to divide it up?"

"Well, I have a suggestion on how to get started."

"What?" McNaulty snapped back.

"Remember the playing field you met me at? The one next to my old junior high?"

"Yeah, of course. What about it?"

"Be there. Nine tonight. Be there or else…" I hung up before he had a chance to reply. My next call was to Sakol. He picked up on the third ring.

"You talk, I listen." His normal greeting.

"It's Matt."

"How things?"

"Well, now that I ain't in jail, things are pretty good." I got to the point of my phone call. "Sakol, I need a really big favor."

"What?" His voice had a note of caution in it.

"I need for you to be in the bushes tonight when I meet a couple of people."

"Bushes? Bushes? What are you talking about, Matt? And who are you meeting that you need backup?" There was no funny accent now.

"A couple of guys from Crescent." I heard Sakol suck in his breath.

When Sakol answered he sounded a bit frightened. "I asked you not to mention that subject again. What are you doing, Matt?"

"That subject has come up again and I need help. I'll explain after everything is over. I need you and I need for you to be armed."

"I'm always armed."

"Okay. Here's the address I need you at." I proceeded to tell him where the school was and where I wanted him to hide. I finished with, "Please be in position before nine. See you tonight." I could hear him imploring me not to hang up as I pushed the button to end the call and then I pushed the button again to turn off my phone. There was nobody I wanted to talk to.

Now it was show time!

CHAPTER 23
EXPOSED

I used the motorcycle again for my meeting with what I now considered the bane of my existence. It was a cold night, but clear, and the stars were shining brightly. This time when I reached the field I continued on across the weed-choked grass and rode until I reached the bottom of the dilapidated stands. Once there, I put the kickstand down and turned off the motor. The field was completely silent except for the sound of the cooling Harley. I looked around to see if I could see anybody, but the hills surrounding the field were all wrapped in the various stages of dusk.

I proceeded to climb up as high as I could get on the bleachers and once there, I looked around again but I couldn't see any sign of Sakol. I didn't know if this was a good sign or not. I really hoped he was out there hiding someplace in the gathering shadows.

While sitting in the stands waiting for the two of them to show up, for a moment I wished I still smoked. Back in the day when I was over in Nam, we paid a buck seventy for a carton of smokes! Yeah, you got that right, seventeen cents a pack. Almost everybody smoked. I thought a cigarette would have tasted really good about now, or at least helped calm my nerves. But then I remembered how difficult it had been to put down the nasty habit and I decided it was best I not even consider trying one. I had heard too many times how a person had quit and then years later tried one and within a couple of days they were hooked again. I had worked way too hard to throw all that away.

I watched as a big dark Suburban finally came rolling across the field. When it stopped, the colonel and flyboy got out of the back seat. I found it interesting to see that the colonel was back in full uniform this evening. He started to climb up on the stands when I said, "Stay down there please. I want both of you down there where I can keep an eye on you."

The colonel snapped back at me, "What is this shit, Preston?" We had a deal."

"Oh yeah. About that deal. I got to thinking it over and after all I've been through... No, let me rephrase that, after all you assholes put me through I feel I'm entitled to some of the money. Remember, I was the one who found the key."

"How much?" flyboy inquired. I was happy to hear him speak since he was the one I really wanted to talk to.

"How much? Well, let's see." I paused and then looking straight at flyboy, I said, "As I recall, the last time we spoke you told me you didn't fly anymore. Is that correct?" Flyboy nodded. I asked him again, "Sorry, I missed what you said, did you say you don't fly anymore?"

This time he spoke to me, "Nope, like I told you at your place, since I got out of the Army I've never been inside a chopper. I had a chance to fly a chopper once, but I passed. I figured I'd flown enough to last the rest of my life." McNaulty was looking at him wondering why he was having this conversation with me. "But what has that got to do with any of this shit?"

I remembered when Walter had told me where the Crescent mission had departed from. As an offhanded question, I asked suit, "I always heard Cam Pha was a motherfucker to fly in and out of, what with all the big hills surrounding it. How'd you ever get that big son of a bitch Cobra out of there and then back in with all that stuff on board?"

Suit was still for a few seconds and then shook his head. "It was a tight spot, but I got choppers out of smaller places than that. The chopper went in and out without too much trouble." His voice started to turn a little surly. "Preston, what the hell does this have to do with why we're here? How much do we have to give you to get you to go away?"

The hair on the back of my neck stood up. First off he kept calling them choppers, which according to my old buddy Johnnie, no military helicopter pilot would ever do. Next, a Cobra was a dinky little helicopter. If the mission had actually been flown by this cat, he would have known he flew a Chinook helicopter or a Huey; the Cobra was a light attack bird.

And last, I had picked a town that was in the far north of what was at that time North Viet Nam, a town we never, ever had any military people even close to, let alone stationed in. I wondered who this clown was. This man had never been in Nam and I knew he had never flown any kind of a bird. What was the colonel trying to pull? I looked at the colonel and in a calm voice, asked, "Excuse me, who the fuck are you really? And who is this fake pilot?"

The colonel gave me a startled look and then barked, "What are you talking about? You know who we are. My name is Jacob McNaulty and this is Burt James."

I pointed at McNaulty, "Well, you might be who you say you are," I pointed at his partner, "but that's not Burt James, helicopter pilot." I looked at the dumpy little dude. "Who are you really?"

"I'm Burt James. I served with the colonel in Viet Nam. Why are you asking all these questions now?"

"Because, I have a good friend who actually flew helicopters. Our military was never anywhere close to Cam Pha. Also, a Cobra is a light attack bird, it only carried two people and would never have been used on the Crescent mission. And, my friend, I know for a fact that no helicopter pilot alive would ever call them choppers. They are birds or planes, but never does a real helicopter pilot call them a chopper. That's three strikes! You're out. So, now the question is, bucko, who the fuck are you?"

The fat little man quickly backed up a couple of steps and pulled a gun from the inside of his coat. First he aimed it at me and when the colonel moved, he turned the gun on him. "Stand still or I'll shoot you."

"What's going on?" the colonel barked.

I butted in and addressed my comment to the fake pilot. "Are you going to tell us who you are? Oh, and by the way, the reason we're here at this field is because there are several Seattle cops hiding in the bushes around this stand. The best thing you can do is put down your pistol and tell us what's going on."

The little man pointed his gun towards me. "I don't believe you. You're bluffing." At this point Sakol, along with half a dozen other officers all with rifles, stood and pointed them at the supposed pilot.

"Look around you." I hoped the relief I felt wasn't present in my voice. "You don't stand a chance. Put down your gun before somebody gets hurt."

The colonel shouted, "Put that gun away, James, now! And what the hell is going on here? I demand somebody tell me what's happening, now!"

"It would appear your fat little buddy there is not who you think he is." I looked at the short man, who had put his gun on one of the seats in the bleachers. "Are you going to tell us who you are?"

The little man sat on the bleacher and with his hands between his thighs and his head down, proceeded to tell us the story about his brother's death, the switch, and why he was trying to get some of the money. He ended his tale with, "The government owed my sister and me something. Because of his tour in Viet Nam he was exposed to something that brought on cancer and he's dead. He trusted the Army and they killed him." He turned his head to face the colonel. "You killed him. Just as if you had put a bullet in him. You used him and then sent him home to die. The fact that it took this long to happen has no bearing on anything. It just took longer than if you'd used a bullet. Some of that money is mine."

By now the cops were standing in a loose circle around the three of us. Sakol stepped up to me and asked, "What are we going to do now?"

I smiled at him and replied, "By the way, thanks for being out there for me. As for what are we going to do? Beats the shit out of me. I wish I had an answer."

As soon as the words had left my mouth, two more dark Suburbans and a Ford Crown Victoria came careening onto the field. Both of the Suburbans had blue lights flashing behind their grills and the Crown Vic had both blue and red lights flashing. When the cars stopped, men came piling out of the vehicles. Some of them were in uniform and some of them were in suits. A couple of them had on jackets with the letters FBI printed on the back. One of the men in uniform had stars on his lapel. When he stepped into the light I realized this guy was a four-star general. I had to fight the urge to salute. The colonel drew up to his full height and saluted him. The general tossed back a casual salute and told the colonel to stand at ease. The general addressed the colonel, "What's going on here, McNaulty?"

"Sir, it turns out this is not Burt James but his brother, Brad. Burt James died of cancer from chemicals we used in Nam."

The general snapped back, "Don't say that. There is no proof that any of the chemicals we used can cause cancer."

"Meaning no disrespect sir, but you and I both know that's total bullshit. Chief Warrant Officer Burt James died from cancer. That cancer was caused by what he did over there in Nam. At least give him that much respect."

The general's cheeks turned red and he looked down at the ground. I could tell he was not used to being spoken to like that, or used to being embarrassed by anybody in the Army. "Well, that's a topic for another time. What about the gold?"

The colonel replied, "We know where it is and we have the key. We also have the diary kept by Hayward Hollis during his time in country."

The general seemed relieved as he exclaimed, "Great!" Then he motioned towards me, "Has he read it?"

I butted in, "No sir, I have not. I considered it but I decided I really didn't want to have the knowledge. I've tried to put what I did in Viet Nam away and that diary was not something I want to read."

The general glanced over at McNaulty and said, "I don't care, take him in anyway. We have to be sure."

"General, I give you my word I did not read a thing in that diary. Besides, I think the colonel still has something he wants to tell you about that."

The general wheeled and glared at the colonel. I was amazed to watch McNaulty actually shrink before my eyes. "Well McNaulty, out with it. What do you know about all this?"

McNaulty lowered his voice, "Sir, can we speak in private?"

"Why?"

"Well, I don't feel comfortable talking about this in front of," he waved his hand at the police and government people standing around, "all these people."

"No! You're wasting my time. Spit it out. What is this man talking about?"

I decided at that point I needed to speak up. "Sir, if you will allow me…" The general turned his head towards me and nodded. "We haven't met; my name is Preston. After I found the diary, I have to admit, I debated reading it. I finally decided not to but I was afraid the colonel or the fake flyboy there might do something rash if they thought I had. I had three copies of the book made at my attorney's office and those copies are locked away in three different banks where you can't get at them." I waited a moment while the general digested what I had just told him. I continued, "Okay, the deal is as long as I'm safe and nobody is bothering me, those copies stay locked up. However, if you cats decide to mess with me, my lawyers have the authority to make as many copies as they feel are necessary and release them. In addition, if anything should happen to Walter McLaughlin or his family the same thing applies.

"You now have the key, the diary and a fake helicopter pilot. I don't care what you do with any of them. I just demand you get out of my life and stay out. You know what will happen if you don't."

I watched the general's face turn several different shades of red. I wondered briefly if he was going to have a heart attack. I doubt if anybody had ever spoken to him like I just had. He stared at me for a few seconds and then turned on McNaulty. "I don't believe any of this."

McNaulty replied, "It's true sir, I saw the letter from his attorneys."

"How the hell could you let this happen, McNaulty? I want an explanation. I want you in my office at oh nine hundred Monday. I want a written report on my desk by then telling me exactly what happened during this whole fuck up. Do you understand, mister?"

I watched as the colonel drew himself to attention. I could see his eyes grow cold as he stared at the general. "Sir, I have given myself completely to resolve this problem. I came out of retirement to help you fix this." The general started to interrupt and McNaulty held up his hand to stop him, "Please, I told you going in I didn't think we could expect to come out of this without some collateral damage. Considering that we have the diary and the key to the gold, this turned out much better than it could have.

"I asked you if we could discuss this in private and you declined, so be it. I have a good idea what's in that diary. You also know what's probably in that diary. We both understand the fallout if the contents were ever to get out. I pulled your chestnuts out of the fire along with a lot of other people's. I saved your pitiful ass along with a bunch of your buddies and now you have the audacity to stand here and treat me like some lackey." McNaulty's voice now was cold and sharp. "I will not be in your office on Monday. When I get a chance to write up what happened over the past few months, I will. As of this moment, I'm done. Done with you! Done with the service! And for sure, I am done with keeping your sorry ass out of trouble." McNaulty paused and then added, "Or worse!"

The general glowered. One of the suited men who had arrived with the general stepped up. "What do you want us to do, sir?" he asked.

"Get back in the vans. We're going back to Fort Lewis," the general ordered. I watched as everybody returned to their vehicles until just the general, the colonel and the fake flyboy were left. McNaulty nodded towards James, the fake pilot and asked, "What do you want us to do about him?"

The general looked at the short dumpy man and scowled at him. Finally he addressed the fake pilot. "Mr. James, my advice to you is to go back where you came from. There will be no gold. There will be no money. You are lucky we don't bring charges against you. You will never discuss this with anybody. Do I make myself clear?"

The little man never looked up, just nodded that he understood the general's message. The general climbed back into one of the waiting vans and the colonel and Mr. James got back into the vehicle they had arrived in.

When I looked around I realized all of the Seattle police had left except for Sakol. I smiled at him and asked, "I ain't ever going to learn what this was all about, am I?'

Sakol smiled sagely at me. "You velly lucky. You still alive. And so ends lesson, grasshopper." With that, he bowed his head and turned and walked off into the dark.

I climbed back up into the stands and sat down. I remembered I had a small pipe hidden in my bike with some excellent weed stuffed into the bowl. I went down to the bike and then returned to the top of the stands. I decided I was going to break a rule I have for myself. A rule I have never broken before. If I have had a drink or anything to smoke, I never ride my bike. It's dangerous enough when I'm straight, let alone if I'm stoned. Until that moment I have abided by that rule, but that night, I felt I had every reason to make an exception.

As I sat and puffed I had a ton of questions. But,I also realized I really was very lucky to be walking away from what could have gotten very ugly. I was almost charged with the murder of a famous college football star, but the real killer had confessed. I almost got killed because the colonel thought I had read Hollis' diary. Flyboy had almost shot me because I had exposed him as a fake. Yes, Sakol was right, I was a very lucky person.

I leaned back and looked up at the moon. I hadn't even noticed it was full before now. Leaning my head back, I let out the longest howl I could manage.

Sitting there on the top board of what at one time had been the bleachers, I looked back at my old boarded up junior high school and my mind wandered back to people I knew from that time. For some reason the memory of how much crap Jeff had given me when I told him I signed up for typing class came to mind. He had called me a sissy. Oh, and by the way, it's no longer called typing class, it is now known as keyboarding.

I asked Jeff if he was taking any classes where there were just two males in the class and the rest females. His comment and his question were the same, "No shit?" And I used the same two words as my response.

I don't remember if I got any dates out of typing class, but it was one of the best things I ever learned. There's not a day that I'm not on the computer working or sending emails. Typing has served me well. And every time I stop by Jeff's office and watch him hunt and peck with two fingers, I make sure and comment on the sissy class I took and how it never has helped me one little bit in my life. He will then string together several four letter words ending with the demand I leave his office at once. I end with my normal closing remark, "Who loves ya baby?" Which gets me a grunt in return.

As I sat in the stands I remembered happier times. I thought back to my first day attending what I thought was such a large school. I remembered getting lost going to some of my classes on the first day. I remembered the first day of math class the girl sitting across from me. I thought Cheryl was the most beautiful girl I had ever seen in my life. But I was nowhere cool enough for her to even acknowledge my existence.

I recalled how much I hated PE. I wasn't a jock and I was always picked last for any team sports. There's something about being picked last. I've known others who had to endure the same stigma. Not all of us were gifted when it came to playing sports, but somehow the teacher took some sadistic pleasure in watching a few kids always get picked last.

As I sat there looking across the old playing field wallowing in memories, my thoughts drifted to Jeff and the games I watched him play at the old junior high. As I looked across the field, I swore I could see him standing there in his football uniform. I watched as he knelt down and drew a play in the dirt. I saw the center hike the ball and watched as Jeff stepped back, avoiding the rush. I watched as he rolled to his right and then threw the ball. I watched as the ball settled into the receiver's arms and then the receiver stepped over the goal line.

I took another puff and held it for a long time. I leaned back my head and as I released the smoke I let out a mournful howl.

I said, "That was for you, Jeff, and that was for a youth neither of us will ever see again." I laughed out loud.

"Who loves ya baby?"

EPILOGUE

Other than a lone candle flickering on the mantel, my front room was in total darkness. It was late and I had just given Bean her treat after we returned from our walk. I was curled up in my favorite chair with Albert King crying the blues over a lost love. Bean snuggled in and I was looking out over a serene lake. The lights of Seattle lay spread out before me and I was being comforted by my small, but nourishing, Scotch. There was a sliver of a moon left high in the sky and the night was as peaceful as it was beautiful.

My mind drifted over the events of the past few weeks and as I sat gazing out over the beauty of the night lake, I reflected on how happy I was with my life. I know all of us get so bogged down in the daily grind we tend to forget to stop and look around. Over the years I've tried to savor life, but I will admit sometimes things just go by way too fast to really appreciate them. Tonight I was in a reflective mood.

I wondered what would become of the general and Mc-Naulty. Would the diary be destroyed or kept locked away somewhere? I had no idea what the diary contained, but I would think the smart thing to do would be to destroy it. In a way I felt sorry for the twin brother. He seemed like such a lost soul. I'm sure he felt he was owed something because his brother had died from things that had happened to him in Nam, but then that applies to a lot of other guys as well.

As for the gold, I'd heard enough stories back in country about how a guy could make money in the black market. Stories about how to take your earnings and put them into valuable things that would be easy to smuggle back into the US. I think I was actually more curious about what was in the deposit box than the diary. I doubted if the fortune was still in the form of gold, but as to what it was, I had no clue. Something more for my little brain to chew on.

I was stirred out of my pleasant place by the obnoxious sound of my cell phone intruding on my reverie. I wondered who was calling me so late at night. I answered. "Talk to me."

"Matt, it's Gladys."

I'm always happy to hear her voice. "Hi babe. Whatcha doin'?"

Her voice sounded a bit depressed and I could tell she was down. I heard her sigh before she told me, "I'm outside your building. I'm feeling a bit lonesome and I was wondering if you wanted company."

Any time I spend with Gladys is a great experience and her company would fit in well with my current mood. "I'd love some company, especially yours. Call me from the lobby and I'll send the elevator down for you."

"It will be just a few minutes. I'm right outside the building."

I considered turning on some lights, but finally decided candlelight was most appropriate for my visitor. I set Bean down on my seat and went off to light a couple more candles. About the time I had four of them lit, the phone buzzed for me to send down the elevator for Gladys. Bean climbed out of the chair when she realized we were going to have a visitor. It's funny how animals learn what certain behaviors mean. She knew if I was sending the elevator down, some-body was gonna come back up shortly.

I heard the elevator stop and as the doors slid open, out stepped Gladys and Sharon. As the two women exited the elevator, they stopped and looked at each other. With a ner-vous laugh, Gladys asked Sharon, "Is this your floor?"

"Yes, I was coming over to visit Matt."

Even in the candlelight I could see Sharon was getting red. "Oh shit! I'm so sorry. I know I should have called first." Sharon looked at me and grinned. "Well, I guess we're even. Me with George and now you with…?" I stepped forward and introduced everybody. Sharon turned and started to push the elevator button. Looking back over her shoulder she told us, "It was a really crappy day at work. Big accident out on I-5 with four kids really messed up. Looks like three will live, but the baby…" She hiccupped and I watched a tear roll down her cheek. Her face was so sad as she took a deep breath and continued, "It was touch and go for all of them. We lost the baby and I just wanted some…"

Gladys stepped forward and as she interrupted her, she put her hand on Sharon's arm. "How about you stay for a while and we all have a drink? I'm sure Matt," Gladys looked over at me as she finished, "would love to have us both stay a while. Right, Matt?"

What was I going to say? Two lovely women who had dropped in out of the night unexpectedly, of course I wanted them to stay. I asked them what they wanted to drink and went off to get them. When I returned both of them were sitting on the couch that looks off across the lake.

Bean had grabbed the perfect spot and was now sit-ting between them. She was in heaven having both of them stroke her body. I handed them their drinks and then went over to my chair. I put my feet up on the ottoman and hun-kered down. Candlelit shadows danced across their faces and I watched as they got acquainted. Gladys knew what

Sharon did for a living but Sharon knew nothing about Gladys. When Sharon asked, Gladys told her straight out, "I'm an exotic dancer. I work at Robbie's."

Sharon leaned forward, put her hand on Gladys' arm and asked with excitement, "Are you serious?" Gladys nodded. "That's really interesting. I'll confess a secret to you, I always wanted to dance in front of some men and take my clothes off." Sharon looked down at her lap, obviously embarrassed at this intimate disclosure. I'll admit, I was surprised. This was news to me.

Gladys patted Sharon's arm in return as she told her, "Tell you what, any time you want to give it a try, I'll make the arrangements and you can come to Robbie's and do it. I'll bet we can put enough makeup on you and change your hair so that even your own mother wouldn't know you."

"Oh, I couldn't. I'm a really crappy dancer."

I piped up, "You should see what some of the gals there call dancing. Moving from one foot to the other and taking off your clothes is not dancing."

Gladys scowled at me, "Matt. Stop!"

"Well, you know the main reason I noticed you was because you were actually dancing."

"And here I always thought it was my body that drew your attention," Gladys shot back. Now it was my turn to turn red and Sharon started to laugh.

"Well, it's something I'll have to think about. And something I'll have to have several drinks before I could do. Hey, speaking of drinks..." Sharon held up her glass and shook it, the ice cubes rattling against the sides of the empty glass.

Both ladies' glasses were empty so I grabbed them and headed off to the kitchen to make new ones. While I was gone I could hear them chattering away and I wondered what they were talking about. After passing out the new drinks I returned to my chair. Sharon took a sip and then let out a deep sigh. "I'm really sorry to intrude on the two of you. I know I should've called, but I just didn't want to go back to the houseboat and be alone after the day I had."

Gladys leaned forward and put her hand just above Sharon's knee. "I understand. My day kind of sucked too. One of our girls has been trying to break a drug habit. We thought she was making headway but today they found her over-dosed in her car in the parking lot behind Robbie's. I know we all have our demons. She was working so hard to get hers under control. She had grown up in an abusive home, she got into an abusive marriage and she was trying to get free. She had turned to drugs to deal with her problems only to find out it just made things worse. I spent so much time with her… I tried so hard…" Gladys sobbed and Sharon quickly reached out and pulled Gladys into an embrace. I watched as Sharon patted Gladys on the back and stroked her hair. It took a few minutes before she finally calmed down. Gladys smiled weakly at Sharon. "Thanks. I really wasn't going to cry. I made myself a promise that I wasn't going to cry, and now look."

Gladys started to push herself up off the couch. Sharon looked at her and asked, "Where do you think you're going?"

"I'll leave so the two of you can be alone."

Sharon shook her head back and forth and replied, "No, I was the rude person, I was the one who didn't call ahead so I'm the one who should leave. I'll go." Sharon looked over at me, "I'm sorry, Matt."

Gladys was still sitting on the edge of the couch and she looked long and hard at Sharon. When Gladys looked over at me she smiled and winked. Her smile was one of total mis-chief. "Sharon, your day sucked," Sharon nodded. "My day sucked," Sharon nodded again. "I have a wonderful idea." Gladys smiled at us.

"Oh, and what's this wonderful idea?" Sharon asked with a bit of trepidation.

"Well, I have an idea where neither one of us has to leave…"

Oh shit!

But that my friend is another story.

THE END

ACKNOWLEDGMENTS

Thank you to my editor Ellen Campbell for stepping up to the plate and repairing what I have written. When the editing was first started, Ellen was unable to finish and I was forced to muddle on without her. But now she is back at the helm and has fixed this novel. Thank you and I missed you while you were absent.

I would like to thank Kevin G Summers for another great cover and once more for his expertise in formatting and preparations of the manuscript. I am so glad there are people in this world who can get those little bytes and electrons whipped into shape to do their necessary things so an author's stories can be read. Thank you, Kevin for your patience while I kept making so many revisions and you kept formatting. I promise, I'm done now!

I would like to thank all of you who read the original manuscript before it was edited and cleaned up. At the risk of missing somebody, I will not name them, however, they saw something in my works and they felt the novel should be finished. Without your positive reinforcement, continuing pressure and reassurance, I would never have allowed this to be published.

I want to acknowledge my current Cocker Spaniels all of whom play a part in the character of Beanie in this book. They have done a wonderful job just in filling the holes left by Buttons (BJ).

Finally, I wish to express my gratitude to my wife, Sandy, who was so instrumental in the development and writing of both *Houseboat* and *Code Name: Crescent*. It is always assumed that a wife is supposed to support and encourage her spouse, however, I feel she has gone way past that. It is no exaggeration to say that without her, neither *Houseboat* or *Code Named: Crescent* would exist today. Thank you.

Pull back the covers my darling... I am on my way.

ABOUT THE AUTHOR

Paul lives in North Fort Myers Florida with his wife and biggest fan Sandy, and their three beautiful American Cocker Spaniels, (Mas, Bean and Sam) whom are better now as "The Kids".

Born and raised in Seattle and now transplanted to Florida, in addition to writing Paul keeps busy involved with community events and working on a model train layout. A graduate of Western Washington University in Education, Paul taught for 4.5 years and became self-employed when he left teaching. Over the years Paul has owned and operated several businesses, where he met many interesting people who always seem to confide in him hence the varied knowledge of people that he uses to create his fascinating characters.

Code Name: Crescent grew out of a trip through Illinois in the winter which is partially described in the prologue of this book. From the prologue grew this story, covering old characters introduced in *Houseboat* and new ones introduced in this novel. As always, this grew out of bits and pieces and when *Houseboat* was published, more time and energies were focused towards finishing this book.